Ireland's
Haunted
Women

D1341301

POOLBEG

All proper names cited in the text are fictitious and their resemblance to actual persons, either living or dead, is coincidental. Likewise, names of dwellings, street names and localities have been invented for purposes of narrative and do not refer to actual places.

Published 2010
by Poolbeg Books Ltd.
123 Grange Hill, Baldoyle,
Dublin 13, Ireland
Email: poolbeg@poolbeg.com

© Christina McKenna 2010

The moral right of the author has been asserted.

Copyright for typesetting, layout, design
© Poolbeg Books Ltd.

A catalogue record for this book is available from the British Library.

ISBN 978-1-84223-445-7

All rights reserved. No part of this publication may be reproduced or transmitted in any form or by any means, electronic or mechanical, including photography, recording, or any information storage or retrieval system, without permission in writing from the publisher. The book is sold subject to the condition that it shall not, by way of trade or otherwise, be lent, resold or otherwise circulated without the publisher's prior consent in any form of binding or cover other than that in which it is published and without a similar condition, including this condition, being imposed on the subsequent purchaser.

Typeset by Patricia Hope in Sabon

Printed by
CPI Cox & Wyman, UK

www.poolbeg.com

NOTE ON THE AUTHOR

Christina McKenna grew up in County Derry, Northern Ireland. She gained an honours degree in Fine Art and a further postgraduate qualification in English from the University of Ulster in 1986. After graduating, she taught abroad for several years. Her paintings have been exhibited in Ireland and on the Continent. She now lives in Warrenpoint, County Down.

ACKNOWLEDGEMENTS

My grateful and heartfelt thanks go to all those women (and men) who trusted me with their stories. You know who you are. To everyone at Poolbeg Press, especially Brian Langan and Paula Campbell, who saw the potential in my initial proposal and took the plunge. To my editor, Gaye Shortland, for her constructive criticism, astute observations, and generosity of spirit. And last but not least, to my husband David for his unfailing love and support.

To Mr Kiely as ever

Contents

Introduction

For those who believe, no proof is necessary. For those who don't believe, no proof is possible.

STEWART CHASE

This is not just another ghost book. This is no reheating of oft-told tales handed down from generation to generation, or stories borrowed from other collections. It is, rather, a personal exploration of the ghost in modern Ireland. The cases that follow are told here for the first time. I have collected them from women up and down the country, from all corners of the island.

Does the ghost of contemporary Ireland differ much from its predecessor? Well, yes and no. It would appear that the "traditional" Irish ghost has become more elusive, having failed to keep pace with the march of our post-industrial society. Who has seen or heard the banshee in recent years, or caught sight of the "Little People" making merry mischief in the moonlight under a hawthorn tree? Likewise the ladies in white and phantom carriages seem to have made themselves scarce. On the other hand, poltergeist activity has remained virtually unchanged down the centuries; scenes of past wickedness continue to haunt the living; the spirits of the deceased stubbornly insist on returning when least expected.

Few subjects divide opinion as ghosts do. Do they exist? The sceptic will scoff; the believer will defend an encounter with a zeal verging on the religious. For at the end of the day – traditionally the time when ghosts begin to appear – belief in ghosts can be considered as an extension of religious belief. Their existence would seem to confirm the reality of an afterlife. It is no coincidence therefore that, generally speaking, the believer and non-believer are to be found in those opposing camps: the religious and the atheist.

But the ghost is more complex than an "apparition", a "phantom", a "revenant" and other such words that attempt to describe it. It is more than a semi-visible or translucent entity. Contrary to popular belief and folklore, it's unlikely to be found in a cemetery. The ghost tends to haunt places it has known in life. Which is why we're infinitely more likely to spot a ghost in a house or other building, on a battlefield, or at a murder scene, all of which are places where the ghost's mortal counterpart lived for a long period or died a violent death.

We have come a long way from headless horsemen, pookas, haunted graveyards, fairies and the like. The modern ghost is a little more sophisticated than that. He or she – no, let us from here on in refer to the ghost as a sexually neuter entity – *it* has to be sophisticated. Put simply, we live in an age where even young children are savvy enough not to be fooled by fairy tale and superstition. If the ghost is to be taken seriously it must work very hard indeed to convince us of its authenticity.

Ghost-hunters know this more than most. They are, in the main, gifted amateurs who devote their spare time to unravelling the mysteries of the ghost and haunted site. They have little time for the sensational, and the trivialization of what is for them a very serious subject. "I have always maintained," says Troy Taylor, founder and president of the American Ghost Society, "that researching ghosts and hauntings is much more like detective work than it is like the antics that you see in movies and on television from so-called ghostbusters and dubious psychic investigators."

I wish to make it clear that I am neither a ghost-hunter nor a psychic. Rather I consider myself to be a neutral observer, albeit a very inquisitive neutral observer. I have come up against the paranormal on two occasions in my life, once as a child and later as an adult. And although the poltergeist that plagued the parental home in childhood and the ghost I saw many years later were very real to me, I still wonder about the objective reality of both encounters and what they signified.

Of the two, it is the poltergeist experience which, even now, all of four decades later, remains the more memorable and credible of the two. This is not only due to the fact that it was such a terrifying ordeal, but because the typical range of poltergeist activity – the thumpings, rappings and scratchings – were so myriad and prolonged as to be indisputable not only for those immediately involved but for other independent witnesses as well.

By comparison, the ghost I saw in later years did not scare me half as much. I woke up one night feeling sure that someone had put their hand in mine. It had not felt life-threatening or even unfriendly. Rather the touch had felt comforting and I was not in the least bit afraid.

3

I was awakened a second time the following night. Close by my bed a man attired in old-fashioned clothing stood gazing down at me. I knew instinctively that he was the owner of the hand. When I switched on the bedside light he disappeared.

Was he my guardian angel, my spirit guide – or had he been part of a dream? All are possibilities. Yet I would still vouch that he was "real" and that I observed him whilst awake.

When I look dispassionately at both those episodes and the wider context in which they occurred, I see that they share something of significance. The phenomena manifested during periods of disruption and change in my life.

I was reminded of this while investigating the cases contained in this book, and particularly those involving children. "Edel Delahant and the Family Poltergeist" is a classic example, bearing as it does many of the hallmarks of my childhood experience. There are pubertal children, an elderly relative coming to stay for a period under the same roof, and the affair culminating in the death of that relative. Similarly, in "The Dead Girl Who Sought Revenge" Kelly was undergoing a period of great change: moving away from home, going to university, having to make new friends. Did she have a vivid waking dream or see an actual ghost, a spectre similar to that which I witnessed? Who is to say?

As is the case with that which "lies outside the physical" we look for clues and try to rationalize what is, in the end, irrational, unfathomable and impenetrable. Many people suffer major crises in their lives and never experience the paranormal, while those leading what would appear to be ordinary, uneventful lives can suddenly come under attack. "The Little Shop of Hauntings" is one such case. "The Haunting of Aisling, age Eight" is another.

I present the cases that follow as accounts told to me in good faith and I've endeavoured to remain non-judgemental in each instance. You, the reader, must decide for yourself what to accept as truth and what to reject as delusion, false memory – or possibly even deception.

A Whole History of Ghosts

As children tremble and fear everything in the blind darkness, so we in the light sometimes fear what is no more to be feared than the things children in the dark hold in terror.

LUCRETIUS, "On the Nature of Things," ca. 60 BC

Belief in ghosts goes back a long way, and it would appear that the ghost has been with us since the Bronze Age. The scribes of Mesopotamia (in what is now Iraq) were etching tales of mysterious spirits onto their clay tablets thousands of years before the birth of Christ.

The ancient Greeks were likewise familiar with the paranormal. Old writings tell of both good and evil spirits – even vampires – that returned from beyond the grave to haunt the living. It is striking that so many of those ancient ghosts seem to conform to what we know of our modern visitants. There is humour too: Pausanius, writing in the second century, recalls a famous bout between a celebrated boxer, Euthymus of Locris, and a ghost. The human won, thereby rescuing a princess, whom he later married.

At about this time Pliny the Younger, that celebrated Roman man of letters, when writing to the senator Lucius Sura, told him he wished to know his sentiments "concerning spectres, whether you believe they actually exist and have their own proper shapes and a measure of divinity, or are only the false impressions of a terrified imagination?" He went on to describe various hauntings. One in particular caught his imagination. It concerned a rented house in Athens, which was "large and spacious, but ill-reputed and pestilential".

In the dead of the night a noise, resembling the clashing of iron, was frequently heard, which, if you listened more attentively, sounded like the rattling of fetters. At first it seemed at a distance, but approached nearer by degrees. Immediately afterwards a phantom appeared in the form of an old man, extremely meagre and squalid, with a long beard and bristling hair, rattling the gyves [shackles] on his feet and hands.

Since the "old man" had the tendency to show up every time a new tenant moved in – so causing them to flee – the landlord found himself frequently out of pocket. Lowering the rent made little difference. Things changed, however, when a seemingly fearless philosopher named Athenodorus appeared. The story of the ghost intrigued him and he took up the tenancy.

The philosopher was visited, true to form, by the ghost, which led him out to the courtyard. It pointed to a spot on the ground, before vanishing. The following day Athenodorus had the particular place dug up. "There they found bones commingled and intertwined with chains; for the body had mouldered away by long lying in the ground, leaving them bare, and corroded by the fetters. The bones were collected, and buried at the public expense; and after the ghost was thus duly laid the house was haunted no more."

Clanking chains were a common feature in old tales of the supernatural. Prisoners were usually shackled in bygone days and it was important that even in death wrongdoers could not be seen to escape. In Charles Dickens's *A Christmas Carol*, Marley's ghost appears to his old skinflint partner, Scrooge, rattling his fetters. In *The Canterville Ghost*, Oscar Wilde has fun with his readers by drawing on the whole gamut of paranormal clichés: ghastly apparitions, shrouds, bony fingers, creaking floorboards, demonic laughter and rattling chains. When Reverend Hiram Otis, the new incumbent at Canterville Chase, hears the clanking ghost of Sir Simon, he jumps out of bed and offers the spectre a jar of Tammany Rising Sun Lubricator to oil his chains.

The clanking ghost of old may have long disappeared, together with our very own banshee (*bean sidhe*: "fairy woman"), our "Lady of Death", yet our fascination with the afterlife in these more enlightened times is still as strong as ever. This fascination reached its apogee in the mid-nineteenth century when the Fox sisters of Hydesville, New York, claimed they could communicate with the spirit world by interpreting the rapping sounds made by a noisy ghost. The spirit was said to be that of a peddler who'd been murdered in the house and buried in the cellar. Although the girls, Margaret and Katherine, had their detractors and were often accused of trickery, human remains were later unearthed in the cellar, thus lending a degree of credence to their claims.

The Fox sisters were pivotal in the rise of the modern movement of spiritualism. They ushered in the era of the séance, together with its interlocutors or mediums, who purported to communicate with the spirits of the dead. For the first time in history there was "evidence" that we could survive death.

Such grandiose claims by the Fox sisters and the mediums who followed in their wake could not go unchallenged. The Society for Psychical Research (SPR) was formed in London in 1882 by an eminent group of scholars and scientists. Their aim was to subject the claims made for paranormal phenomena to the same rigorous probing and scrutiny as those applied to scientific research.

Today we have groups such as the Irish Paranormal Alliance (IPA) and the Northern Ireland Paranormal Research Association (NIPRA), which continue this valuable work, applying similar high standards of investigation. The NIPRA's founder member Warren Coates and his team have been kept busy for the best part of two decades. The group works alongside a priest and minister and find that their services are in greater demand during the winter months. "It's not that the spirits take summer holidays," Warren quips. "It's simply because people spend more time indoors and so are more aware of noises and changes in atmosphere. And of course the spirits need darkness to communicate better and make their presence felt."

It remains only to be seen if our modern ghost stories contain borrowings from those that have gone before, down through the centuries. The other explanation is, of course, that ghosts and hauntings possess – and have always possessed – common elements. It could be argued that, because such matters are non-physical and therefore outside time, it follows that the ghost will remain unchanged even though our societies and cultures are in a constant state of flux and renewal.

Ghosts in Other Cultures

Belief in an afterlife is common to all cultures. Even Neanderthals seem to have believed in survival after death. Archaeologists have uncovered multiple graves at single burial sites, together with evidence of flowers and animal antlers buried alongside human remains. This suggests that those early primates believed that some sort of future existence awaited their resurrected dead.

In many cultures, the spirit world is accepted as fact, and ghosts come in many guises. The North American *windigo*, feared by the Algonquin nation, is reputed to be part animal and part human, and said to make pacts with evil spirits to kill people. It dwells in forests and is especially fond of feeding on the flesh of children.

Yet other Native Americans, the tribes of the Great Plains for example, consider it a normal part of life on earth that humans should interact with ghosts and spirits. Oddly enough, the Cheyenne do not accept that a ghost is the spirit of an individual but nevertheless believe in individual souls. They hold that the soul, or *tasoom*, is the essence of the human being, and continues to live on after death.

9

In some parts of Africa the ghost is seen in a very different light. The Kikuyu people of Kenya believe that we all have a spirit, or *ngoma*, that becomes a ghost upon a person's death. If somebody is murdered then that person's *ngoma* will haunt the murderer for the rest of his life – or until he turns himself in to the authorities. Ghosts are everywhere for the Kikuyu; even certain trees have their own spirits, entities that demand food offerings lest the local people suffer calamities.

The Japanese have a whole phantasmagoria of grotesque spirits to contend with. There's the demonic *toyol*, which appears in the form of a mischievous green baby with red eyes, and will do the bidding of whoever summons it. It is said to suck on the big toes of people while they sleep and steal if commanded. It is not all bad, however: it will lay claim to only *half* of the victim's property or wealth.

Along with the *toyol* there's the *shojo* and *umi bozu*, popular Japanese sea-ghosts. The *shojo* is a licentious spirit with red hair, which can be coaxed away from its wild partying by offering it rice wine: sake. The uglier *umi bozu*, bald with huge, hideous eyes, is said to haunt sailors.

In the Middle East belief in ghosts has greatly diminished since the days of ancient Sumeria and Mesopotamia. This is due in part to the influence of the Muslim Qur'an, which appears to rule out the possibility of the dead returning, for whatever reason, to haunt the living. We read that "there will be a barrier between them [the dead] and the world they have just left till the day they are raised to life again". Nor can the living speak to the dead: "Verily, you cannot make the dead hear and you cannot make the deaf hear the call when they turn their backs and retreat." (However, there seems to be one exception to this "rule". According to Islamic lore the Prophet Mohammad declared: "After the deceased is placed in his grave and his companions turn to leave, he hears the shuffling of their feet as they walk away. Then there come to him two angels.")

All this is in contrast to the beliefs of the Tuareg of the Sahara. Although Islam has largely supplanted the animistic beliefs of this nomadic people, some of their ancient superstitions endure to this day. One of the most curious is the Tuareg reluctance to mention the names of their deceased, a practice shared with many Asian peoples. It appears that they fear the return of the dead person's ghost, believing that the mere utterance of his name will summon the spirit from beyond the grave. In fact, youths are completely forbidden to speak the names of deceased ancestors, especially those on their father's side. They believe that the spirits of the dead roam freely but particularly in the vicinity of burial places, which the Tuareg avoid. Spirit possession is common, music often provoking it but, strangely, also considered to be the cure.

And what of the Jews and their ghosts? By far the most fearsome among them appears to be the *dybbuk*. It seems to be a relatively recent ghost, however. We first encounter it in Jewish literature in Poland and Germany in the seventeenth century. According to legend, the *dybbuk* (short for *dybbuk me-ru'ah ra'ah*, which means "a cleavage of an evil spirit") enters a living person and cleaves to his soul. It can cause mental illness and will speak through the mouth of the afflicted human.

In closing it's worth mentioning that we Westerners are largely alone in rejecting the possibility that ghosts are confined to humankind. For example, the Eskimo of the

Arctic Circle take great pains to ensure that the spirits of the animals they hunt do not return to haunt them. No longer practised, the great Bladder Festival was celebrated in December and was a high point among the Inuit and Yu'pik peoples. During the hunting season the bladders of all slain animals – whales, polar bears, seals, walruses and others – were preserved. At the time of the festival the bladders were taken to an assembly-house and rituals enacted. Men were forbidden to engage in sexual intercourse with their spouses throughout the five days of festivity. Why? They believed that failure to "perform" satisfactorily might incur the wrath of the ghosts of the slaughtered animals . . .

Do Ghosts have a Purpose?

One of the most memorable scenes in the history of English drama must be the ghost scene in Shakespeare's *Hamlet*. It occurs shortly after the curtain rises. A sentry takes over the watch atop the battlements of the royal castle at Elsinore, Denmark, and we learn that an "apparition" has been seen on two consecutive nights. It's the ghost of the dead king, Prince Hamlet's father. When the prince questions it he learns that his uncle murdered his father. The ghostly visitations had a purpose: Hamlet's father wished for his son to avenge his death.

So much for the fictional ghost. Whether "genuine" ghosts interact with the living for a defined purpose remains a vexed question. A celebrated Belfast ghost of the seventeenth century is reputed to have, like Hamlet's father, sought to right a wrong. James Haddock, who lived to the south of the city, died in 1657. He'd made a will, bequeathing part of his land to his wife and the rest to his son on his coming of age. But the widow married James's executor, who altered the will. It now favoured his own son in place of James Haddock's.

Some time later a friend of the deceased was riding from the village of Hillsborough to Belfast. On crossing a bridge he encountered the ghost of James Haddock; it urged him to contest the altered will in court. For a month long, the ghost continued to manifest until its wish was granted. It even made a brief – and spine-chilling – appearance in the courtroom. The judge ruled in dead James Haddock's favour, whereafter the ghost departed for good.

Marsh's Library, adjacent to St Patrick's Cathedral, Dublin, also hosts a ghost with a purpose – that of its founder, Archbishop Narcissus Marsh (1638–1714). According to contemporary records, Marsh's niece Grace, who lived with him, eloped with a curate and married him in a pub in Chapelizod. She left word that she'd written a note to her uncle, begging his forgiveness, and had slipped it into a book in his great library. But in life he never found the note, and it's said that he still haunts the library, tossing books from the shelves, in his fruitless search for it.

While researching this book I encountered only one clear instance of a ghost with an intention, the strange case of "Hazel Quinn".

There are those who argue that ghosts have no purpose whatsoever. Others contend that the motivation behind ghostly visitations – or actual meddling – can vary from the benign to the malevolent. In their book, *Death: the Final Mystery*, the psychical researchers Lionel and Patricia Fanthorpe state that:

Nearly half a century of research into most aspects of the paranormal has led us to the conclusion that anomalous phenomena can be positive, negative, or neutral – rather like the human race itself. If ghosts are demons in disguise, many of them must be singularly good-natured demons, and the majority of the rest are so bland and ineffectual as to be practically innocuous.

The same authors are in little doubt that ghosts do exist. They conclude that after careful research and evaluation "there is enough strong evidence for genuine contact with departed human beings to make survival not only reasonable but probable."

Why Women?

In 2006 I co-authored *The Dark Sacrament*, a book dealing with exorcism in Ireland. During the research I was struck by the number of women involved; it was clear that they greatly outnumbered the men who had fallen victim to oppression by paranormal forces. Try as I might, I could not account for this, nor did I find a satisfactory explanation in the literature.

Could it be that ghosts appear to men and women with equal frequency – but that women are more likely to share their experiences? After all, men tend to discuss their private lives less readily than do women. Or perhaps it's because most men tend to suppress their "feminine" side – what Jung called the *anima* – so that the creative, intuitive and visionary area of their subconscious mind is rarely acknowledged.

It's an interesting topic for debate. Whatever the truth, the fact remains that my portfolio of cases involving women far outweighs that of those involving men.

The women I spoke to in the course of my research are from all walks of life. They are young and old, single and in relationships. Interestingly, the cases also include women of several religious persuasions and none. This last would seem to indicate that ghosts do not necessarily appear to the devout. They do not seem to differentiate between the believer and the sceptic.

This is not to say that religious belief has no place in haunting. Several women I spoke to were convinced that their "sightings" were the result of a lack of devotion; they believed that by neglecting their prayers they had somehow opened a door into the other side, and that the entities that came through that door had been sent to confirm the reality of the "heavenly realms". Who can say that they are mistaken?

There were many similarities between the cases recounted to me. For it is a fact that, when it comes to the great drama that is the paranormal, although the characters and settings may change, the capers and routines of the ghosts will usually remain consistent from one act to the next.

Even though the ten cases presented here have common elements, I believe that together they present as diverse a range of hauntings as is possible within the context of familiar and everyday situations.

Ultimately, the ghost is and remains an enigma. It frightens us because it represents the unknown. Friend or foe, benign or malignant? We simply do not know.

A Ghost Book for our Time

This book was never intended to supply answers. I do not have them. I might go further as to say that nobody has answers; what passes for knowledge of the nature of the ghost is largely speculative. For every theory there's a counter-theory; for every "proof" there is lingering doubt.

My intention is to lay before the reader examples of ghostly activity in modern Ireland. The accounts you'll read are of hauntings that occurred in recent years, from the early 1990s to the present.

The women I interviewed spoke to me in the under-standing that I would treat their stories in confidence. To this end I have changed the names of all those involved. Moreover, I have transposed the localities to avoid identification. Lastly, for the sake of the narrative, I've recreated various conversations in a somewhat different form from the originals, while retaining their substance and import.

Christina McKenna
Warrenpoint, 2010

1

Róisín and the Ghost that Drew Blood

*Perhaps other souls than human are sometimes
born into the world, and clothed in flesh.*

J SHERIDAN LE FANU, *Uncle Silas*

The room was cold . . . so very, very cold. Michael and Róisín lay side by side in the narrow divan bed. Róisín was curled up in the foetal position, Michael was sprawled on his back; both were fast asleep. They were young and newly met and in love.

All was quiet in the bedroom of the house in William Street in the city of Limerick on that winter's night. All quiet, save for the ticking clock beside the bed and the rain that had been falling steadily through the thick February darkness.

Outside nothing stirred. The row of terraced houses and shops, curtained and locked against the night, looked as drab and neutral as any row of old buildings in any Irish town centre. However, behind the door of one of those houses something deadly was about to be enacted.

Róisín stirred restlessly and her eyes snapped open – suddenly, abruptly and seemingly without due cause. They locked on the illuminated hands of the clock. She saw that it was 5.10 a.m. A terrible dread gripped her. Something horrifying was about to happen. She could sense it. She could feel it. *Get out of the room,* something urged. *Get out of the room!*

She tried to move. But her body wouldn't obey. It couldn't obey. She was paralyzed from head to toe as if trapped in a block of ice.

Fully alert now, she was conscious of Michael slumbering beside her. Could see the pre-dawn light stain the window, hear the ticking clock and relentless rain and the pounding of her own heart. But something "other" was in the room with her, an invisible other. Róisín sensed that the worst was yet to come.

When it did come, only seconds later, it was terrible in its suddenness. She gasped. Brute hands were clasping the sides of her head, pressing, as though intent on crushing her skull. The pain was excruciating. She couldn't breathe. She couldn't speak. She couldn't move.

I'm dying, she thought. Oh, my God, this is what dying must feel like!

The invisible fingers began tightening even more. Her skull was about to crack open. She was screaming but no sound came. The hands were now about her throat, gripping and squeezing the very life out of her.

She prayed for death to come quickly. She let her eyelids close in defeat.

Keep your eyes open, a voice in her head was commanding her. *It's the only way you'll survive. Keep your eyes open!*

The urge to die was strong, but the urge to live must prevail.

God, help me! she silently begged.

All at once the window fell away from view as if a blind had been snapped down. She was in darkness. Her eyes were shut tight. With a fierce act of will she tried to open them. But each attempt sent burning pains shooting through her body, from head to toe. She was under attack. She was fighting for her very life.

Open your eyes! Open your eyes!

God help me, she implored again. God, help me!

Then abruptly the weight on her eyelids began to ease; little by little, bit by bit, and the darkness was giving way to a lustre of window.

Something miraculous was happening.

A glorious lightness was beginning to creep up from her throat. The pressure on her head was beginning to ease. Ever so slightly, yes, but it was there: a tingling sensation. Gentle, reassuring.

Her eyes were fully open now and she tried to stir. But no, movement was not yet possible. Her entire body was still locked fast, as before, in the foetal position.

I'm being held like this for a reason, she told herself. Something's going to happen. I can *feel* it.

She waited.

The pain in her head had abated. The clock was ticking and the rain was murmuring and Michael was sleeping beside her.

And she waited. Waited to bear witness – that was how she thought of it now; a part of her was insisting that she look, listen, and remember.

Then they came.

There were two of them, human-shaped, one behind the other. Róisín saw a white figure pursued by a towering, dark form. They passed in front of the window, the light from outside rendering them clearer still. The white figure appeared to be trying to escape. The dark shape surged behind it, menacing in its great bulk, its evil filling the room like toxic gas.

Róisín prayed the dark entity would not come near her. She *knew*, she just *knew* that if it did, she'd die.

But mercifully, within moments both apparitions had vanished, passing into the wall. With their passing she found her limbs loosening.

She was released.

The clock read 5.30 a.m. She reached out a trembling hand to switch on the bedside lamp and turn to the still-slumbering Michael.

Róisín McCabe will never forget that dreadful night. Now, all of seven years later, the twenty-eight-year-old still shudders at the mere recollection of it.

"That was just the beginning of it," she tells me. "I was tormented for months after that."

Tormented, or indeed, *haunted*. For that's what Róisín suffered in the aftermath. That February night in Limerick pushed open a door into a dark and frightening world. The ensuing nightmare would finally end much, much later, a thousand miles away in a church in the southeast of Spain.

But let us return to William Street and the night in question.

Michael sat up. He rubbed the sleep from his eyes.

"What is it? It's not time to get up already, is it?"

"No, I . . . I just . . . I think . . ." Róisín struggled to explain what had occurred, "I just had a . . . nightmare . . . I –"

"Jesus!" Even in the light from the bedside lamp he could see something was very wrong. "What happened to you?" He scrambled out of bed and switched on the main light.

The light revealed it had been no nightmare. Róisín saw that there were red smudges on the bodice of her nightdress; even as she looked, little spots of blood continued to seep through the material.

Her upper arms and chest were covered in scratch marks. It looked as though she'd been thrust into a hedge full of briars.

"God, we'd better get you to the doctor!" Michael said. "Did you do that in your sleep?"

Róisín had great difficulty in describing what had just happened, but she did her best, hoping that Michael would not think her crazy.

"Nah, that was a nightmare," he said, trying to reassure her. "Sometimes dreams can seem very real."

"That may be, but it doesn't explain how I got all these scratches, does it?"

"You must have . . . you must've been itching in your sleep and scratched yourself."

Róisín splayed her still-trembling hands. "Look at my nails. I chew them, remember? How could I scratch myself?

21

No, Michael, it wasn't a dream. It was real. And no, I'm not going to the doctor. If *you* don't believe me, what's a doctor going to think? He'll have me committed." She began to cry. "God, it was awful! You can't imagine how awful it was. I thought I was going to die."

"Look, all right, I *do* believe you," Michael lied, putting a comforting arm about her. "Tell you what: we'll get you fixed up then go out and get a nice breakfast at Doolan's. How's that?"

Later that morning, after a walk in the fresh air and several cups of strong coffee, Róisín began to feel slightly better. She knew what she'd experienced was very real. It was definitely not a dream. Nor was she losing her mind. The scratches proved that – as did the clock. Throughout the ordeal she'd been fully conscious of the time.

She tried to hide her fears from her boyfriend. They'd only been going out for a few months and she didn't want to jeopardize the relationship. There was only one person she could confide in: her mother, who lived just a few streets away. She'd call her after Michael had gone to work.

As it turned out, she didn't need to ring her mother, because at around ten o'clock Róisín's mother rang *her*.

"God, are you okay, Róisín, love?"

"Oh, Mum . . . yes, well . . . yes, I'm fine, I –"

"Thank God for that. You didn't hear the news, then? I was worried sick. A young woman was murdered two doors down from you last night. It put the heart across me 'cos I thought it was you."

Róisín was shocked beyond words.

When she visited her mother and showed her the scratches she was really taken aback at her reaction.

22

"You know the last time I saw you like that was when you were a baby."

"What? How d'you mean?"

"Yes, you woke us up one night, screaming your little head off. And when I lifted you out of the cot you were covered in scratches, just like that. Your father, God rest him, thought a rat had got into your cot when he saw the state of you. We lived in an old damp house then, so it was possible, I suppose. But when I took you to the doctor he said that was very unlikely. Then when I heard that old Mrs Toner had died in the night I put two and two together."

"Mum, you're scaring me and you're not making any sense. What are you saying?"

"Your grandmother had 'the gift', you see – or second sight, if you like. She knew when bad things were going to happen, and they say it skips a generation. She could hear the banshee, and when you got to about seven you started hearing it too."

"What? My God, Mum!" Róisín burst into tears. "I can't believe what I'm hearing!"

"Look, love, that's why I never mentioned it, because I knew it would upset you."

"Well, tell me *now*. I have a right to know."

Mrs McCabe sighed and chose her words carefully. "It's in the past and it was a long time ago. But if you must know, one night you came into your dad and me in the middle of the night because you couldn't sleep. There was a lady crying beside your bed, you said, and when you asked her why she was crying she told you that young Stephen Neary was going to die. Well, later that day little

Stephen *did* die. But your father and me never mentioned it to a soul. The child had leukaemia, so it was expected. But I knew you had the second sight for sure after that happened."

"But why didn't you tell me about these things before, Mum?"

"I didn't want to worry you, sweetheart. I worried enough for the both of us. And besides, what good would it have done? There are some things we're not meant to understand. Just pray for the soul of that poor young girl. You were there to 'help her over' by taking on some of the awful pain she must have suffered at the end. So don't look on it as a bad thing."

"It's one hell of a scary thing, Mum, and I don't want any part of it. God, I don't want to go through anything like that ever again. Why in God's name has it started up again?"

"You just happened to be near where a bad thing happened. You're more sensitive than other people. You sense when bad things are going to happen. So, you know, maybe it's best if you move out of that house. You can stay here until you get sorted out."

"Oh, don't worry. I wouldn't stay in that place another night."

Róisín waited until Michael returned from work before going back to the house. Since they shared the house with three others, moving out was easy enough – just the clothes from the wardrobe and chest of drawers, some photos from the bedside locker and several personal belongings.

And the clock. Somehow she couldn't bring herself to touch it. How could she look at it ever again without being tormented by the memory?

The bedding was hers as well, but again, she couldn't go near the bed. Michael bundled the sheets and duvet into a bin bag in preparation for the skip.

They shut the door on the bedroom, Róisín praying silently that the next tenant would have a less traumatic time of it.

Finding another place proved simple enough. There were lots of rentals available in the town due to the high influx of foreign nationals. They viewed three places before settling on a small semi-detached house on the outskirts of town.

"I didn't want to live in a terraced row again," Róisín tells me. "The murder happened just two doors down and I kept thinking maybe if I hadn't been so near it I wouldn't have gone through all that. You never know who you're close to in a terrace. Ideally, I wanted to live in a detached house, but that was way out of our budget. We were saving up for our own place anyway. Our new place seemed a good bet. There was an elderly lady living next door who seemed very decent and we had a little garden."

The couple were very happy with the move and after a week had completely settled in. Róisín's slumbers, however, continued to be disrupted. She had no trouble falling asleep after a hard day at the office, but seemed always to wake up too early in the morning – around the dreaded hour of five – then could not get back to sleep again.

"This is hard to describe," she says, "but since that night there seemed to be a dark cloud hanging over me. I thought it would disappear with the move, but it didn't. There was an oppressiveness in the air, no matter where I was – at home, at work, even when I was out enjoying myself with Michael or my mates. It was as if something was following me. Then odd things started to happen. Little things to start with."

The "little things" she refers to were easily enough discounted at first. Her photographs would be rearranged on the mantelpiece. Maybe Michael had done it, she reasoned each time, yet when she put it to him he denied it. An ornament would go missing and turn up again out of the blue. One morning she found the contents of the fridge lined up neatly on the kitchen table as though awaiting an inspection.

"Michael, I think there's something in this house. And I know you've noticed it too and you're pretending you haven't, just to spare me."

They were having breakfast. Róisín was exhausted as usual after another unsettled night.

"Look, you're not sleeping well and that can play tricks with your mind," he said. "Take the photographs, for instance. You might have rearranged them and not even been aware of it. Same with the fridge. You could have come down here last night for a drink and forgot to put the stuff back. You told me once that you were a sleepwalker when you were younger."

"That was ages ago. I *wasn't* sleepwalking. I know I wasn't. I hardly get any sleep for a start, let alone have time to rearrange pictures and clean out the fridge. You think I'm going loopy, don't you?"

"No, love. I don't think you're going loopy. But what I do know is that you need your sleep. Now take the day off and I'll call in to your boss on the way. Didn't you say you're always pretty slack at this time of the month?"

Róisín knew that protesting was futile, so she agreed, to keep the peace.

Michael left soon after and she climbed the stairs to the bedroom. It was the first time she'd been alone in the house and she felt a little uneasy.

She crossed to the window and opened the curtains. The rain was clearing, by the look of things, but it was going to be another grey day. Her new neighbour, Mrs Coyle, was putting bread out for the birds and she waved to her. It was good to have someone close by. Thus reassured, she drew the curtains again, and slipped beneath the bed covers.

She drifted into a light sleep, the sounds of traffic out on the main road fading away and taking her anxieties with them. A faint rumble from downstairs gave her a start, but it was only the fridge having one of its fits. She turned over and waited for sleep to come again.

Then there came a sound that could not be discounted. Róisín sat up immediately. She'd heard one of the downstairs doors creak open.

"Michael, is that you?"

He had his own key. Maybe he'd forgotten something. She got up and went out to the landing. She always closed doors. It was a habit from childhood. To keep the heat in, as her mother would say.

"Michael, are you there?"

Down the hallway the door to the living-room stood open. Even as she called out to Michael, she knew it couldn't be him – or anybody else. She'd put the chain on the front door after Michael left, and she saw that the chain was still in place. This fact alarmed her further.

There was someone, or something, in the front room.

She dashed back into the bedroom and slammed the door. What to do?

She'd ring her mother and ask her to come over. But her handbag was downstairs and her mobile was in it.

The doorbell rang. Thank God, she thought: maybe it's the postman! Her fear turned to hope and she rushed downstairs, making sure not to look through the open door of the living-room.

Old Mrs Coyle stood on the doorstep, holding a plate covered in tinfoil.

"I was just baking some scones and thought you'd like some."

"How very kind! Won't you come in for a cup of tea?"

She prayed Mrs Coyle wouldn't refuse. She really needed to face whatever was waiting for her in the front room and was not going to do it alone.

"Well, y'know I was just –"

"Please, it's no trouble and I could do with the company."

"All right, just a small cup then, dear."

"We'll sit in here," she said leading her through. "It's nicer."

There was no one in the room. There was nothing out of place as far as she could see. All seemed normal. All, that is, apart from the coldness. It was practically freezing.

Mrs Coyle hugged herself. "Oh, it's very cold in here. You need the heating on in this weather, dear."

"That's odd," Róisín said. The heating had come on an hour earlier and was not due to switch itself off for another hour. She crossed to the radiator. It was on full. "Oh, I forgot to turn this one on," she lied, trying to keep the fear out of her voice. "Let's have our tea in the kitchen."

After Mrs Coyle departed, Róisín left the house and spent the rest of the day at her mother's.

She returned home a half-hour before Michael. Her mother had set her mind at rest, and being out of the house helped her to put things into perspective. Imagination can play tricks when one is stressed and she'd been very stressed over the past few weeks. Her mother had also given her a novena to say.

Back at the house, she went into the front room again and all seemed normal. The chill had gone. She recited the prayer aloud and placed the leaflet on a small table beside the fireplace. She intended to recite it every day, and felt good that she was being proactive as opposed to feeling helpless.

"Nothing unseen can hurt you," her mum had said and Róisín knew she was right. Her biggest enemy at present was her own fear. With that in mind, she decided not to tell Michael about the door or the chilliness of the room.

She returned to work the following day and was glad of the distraction.

A week passed and nothing untoward happened. She said the novena faithfully every night and believed it was working. Little things continued to niggle her, however. Her keys or handbag might disappear and then show up again in the most unlikely places – in the airing cupboard or on top of the wardrobe. The doors she always closed before leaving the house would sometimes be open on her return. She tried to ignore these things by calling to mind her mum's wise mantra, and saying it aloud whenever she felt afraid: "*Nothing unseen can hurt me.*"

Then one evening something happened which simply couldn't be ignored or ascribed to an overactive imagination.

She had arrived home to an empty house. Michael's business hours didn't always tally with hers. Relieved, she noted that all the doors downstairs were shut, just as she'd left them that morning.

She went though to the kitchen and put the kettle on. As she waited for it to boil, she stood gazing out of the back window. It was a crisp March day and a sharp breeze was playing havoc with several lines of washing. Rain began spattering the windowpanes and she saw Mrs Coyle hurry out to rescue her own washing.

Róisín rushed out to help her.

"Wait, Mrs Coyle! I'll give you a hand."

The old lady turned from the clothes with a look of surprise. "Goodness me, dear! I thought you were laid up in bed."

Róisín frowned. "No, why would you think that?" She unpegged a couple of items and handed them to her. "I've just got in from work."

"That's odd. I thought I heard you going up and down the stairs and at lunchtime when I was putting the washing out, I saw you at the bedroom window in your nightdress. Well, at least I *thought* it was you. I waved but you just turned away. I knocked on the door, thinking you might need something, but you didn't answer."

A fret of fear gripped Róisín. What was the woman talking about?

"Must have been my ghost," she joked, but she could see that Mrs Coyle was serious.

"That's odd. I could have sworn it was you. Oh, well, I'd better be going. Got the bingo at seven."

"Right you be then. Hope you win."

Róisín returned indoors and sat down at the kitchen table. The electric kettle had switched itself off, but she no longer felt like having tea. What was Mrs Coyle talking about? How could she have seen her at the window? She'd been out all day. And how could she have heard somebody on the stairs? It was ludicrous.

As she sat contemplating the absurdity of it all she became aware of a strange smell. A smell of burning. She checked the cooker – needlessly, because she knew she hadn't turned it on. But the smell wasn't in the kitchen. It was in the hallway, and she followed it down the corridor. It grew stronger as she neared the living-room door.

What on earth was she going to find in there? But this was no time to waver. The house could be burning down.

She flung the door wide.

There was no fire, however. The room was just as it should have been, but the odour was overpowering. As if someone had been burning paper. Róisín had never lit the open fire; nor had the previous tenant; a pot of dried flowers sat in the grate. So where, she asked herself, was the smell of burning coming from?

She ventured in.

There was something on the little table to the right of the fireplace. She moved gingerly towards it.

She cried out in horror. The novena to the Divine Mercy, the one her mother had given her and which she'd

31

been reciting faithfully night upon night, lay burnt to a crisp beside the reading lamp.

She backed out of the room and slammed the door.

"You have to get Father Ryan to bless the house. I'll give him a ring. That's the best thing."

Róisín was at her mother's again, having fled the house. She'd rung Michael at work and was waiting for him.

"No way am I going to be there on my own again, Mum."

"Look, after the blessing everything will be as right as rain. Father Ryan is very powerful with that kind of thing. You don't know what happened in that house in the past, so it's best to be on the safe side."

But Róisín knew in her heart that the house had nothing to do with it. Ever since the night of the murder her life had not been the same. No, she decided, the house was neutral; she – and she alone – was being targeted. It was as if some mysterious force was pursuing *her*.

Father Ryan came the following evening. He was a stern man not given to small talk. Equipped with a prayer book and a bottle of holy water, he went from room to room, reciting prayers and making the Sign of the Cross. Róisín, her mother and Michael followed in his wake.

He left the blessing of the front room until last. Upon entering, he crossed to the small table where the remains of the burned prayer leaflet still lay. He prayed over it. Then, turning to the couple and blessing them both with holy water, he said the final prayer.

"Oh, Lord Jesus Christ," he intoned, "keep Róisín and Michael safe. Protect them from all harm and guide them by the light of your love, in the Name of the Father, and of the Son and of the Holy Spirit, Amen."

And that seemed to be that. He removed his stole.

"Well," he said, throwing a glance at the burned prayer. "You can do away with that ash now."

"Yes, Father," said Mrs McCabe. "We just thought it better to leave it there so you could see for your–"

"Yes, that was the thing to do, Mrs McCabe."

"I'll get the dustpan, so," she said, scurrying out.

Róisín always found herself to be both amazed and peeved at how docile her mother could become when within praying distance of a priest. She herself had given up on the Church a long time before, having had a surfeit of it during her schooldays.

"Father," she said, "d'you think things'll be all right now?"

"Well, that depends on yourself and . . ." – he turned his head – "your young man."

"Michael," said Michael.

The couple exchanged glances. Róisín's ire was rising. "On *us*? How on earth–"

"I think, Father, what Róisín means to say," Michael cut in, not wanting a tense situation to get worse, "is that we haven't done anything wrong. Róisín didn't invite all these ghostly things to visit her. She's not responsible."

"Even so. Are ye not living under the one roof now?"

"Yes, we are!" Róisín's anger had made her forthright. "And what's that got to do with anything?"

"Well, now, it's better to be married than living in sin. That's all I'm going to say and –"

Father Ryan didn't get to answer, because at that moment Mrs McCabe appeared, armed with the dustpan and shovel.

33

"I'll be off now," he said. "Keep up the prayers. That's all we can do."

Mrs McCabe dropped the dustpan in a fluster. "Oh, I'll see you out, Father. It was very good of you to come at such short notice." She took her purse from her handbag and followed him out to the doorstep.

Róisín wanted to scream but just about managed to remain calm until her mother, too, had departed a few minutes later.

"Typical!" she spat, venting her frustration on Michael. "Have these priests nothing better to do but interfere in people's private lives? Just because they're not allowed to marry means we *all* have to feel guilty." She stormed about the kitchen, preparing supper and rattling the pots and pans.

Michael listened quietly, knowing she had good cause to be upset.

"Look," he said, "I'm just as angry as you. But you know, maybe he's done some good here, so let's just wait and see."

Róisín relented. "Yes, I know," she sighed. "I'm sorry."

That same night she went to bed and slept soundly till morning. The next night was the same. Father Ryan's blessing was working. She regretted having ridiculed him. Four weeks went by without any further ghostly manifestations or audible bumps in the night. Róisín's life had returned to normal.

Or so she thought.

One night towards the beginning of April she woke with a great sense of unease. She was sure she'd heard something out on the landing.

She switched on the bedside light. The clock read 4.30 a.m. Michael was fast asleep beside her. She always envied his ability to fall into a deep slumber as soon as his head hit the pillow. A slumber that could only be broken by the alarm going off at seven.

She lay very still and held her breath.

She was convinced she'd hear it again. But there was nothing. The house was quiet but for its usual murmurings: water dripping through pipes, the wind at the window-pane, the hum of electrical appliances below in the kitchen.

Satisfied that she'd merely imagined the sound, she got out of bed to use the bathroom.

Before switching on the landing light, however, she noticed a seam of light coming from under the door to the spare room. Odd. Michael was obsessive about pulling out plugs and turning off all lights last thing at night. It was one of his better household habits. He must have overlooked it.

She pushed open the door and shivered. It was cold, but that was understandable: the heating was rarely turned on in the spare room – it was little more than a storage room. There were several cardboard boxes set along one wall. They contained bric-à-brac that she hadn't got round to unpacking.

One of the boxes was open. Strange, Róisín thought. They'd all been taped shut. Not unless Michael had been looking for something. She crossed over and got down on her knees to close it. But as she was getting up again she caught sight of herself in a wall mirror.

She tensed, senses alert.

She was not alone in the room; she knew that with a near-certainty. There was something "other" with her. She could feel it: a presence. A presence two or three feet behind her.

She tried to move but her body was so stricken with fear that she slumped back onto her knees again. She stared with horror at her image in the mirror. Her face was contorted in terror, her mouth open in a scream, but no sound emerged from her throat.

She tried to shut her eyes against her reflection, but couldn't. She was being held prisoner, yet again.

Slowly, behind her, a shape began to rise. A dark, murky shape as of roiling dense black smoke. It was swirling and swelling, rising higher and higher. Within seconds it was towering above her and had resolved itself into a form. The form of a huge man. It was the dark figure she'd seen in her bedroom the night of the murder. The figure she'd prayed would not come near her was right behind her.

Every nerve and sinew in her body was wrung tight. She was paralyzed. She couldn't move. She couldn't breathe. But she could *smell*.

The odour was overwhelming. She thought of the charred prayer. But this was not the smell of burning paper. It was worse than that. It was a strong, acrid stench mixed in with something like hearth smoke.

The last thing Róisín remembers was the image of herself disappearing in the mirror as she passed out.

Next she knew, Michael was standing over her, shaking her awake.

It was seven o'clock and the alarm had just gone off.

She'd been lying unconscious on the floor of the spare room for the best part of two hours.

"I couldn't stay in the house after that night," Róisín tells me. "I was always on edge and even more so when details of the murder in William Street started to come out. The poor girl was a foreign national. She was around my age and she'd been strangled. I was devastated."

She fingers a little pendant on a chain around her neck and smiles. "Then I was given this," she says. "The Caravaca Cross. It gives me protection and drove all that stuff out, but I had to go a long way to get it."

Róisín was on the verge of a nervous breakdown. But she resisted the urge to see a doctor. How could a doctor help her? Michael, driven to distraction himself, came up with a suggestion. A holiday, he reasoned, would do them both good.

"We'll go to Spain," he said. "We can stay with my Aunt Liz in Alicante. She has a big house there. She and my uncle bought it as a retirement home but he died last year. She'll be glad of the company. We can get a cheap flight so it'll cost next to nothing."

"If you think it's okay. . . ." she said. "As long as we're not imposing."

He laughed. "We won't be."

Aunt Liz picked them up at the airport. She was delighted to see her nephew and quickly made friends with Róisín. The three spent a lively weekend in the holiday town. Róisín almost forgot her ordeal. At least, she thought she had, until Liz took her to one side on the third day.

"There's something the matter, isn't there?" she said. "I can tell."

Róisín broke down. She had to confide in somebody, she said. No one but Michael would believe her.

But Liz did.

"Have you ever heard of Caravaca?" she asked.

"I haven't, no."

"It's about three hours' drive from here," Liz told her. "Up in the mountains. People from all over the place go there, on account of the cross. It's supposed to have great powers."

She went to a drawer, rummaged about, and returned with a small object. It was a gold crucifix but it differed in important respects from those Róisín had known from childhood. There were two crosspieces, one to which a miniature figure of Christ was affixed and another roughly halfway from the top to the foot. An angel stood on each side of the cross and appeared to be holding it.

"It goes back to the thirteenth century," Liz said. "The story goes that it was given to a priest who converted a Moorish king. This was when the Moors still ruled Spain."

"They were Muslims, weren't they?" Róisín said.

"That's right. They came across from North Africa." And she related the story of the cross and how it came to be given to the Moorish ruler of a province of Spain.

In or about 1231 a missionary named Father Gínes Pérez was travelling through the mountainous region of Murcia. His sacred duty: to convert the Muslim invaders to Christianity. In some respects he was successful. Yet he was fully aware of the dangers; proselytizing was a capital offence in Moorish Spain. Somewhere about March of that year the priest was captured red-handed, and brought to the royal palace at Caravaca.

Father Pérez feared the worst and made his peace with God. But the king, Zeyt-Abu-Zeyt, was intrigued by Christianity. He'd heard much about its rituals and wished to know more about them, perhaps even have one enacted in his presence. To this end he had Father Pérez summoned to his quarters and commanded him to say a Mass.

"I cannot," the priest told him. "I need my equipment for that."

King Zeyt had someone bring the priest what was needed, and all was assembled in due course: a chalice, a paten, a missal, bread and wine, and vestments. All that was missing was a crucifix. Without it, the priest said, it would be impossible to celebrate a proper Mass. A fresh search was made but to no avail: in the Moorish town there was no crucifix to be found. Disappointed, the king was about to dismiss the priest when he happened to look out of the window. To his amazement, he saw two angels descending from on high carrying between them a golden cross. Unlike the conventional cross it had an extra bar in the middle.

The miracles did not end there. It is said that Jesus himself appeared during the consecration as a beautiful little child. The king was so impressed he converted to Christianity that very day.

Liz placed the tiny object in Róisín's palm.

"There it is. They say that if you have a Cross of Caravaca you'll never die an unnatural death. That was my husband's. He died in his sleep, God rest him."

Róisín nodded and handed back the cross. Liz returned it to the drawer.

"But we'll get one for you, Róisín," she said. "We'll go to Caravaca and see Monseñor Ansaldo. You'll like him. He was a great friend of my husband's."

"We'd left Alicante behind us," Róisín says, taking up the story again, "and were travelling roughly south on the A7 motorway. It might have been anywhere, if it wasn't for the signs pointing us in the direction of places with names like Cartagena and Almeria. I'd only been to Spain once, years ago, when I went with two girlfriends to Torremolinos for a week. We didn't see much of Spain then, apart from the beach and the clubs.

"This was very different, of course, and I suppose one motorway is very much like another. Some of those Spanish drivers scared me half to death but Liz took it in her stride. She's a very good driver. My only quibble was that she had the air-conditioning on full the whole time and I nearly got frostbite sitting in the back. Michael laughed at that. Imagine somebody suffering from frostbite in Spain in August! So Liz turned it down for the rest of the journey.

"I honestly didn't know what to expect. Liz told us that her husband, Jaime, came from a place near Caravaca. His people were farmers and quite well to do. They'd met in Alicante when Liz was there on holiday and Jaime was on a business trip. It was all very romantic. He was a widower in his seventies; his wife had died about ten years before. He was into property in a big way so when they married they had the pick of the houses in the city. Liz's house, the one we were staying in, was to be their retirement home."

They left the motorway at Alcantarilla and headed west in the direction of Caravaca. In the distance rose the mountains, blue and purple in the summer heat haze. It was wild country, with little sign of habitation. Róisín considered that very little must have changed since the Moors ruled there all those centuries before. They passed a house set in something resembling a desert oasis, complete with palm trees. The house was blindingly white and its architecture owed more to North Africa than to southern Europe. It stood aloof in terrain that was becoming increasingly wild and rugged.

They skirted the town of Cehegín and a strange sight rose on their right. It was a huge sculpture of two white legs cut off at mid-calf. It was set incongruously on a mound in the middle of a roundabout.

"It's a monument to the workers of the area," Liz explained. "It's a man's foot and a woman's foot."

"I see," Róisín said, even though she didn't. She was beginning to feel that they were venturing into strange territory. It no longer bore any resemblance to the Spain she'd been accustomed to. No tourists, no brash billboards.

The Taibilla mountain range was rearing up ahead. It was mid-afternoon and the sun was creating a heat haze. Róisín was feeling as far removed from a dark, Limerick night as it was possible to be.

She'd no need to ask whether they'd reached Caravaca because the town had been rising out of the shimmering landscape for some time. As they drew nearer, Róisín could plainly see the Moorish citadel atop the hill the town had been built on. Its walls were of pale stone and looked as though they could have withstood any army ever ranged against them. Beyond the battlements she could make out an ornate church or basilica, and beyond that again what must have been a palace at one time. She'd been prepared for a spectacular place but the town and its beautiful mountainous setting almost took her breath away.

Liz negotiated the narrow streets with an ease that told Róisín she'd been here many times before. They climbed ever higher and soon the modern shops and houses made way for the medieval part of town. After a time Liz stopped the car in the shade of ancient fortifications. She pointed. A huge cross stood atop an old church. Its shape was unmistakable: the upright crossed by two bars instead of one. Except that here there was no figure of the crucified Christ, or of the two angels who'd brought the original cross to the palace of the Moorish ruler.

"That's the Church of the True Cross," she said.

"The monsignor's?"

Liz shook her head. "No, but he says Mass there on occasion. Especially when there's a High Mass. I've arranged to meet him in his parish house, if that's all right with you . . ."

Róisín assured her it was. She told me that she was having mixed feelings at that moment, and was nervous.

"The whole town seemed to be one big shrine," she says. "Everywhere you looked there were churches or statues. And the Caravaca Cross was everywhere. But it wasn't as commercialized as, say, Knock or Lourdes. You didn't see supermarkets selling holy pictures and rosary beads. I suppose it's because not that many people know about the cross. I know I didn't until I met Michael's aunt."

Monseñor Ansaldo was a charming, elderly priest: tall and thin with sleek silver hair. Róisín thought he reminded her of an old film star but was unable to remember who it was.

"He was very respectful," she tells me. "A real gentleman. He spoke very good English too and that put Michael and me at our ease. We'd expected that Liz would have to translate everything. But she'd phoned on ahead and the monsignor knew we were coming. He also knew a little bit about what had been going on in Limerick. He invited us to have coffee with him in the 'salon' as he called it."

It turned out to be a conservatory of sorts at the rear of the parochial house, half indoors and half in the open air. It was a place of great tranquillity. Few sounds of traffic permeated from the town and the garden was filled with birdsong. From time to time a church bell would ring, sometimes in the distance, sometimes close at hand.

Monseñor Ansaldo questioned Róisín very carefully on the nature of the ghostly manifestations she'd been experiencing. He became very agitated on learning that her "psychic" powers began to show themselves when she was no more than an infant. He seemed to think that this was significant. He asked her to describe as best she could what had occurred on the night of the murder, and the further manifestations she'd experienced in the spare room of her new home.

"I didn't want to go into a lot of detail," she says. "The memories were still very raw. But he pressed me to tell him as much as I could. He didn't actually use the word 'evil' when we discussed the black shape that was chasing after the white one, but I could see him frowning all the time and I think I guessed which way his thoughts were turning. So I came right out and asked him.

"Evil spirits?" he said. "Perhaps. We don't know much about such things. There are many things we cannot explain. But I do not think I would say 'evil', no."

Róisín was convinced that the kindly priest was trying to put her mind at rest. But he had a suggestion to make.

"We will go into the church," he said, "and I will give something to you that I know will help you. I gave one to my old friend, God have mercy on him." He was looking pointedly at Liz, and Róisín guessed what he was referring to.

"A cross?" she said.

He nodded, smiling. "*Sí, la Cruz de Caravaca*, the Caravaca Cross."

The church adjoined the parochial house. It was beautiful, Róisín recalls, an ornate building that represented the full flowering of the Spanish rococo style of architecture. Its interior was deliciously cool, a stark contrast from the still-hot afternoon sun. When they entered through a side door – Monseñor Ansaldo, Aunt Liz, Michael and Róisín – the church was deserted except for an elderly woman lighting a candle at a small shrine to the Blessed Virgin. She glanced around as the four entered, acknowledged the priest with a nod, turned, made the Sign of the Cross, and resumed her devotions.

Monseñor Ansaldo beckoned his visitors to follow him as he made his way to the central aisle. He genuflected before the altar; they did likewise. He opened the little gate and signed for them to enter the sanctuary.

"Please, wait here," he said. "I will be back in a moment."

Róisín watched him go to what she assumed to be the sacristy. He returned presently. A tiny, gold-coloured object glittered in his palm, its ornamentation reflecting the light that fell in through the stained-glass windows.

"Here it is," he said. "The Cross of Caravaca."

It resembled the one once owned by Liz's husband. It was much smaller, though: Róisín judged the cross itself to be no more than three or four centimetres in height. Its loop told her it was designed to be worn as a pendant.

With his back to the altar the priest took her right hand and placed the cross in her palm. He folded her fingers over it. He didn't need to speak; the gesture was unmistakable, no matter what the language. This was a valuable object and must be kept safe.

"Please kneel down," he said.

Róisín, Michael and Aunt Liz needed no urging. They knelt and bowed their heads, Róisín keeping her fingers pressed tight about the cross. So tight, in fact, that when she released them some time later she discovered a red, cruciform weal where the pendant had pressed down into her flesh.

Monseñor Ansaldo placed a hand lightly on her head. He began to pray aloud. The words were Spanish yet Róisín recognized them by their cadences and certain similarities to their corresponding English versions. They were the Glory Be, the Lord's Prayer and the Hail Mary. The latter were repeated several times. It was as the priest intoned the final "amen" that the situation in the church changed drastically. There was a sudden scream from close at hand.

"It was the old woman," Róisín says, and even several years after the event it's clear that the event disturbed her greatly. She fingers her Caravaca Cross nervously as she recalls it. "The woman who was lighting the candle. She let out an unmerciful screech and was shouting something I didn't understand. Liz told me later that she was blaming us, 'the foreigners' as she called us, for bringing something bad into her parish church."

The woman had left her place by the Marian shrine and was pointing upwards, above the heads of the priest and visitors. Róisín and the others followed her pointing finger.

"She was pointing up at a cloud of black smoke," she says, "of the kind I'd seen that night when I saw the figures, the one in white being chased by the one in black. I simply knew I was seeing the same thing. It had followed me there from Limerick.

"It seemed to hover right above where I was kneeling. It was swirling around and making darting movements, like it wasn't sure where to go. But it seemed to make its mind up and began making for the front door of the church. I heard the priest saying words in Latin or Spanish – I'm not sure which – but he seemed to be praying very rapidly. There was something frantic about the prayers and that scared me. In the meantime that woman was still shouting something."

To everyone's astonishment the black "cloud" passed through the stout timbers of the church door.

Róisín turned to the priest.

"What was that, Monsignor?" she asked.

She noticed that his normally dark face had gone pale. He was staring at the door and shaking his head. The elderly woman was heading for the side exit, the one the four had used to enter the church. They heard the door being shut. A stillness descended.

"I do not know," the priest finally answered. "But it cannot harm you now. It is gone."

The monsignor spoke the truth. Back at the parochial house he had the maid bring drinks. Nerves had to be calmed. Yet Róisín had felt a calm almost from the moment the black shape disappeared. It grew stronger with each passing minute.

She explains that the Spanish priest had no ready explanation for her ghosts. He assured her there are many "unseen things" in the world and could only advise prayer and devotion. Michael and Róisín returned to Limerick and could pick up the pieces of a life that had been disrupted by the paranormal.

"It never came back," she tells me. She reaches again for the pendant, looks at it lovingly and kisses it. "I put it down to this cross. I'm not in the least bit superstitious or anything but I can't deny the evidence of my own eyes. From the moment I got the cross my life was turned around. And I'm grateful for that."

No more ghosts?

"No, no more ghosts," she says with a smile. "They're history, thank God."

Endnote

On the night Róisín suffered her paranormal assault, a twenty-three-year-old East European woman was murdered close by in the same street. She'd come to Ireland in 1999 and was working as a waitress.

Her killer, a fellow national, had only been in Ireland a couple of months. At his trial in November 2004, it was alleged that he was trying to persuade the young woman to become a prostitute in Dublin. Her refusal "annoyed him" and led to her death.

The victim died from strangulation and head injuries at the time Róisín McCabe suffered her paralyzing attack. Róisín continues to wear the Caravaca Cross and there have been no further attacks.

2

The Little Shop of Hauntings

Fear of things invisible is the natural seed of that which every one in himself calleth religion.

THOMAS HOBBES, *Leviathan*

Gemma thought she was going mad. An understandable reaction to the impossible, the bizarre.

She'd left home at the usual hour: a few minutes after 8 a.m. It was a chill November morning when she set out and she hoped to reach the shop before the rain. One of the attractive aspects of her work was that it was just a short drive from her house. She was a woman who liked routine. She prided herself on the fact that she'd arrive at the shop at exactly the same time each and every morning, six days a week.

She would always be the first through the door. It was more than simply a duty for Gemma. She owned the jewellery shop. She was also proud of the fact that it was among the oldest existing businesses in Ballymena, County Antrim; it was established in the nineteenth century by an Englishman by the name of Goldsmith – no relation of the famous Irish writer. Gemma had always considered it to be curious that he'd gone into the jewellery trade; it was as though Mr Goldsmith had decided that his surname had "predestined" him to choose it.

The year was 1992. Gemma's brother Sam had bought the business a decade earlier. It had belonged to an elderly widow whose family had run it before the Second World War. The shop had enjoyed both good times and lean times, the latter primarily during the austerity period of the 1950s.

Sam branched out in 1990, opening a bigger jewellery shop in Belfast. He sold the Ballymena business to Gemma and her husband Donald. Gemma, in her forties, married with two children, had managed the shop for her brother before the purchase. She found the work fulfilling. Moreover, her son Thomas had trained as an engraver and joined her. It truly was a family business.

She'd nodded or called out a greeting to other retailers as she raised the steel grid on her shop front. It had two windows, one being devoted to rings and other jewellery, the other taken up largely with household ornaments and trophies. The latter was a speciality of the shop and Gemma was proud of the engraving skills she could offer, courtesy of twenty-year-old Thomas.

The day, a Monday in mid-November, had begun as any other. Gemma had busied herself in the shop before opening for custom. She'd gone from one display to another, making fine adjustments – she was very particular about things "being in their proper place". She'd checked the float in the cash register, satisfying herself that, on the off-chance somebody might wish to splash out several hundred pounds in cash on an item, she'd be able to offer the correct change.

At five or six minutes to nine, two others entered the premises: Gemma's son Thomas and Rita, the eighteen-year-old assistant whom Gemma was training in the trade. Rita opened the door to the public at nine o'clock sharp.

There had been no customers until a little after ten, when two schoolgirls wandered in, clearly browsing for no better reason than wasting time. Rita had followed them about and got rid of them quickly. A businessman called by some minutes later with a locket he wished to have engraved. Gemma took the order and passed it on to her son.

It was then that she discovered her handbag was missing.

Gemma is a creature of habit. And she had a place for everything, both at home and in the shop. Every morning she'd hang her coat and handbag on the stand just inside the door of the workroom at the back of the shop, and leave her car-keys on the little table next to it. She'd gone through those exact same motions that morning. Yet there was no sign of her bag – and the keys had disappeared as well. Puzzled, she turned back to her son.

"Thomas, have you seen my bag? And my keys?"

"No, Mum," he said without looking up from his desk. As usual he was hunched over a delicate piece of engraving, his big rod-stand lamp magnifier commanding all his attention. She admired his dedication.

Gemma was more perplexed than ever. "Was anybody in here?" she asked. "Besides Rita?"

"No, Mum. Maybe you took your bag out the front."

But she knew with certainty that she had not. All of a sudden she recalled the two young visitors to the shop earlier that morning: the girls who were most likely mitching from school. She went back into the shop.

"Rita, those two young girls who were in earlier . . . did they go into the backroom by any chance?"

"No, certainly not. I had my eye on them the whole time."

Gemma nodded. The assistant was simply confirming what she already knew.

"My bag's missing," she said. "It was . . ."

Her voice tailed off. Her eye had fallen on a shelf immediately behind Rita. *There* was her handbag, with her car-keys right beside it.

Rita must have seen her startled look because she turned round at the same moment.

"How did they get *there*?" Gemma asked.

"You must have put them there. *I* certainly didn't."

Without another word Gemma collected the bag and car-keys and returned them to their usual places.

The rest of the morning was uneventful. She went for lunch at her usual time and returned on the dot of two. No sooner had she taken up her station behind the counter than a young man came in. He wished to buy two wedding rings and already had the sizes. It would only be a matter of choosing the right design. He wanted something "out of the ordinary".

He finally settled on an elaborate pair of gold rings with an intricate design. Each would be engraved with the name of the wearer and the date of the wedding. Gemma promised the young man that the rings would be ready for collection in two days' time. She took them into the backroom for Thomas's attention, placing them in what she called the "in-tray".

A half-hour later, while both she and Rita were attending to customers, Thomas put his head around the door. He beckoned to her.

"Where's the other one, Mum?"

She didn't know what he was talking about. He showed her the docket.

"It says here you want two wedding rings done," he said, "but you only left the one in the in-tray."

His mother, having finished with a customer, joined him in the workroom. Sure enough, there was only one wedding band in the tray: the larger one. The bride's ring was nowhere to be seen.

"I left them both there together," she said.

Thomas chuckled. "I hope you're not going dotty on me, Mum," he said. "First you mislay your bag . . . now this."

"It's not funny, Thomas! I distinctly left *two* rings there."

"Maybe you only think you did . . ."

Gemma, her irritation growing, began a thorough search of her son's desk. She moved papers and other items to one side, began pulling out drawers and checking their contents.

No lady's wedding ring.

"I know I put it here," she said in exasperation. She heard the doorbell jangle twice. "Be a dear, son, and have another look, will you? I'm needed out the front."

Business was brisk that afternoon. Orders were placed, orders were collected. Rita sold an expensive pocket-watch to a clergyman. Gemma haggled with a councillor over a plaque for a commemoration ceremony. She served her fourth customer and opened the cash register to give him his change.

Lying on top of the stack of £10 notes was a wedding ring. It was made for a bride and had an elaborate design.

It was at that moment that Gemma wondered if she were going mad.

"That's not like you," Donald said, on learning that evening of his wife's predicament. "You're always so orderly."

"I know," Gemma said. "And I was as careful today as I always am."

"Maybe you're tired, love."

"I'm perfectly fine!" she shot back. She was still irked by what had happened, and more annoyed with herself than with anybody else.

She thought no more that evening about the curious events. Indeed, when she awoke next morning they were all but forgotten. She went through her unvarying routine and arrived at the shop at her usual time.

Trade was brisker than previous days. The run-up to Christmas was well underway. This was always the busiest time of year. Gemma enjoyed it; it kept her on her toes. She liked to keep herself busy. Marriage and raising a son and daughter had taken up a great deal of her time for many years. She was delighted to have returned to the workplace when she did. Her work fulfilled her.

She was quietly humming to herself about mid-morning when she went into the workroom to check on an order. Thomas was adding the finishing touches to a delicate piece of engraving. He looked up and smiled when she came in.

She was about to ask a question when, quite out of the blue, something very unusual occurred. There was a sudden crash. Or, rather, a series of crashes.

They came from a shelf close to where Thomas was sitting. Incongruously and bizarrely, cardboard boxes were tumbling from the shelf and bouncing off his desk. Two of them struck him before falling to the floor at his mother's feet.

"It was the weirdest thing," Gemma says, "because it was as if someone was standing beside the shelves and purposely throwing the things down one by one."

"My God!" was all she could say.

Thomas was on his feet. He was staring at the toppled boxes that were littering the desk and floor. Several had burst open and their contents were scattered. There were rings, watches, earrings, bracelets, necklaces, pendants and other valuable items. It was fortunate that most if not all had been wrapped in tissue paper or sturdy packaging, otherwise they'd have been scratched or damaged beyond repair. They represented a good part of the stock that Gemma had painstakingly catalogued the previous week in anticipation of the pre-Christmas trade. Horrified, she was down on her knees at once, sifting through the mess, trying to make order out of the chaos. Thomas helped her. Each saw that the other's hands were trembling.

"Christ, what was that, Mum?" he asked. "Was there a draught or something? How could they all be blown down like that?"

Gemma studied the door. It was tightly shut. She always shut it after entering the workroom; you never knew when prying eyes might want to look in there. She and Donald had talked about installing CCTV cameras in the shop and the workroom. But Thomas wouldn't hear of it; he told them he could never work comfortably with the feeling of being watched all the time. No argument could sway him.

"It wasn't a draught, son," she told him.

"Then what was it?"

"I haven't a notion."

Together they inspected the shelf but found nothing wrong; nothing that could have precipitated the fall of the boxes.

She said not a word to Donald that evening about the latest incident; she considered it prudent to keep it to herself.

But next day something else occurred that caused her to break her silence.

She opened up the shop as usual and, following her normal routine, went straight through to the backroom. But, as she was taking off her coat, her subconscious told her that something was amiss.

She looked around and stared in dismay at the rear wall.

The lower shelves were bare.

The shop had been burgled. It was the only explanation.

She went to the shelves and examined them at close quarters. She'd checked the inventory the previous day before locking up for the night; it was second nature to her. The shelves had been well stocked as always.

Suddenly afraid, her first impulse was to call the police. She went to the phone extension on Thomas's desk and picked up the receiver. She hesitated – and replaced it. It wouldn't do to have the RUC coming to her door with sirens wailing. Bad for business. She'd have to make sure it wasn't a false alarm.

A second door led off the workroom. Behind it were stairs that led down to a small corridor with storage space and a lavatory. She pushed open the door.

There were no signs of a break-in. The small window at the back – the one that was barred and always locked – was firmly shut. She switched on the light.

Lined up against the wall facing the toilet were the items that had gone missing from the shelves.

A chill ran through her. She dashed back up the stairs in a panic.

At that same moment Rita came through the door, furling her umbrella, on time as usual. She saw her employer was upset and wondered what was wrong.

"Rita, did you . . . did you move those things from the shelves?" Gemma stammered.

"No, of course I didn't. Maybe Thomas did it before he left. Are you all right, Gemma?"

But Thomas insisted that he hadn't moved the merchandise. All agreed that it was very mysterious.

The mystery was to deepen. In the course of the following days, items went missing from the backroom, to be found again in places where they should not have been. Gemma left her purse on a shelf for a moment and when she returned it had disappeared. Thomas found it in a drawer.

There were noises from the corridor beyond the workroom. Every time Thomas or his mother went to investigate, the noises would suddenly cease.

The incidents increased in number. By the end of the second week they were occurring almost every hour. Gemma had to face a bleak truth.

They had a ghost.

Things went from bad to worse in the ill-starred jewellery shop. There was trouble on two fronts: in the backroom and in the shop itself.

"It started to really upset us," Gemma says. "I was on edge all the time. It was as if something was trying to ruin the business and our reputation. And it had picked the busiest time of year so we'd lose custom at our most profitable time."

Gemma had hoped – and prayed – that the customers would not be involved or inconvenienced in any way. That was to change about two weeks before Christmas.

A gentleman called by with an expensive Rolex. It was decades old but in excellent working order. He wished to make his son a present of it but the boy's wrist was thinner than his own. He requested that some links be removed. Gemma asked him to call back at the end of the day, when it would be ready for collection. She wrote out a docket, went into the workroom and handed the watch to her son.

Two hours later she dropped by to check on another order. She was surprised to see that the docket was still where she'd left it but there was no sign of the watch.

"Where's the Rolex, Thomas? Did you manage the links?"

"It should be there with the rest, Mum."

But it wasn't. This, thought Gemma, is getting beyond a joke. She searched the desk, and the rest of the surfaces in the room, aided by her son. No Rolex.

"We have to find it!" she exclaimed. "He's calling for it at five. Oh, my God! Are you sure you didn't take it out to the shop?"

"I'm sure."

It was no use. They combed every square inch of the premises to no avail. At five o'clock the gentleman returned.

Gemma had to think quickly.

"I'm sorry," she told him. "I know I promised it today but my team is under a lot of pressure."

He was understanding, and agreed to call in again the following day, at the same time. When he did, once again Gemma had to disappoint him. Could he wait another day?

"If I'd known that, I'd have taken my custom elsewhere," he said curtly.

Gemma knew she'd lost a customer.

The Rolex did in fact show up the following day. Thomas found it. Incongruously, impossibly, it had found its way to the bottom of a waste-paper basket.

The ghost was getting out of hand. It turned its attention once again to the shelves and to the back corridor.

All that week, banging and crashing was heard coming from the rear of the shop. It came seemingly out of thin air; no cause was ever found. Thomas was forced to wear headphones and listen to music to block out the din.

The customers could also hear it plainly. Time after time, Gemma and Rita had to pretend they had workmen in carrying out some renovations.

And items continued to go missing. Like the Rolex, many were the property of customers, who wished to have engraving done or small repairs made. A particularly fine engagement ring was missing for days. Its owner threatened to go to the police until Gemma persuaded her that her ring was simply "mislaid" and would show up. It finally did, but not before the customer had spread the word throughout Ballymena that the jewellery shop was "bad news".

Business was badly hit. So badly in fact that Gemma wondered if the shop would survive at all. Drastic measures were called for.

Gemma and her husband Donald are evangelical Christians. She places much store in orthodox belief and is deeply mistrustful of occurrences that seem to lie outside the mundane. In 1992 she had never even considered the possibility that ghosts could exist.

She had to face it now. Donald was in agreement.

"It's not you, love," he told her. "It's the shop. Something isn't right. I think we should get somebody in to look at the place."

"What are you saying? What kind of 'somebody'?"

"Well, we could do worse things than call in a clergyman to say a wee prayer or two."

Gemma didn't at all like the direction the conversation was taking. It was bad enough coping with the shenanigans in the jewellery shop; now Donald seemed to be implying that there could be something *evil* about them, that they required a visit from a clergyman. He saw her disquiet and did his best to ease it.

"That's not what I mean at all," he told her. "My father used to say that ghosts are nothing more than the spirits of unhappy people. He'd say that sometimes the spirits aren't able to adjust to their new surroundings and they kick up a fuss to get our attention. A bit like a child throwing a tantrum when he's out of sorts. So what we have to do is have someone say a few prayers for the ghost. Then he'll leave you in peace."

Gemma was satisfied with that. She would, she told Donald, make a few discreet enquiries among her friends on the church committee. Somebody would know what to do.

Somebody did: her old friend Millicent Smith, who seemed to know everybody within a fifty-mile radius of Ballymena.

"There's a lovely man in Randalstown," she told Gemma. "Very spiritual but very open-minded as well. He does this sort of thing all the time. I'll give him a ring if you like."

Gemma drove to see Reverend John Parris at his home and gave an account of the phenomena that had visited the jewellery shop. He asked whether she'd experienced anything out of the ordinary in her home.

She was prepared for that. "That's the first thing my husband asked, Reverend. He thought I was seeing things or being forgetful. I thought the same thing myself. Until there was so much happening that I knew I wasn't imagining it. And my son saw it too. He heard those noises, and those boxes just seemed to fly off the shelf and strike him."

"It sounds as though it could be a poltergeist," Parris said. "You'll have heard of them, I suppose. They like to play games."

"Is that what *you* think it is, Reverend?"

"I can't say. It could be a number of things. I'd need to pay the shop a visit. You won't mind if I bring a friend, will you? She's what's called a 'woman of discernment'. That means she's blessed by the Lord with the gift of discernment, that she can see things which are hidden from the rest of us. She helps me quite a bit."

Gemma assured Reverend Parris that his friend would be most welcome. She left the house in Randalstown an hour later, with the promise that the minister would journey to Ballymena that coming Friday evening, after the shop had closed for the day.

Christmas was approaching fast. Whatever it was that was disturbing her life and upsetting her trade, Gemma wanted to be rid of it.

Reverend Parris introduced the woman simply as "Thea". Gemma suspected it was short for Anthea. But it's actually an abbreviation of Dorothea, which is Greek for "gift from God", a most apt name for this unusual lady.

I learn this from Reverend Parris, a Church of Ireland clergyman, when I call on him at his home. Although more than a decade has passed since his visit to the haunted jewellery shop in Ballymena, he recalls it with immense clarity. It is he who takes up the story from the time Gemma returned home.

"I telephoned Thea that very night," he tells me in his gentle voice. "We travelled quite a bit about the country in those times. I don't know why but there seemed to be a lot going on that required our prayers."

I judge the Reverend to be close to seventy. He's a fit-looking individual, very refined and with impeccable manners. There's an air of quiet confidence about him – and something indefinable, which I read as spirituality.

I ask first about Thea, intrigued as I am by this unusual ghost-busting team: a Protestant priest and a mystic. He smiles at my use of "mystic".

"It's a common misconception," he says, "that the Christian Church frowns on such things as the discernment of spirits. The fact is that you'll find it mentioned in many places in Scripture. What we as Christians have to remember is that God frowns on such practices as divination, which is trying to foretell the future through cards, Ouija boards and the like. But discernment is a gift from the Holy Spirit and it's only through the Holy Spirit that a person can discern the higher realities. That's what Paul was getting at when he said, 'Do not put out the Spirit's fire; do not treat prophecies with contempt.' He said we should test everything and 'hold onto the good'. By that he meant that we shouldn't reject out of hand what we don't understand."

Thea, Parris tells me, is quick to shrug off her "talent" as nothing more than a gift bestowed on her quite at random, and undeserved. Sometimes the gift of "second sight" is passed down from mother to daughter but he assures me that Thea alone of her family was so "honoured", as he puts it.

"We went to Randalstown as arranged," he continues. "We met Gemma and her husband in a nearby hotel, had a coffee and went to the shop from there. There was still a good bit of activity in the street, many shops being open late because Christmas was on the way."

The shop was silent when Donald let the four in a little after 8 p.m. He didn't switch on the lights in the shop but went instead to the rear and opened the door to the workroom. He turned on the lights there and beckoned to the others.

"It was all a bit melodramatic, I suppose," Parris says, "but Gemma didn't want to attract any attention. There were still a lot of townspeople about and it would have looked a wee bit odd to have a minister going into the shop at that time. You know how people talk. Poor Gemma. She was having a hard enough time of it as it was, without having more tongues wagging."

The Reverend had decided to perform a full Eucharist in the workroom. Having learned from Gemma the extent of the paranormal activities, he thought it merited the sacrament. As far as he was concerned the manifestations were the work of a troubled spirit and he intended to pray for the soul of that departed individual.

I ask whether he at any point suspected that evil forces were at work. He is almost certain that this was not so.

"We must never rule out that possibility," he says, "but from what Gemma told me there didn't appear to be any real ill will against her and the others. Nothing that you'd call malevolent. It seemed to me that whatever it was that was behind the upset, it had set out to annoy – to irritate – rather than to attack or cause accidents. Nobody got hurt, thank God. There was a lot of inconvenience but nobody got hurt. It's worth bearing that in mind."

There was a big round table in the workroom. Gemma and Donald tidied it up in preparation for the Eucharist. It would be a simple affair. The Reverend took from his bag his wooden cross, prayer book, bread and wine.

In effect, Reverend Parris was about to perform a deliverance. An entity, which he believed to be one of the so-called "restless dead", would be prayed for – and politely asked to leave the jewellery shop. There is not much difference between deliverance and exorcism. It's generally held that exorcism is largely a Roman Catholic rite, and that there are two forms: the solemn and the simple. The first is used when it's believed that malevolence is present; the second is by far the more common, and can range from the blessing of a religious object to prayers said over a troubled individual. The deliverance is used principally by non-Catholics. It differs from the simple exorcism only in name.

The stage was thus set. Reverend Parris requested that the doors be left open for the ceremony: the door leading out to the shop and that leading to the rear corridor. As he explained it, there should be nothing to bar the passage of the unquiet spirit when it could be persuaded to depart.

Although she did not reveal them to Gemma and her husband, Thea later gave an account to Parris of the sensations she felt that evening as they prepared to begin the Eucharist. In fact, she'd picked up certain psychic impressions almost as soon as she'd entered the premises. They disturbed her.

"She was getting impressions of pain and suffering," the reverend tells me. "There was also death, and children seemed to be involved in some way. That's how it works with Thea – her images and impressions are very vague and unclear. She picks up more sensations and feelings than anything else."

The service began. Reverend Parris recited the prayers and the three others supplied the responses. The sounds from the street outside the shop were subdued by this time and an atmosphere of serenity seemed to descend on the little group gathered around the table.

But some moments after the consecration of the bread and wine, the Reverend felt a cold draught on the nape of his neck. He'd placed himself with his back to the door leading to the rear corridor.

"I have to say the hairs on the back of my neck stood on end when I felt that breeze," he says. "All the windows were shut and it couldn't have had a natural cause. But there was worse to come. I distinctly heard footsteps coming up the stairs behind me. They were heavy as if made by a big, burly man. I said a quick, silent prayer and continued with the Eucharist."

Unknown to Reverend Parris, however, the ghostly tread on the stair was not the full extent of the haunting. Thea was standing with an uninterrupted view of the doorway. She'd tell him later what it was she saw – and felt.

"It was the figure of an old man," he says. "Not very tall and not very distinct. She said it was wearing a hat; she was very certain of that. She said that it came through the doorway and stopped right behind me. I was completely unaware of it, as were Donald and Gemma. Thea said that she felt what she called 'antipathy' coming from the figure. Not hatred or anything approaching evil, mind you. Antipathy: as though it was annoyed with us. She says that it seemed to fade away slowly again. It couldn't have been there for more than a minute or two."

The rest of the deliverance progressed without incident. When it was over, Reverend Parris and his associate took their leave and returned to Randalstown. The following Monday he received a phone call from Gemma. She was jubilant. The ghost that had plagued her shop for so long was gone. She reported that the atmosphere in the rear of the premises seemed transformed; even her son Thomas seemed brighter and more cheerful as he went about his work.

Christmas came and went. The jeweller's shop thrived. Nothing went missing any more. Customer confidence was restored. The hauntings were behind them.

What exactly had caused the disturbances in the first place remains an unanswered question. Yet there are clues. In the days that followed the deliverance, Reverend Parris looked into the history of the building that housed the jewellery shop with the aid of old borough archives. He discovered that towards the close of the nineteenth century a medical doctor had practised there. It was a tenuous link, and one that, on the face of it, had nothing to do with the paranormal activity.

"You'd think that, wouldn't you?" Parris says. "But the thing is that Thea and I discussed what she'd experienced that evening and it was most interesting. She received the definite impression that that doctor's surgery had been used for illegal operations, including abortions. Whether it was the doctor who performed them or somebody else – somebody unqualified – it was impossible to say."

I wonder if it's possible that whatever it was that was tormenting Gemma had its origins in those operations. The Reverend seems to think so.

"There was certainly an unhappy soul involved," he says. "I believe it has found its rest now. That, at least, is my fervent prayer."

3

Edel Delahant and the Family Poltergeist

The attribution of poltergeist phenomena to PK [psychokinesis] is rather like explaining one unknown in terms of another unknown. Parapsychologists know so little about the limitations of PK that they simply are unable to say whether or not it is plausible to accommodate the variety of poltergeist activities under the concept of PK.

HARVEY J IRWIN AND CAROLINE WATT
in *An Introduction to Parapsychology* (1989)

Poltergeist, parapsychology, psychokinesis – three words: each rather long and each beginning with "P". They have something else in common, as Irwin and Watt noted: they deal with unknown quantities.

Parapsychology is the study of the paranormal, in other words that which lies outside the sphere of orthodox psychology. There are many who regard it with suspicion. As well they might. For, despite the best efforts of the parapsychologists, the type of phenomena they study stubbornly refuses to allow itself to be weighed, measured and classified in the laboratory.

Psychokinesis is the mind's ability to affect matter in the external world. In other words, the movement of objects from one place to another by the power of one's mind alone.

Psychokinetic activity is most usually associated with that oddest of ghosts, the poltergeist or "noisy spirit". The Hungarian-born psychoanalyst Dr Nandor Fodor, who was a colleague of Sigmund Freud for a time, did not even consider the poltergeist to be a ghost proper. He called it "a bundle of projected repressions".

"What would you say," Gerry Delahant began, "if I was to tell you I've asked Granddad to move in with us?" He looked from one girl to the other. "It wouldn't be permanent."

The dreaded moment had arrived. The girls, by rights, had no say in the matter. Susie was eleven and Molly was nine. By rights they had to do what their parents told them. But Gerry and Edel Delahant were not the sort of people who laid down the law with their children. Both in their early thirties, they believed in the minimum of discipline, and favoured gentle persuasion above draconian measures. "My girls are my friends," Edel would say proudly. "It's always been like that. No 'spare the rod, spoil the child' as far as I'm concerned."

The formula seemed to have worked very well. Susie and Molly were loved by all and sundry. Their teachers had nothing but praise for them; they consistently came top in their respective classes. They were extremely well behaved and had never given their parents any trouble.

"Granddad Delahant?" Susie asked.

"Yes, of course," Edel said. "Who else?"

Her own father was well able to take care of himself. More than that: he was one of the healthiest men she knew. Not yet sixty, he'd been a keen sailor all his life. As had Edel's mother. The two lived for the outdoors. As soon as Edel, the last of the children, left home, her parents had fulfilled a long-cherished dream. They'd bought a boat – or "yacht" as her mother liked to call it – and were on a more or less permanent holiday. The last she'd heard from them, they were moored in a harbour in Panama and having "a wonderful time".

Granddad Delahant was otherwise. He was considerably older; in 2003 he was seventy-one. He'd married late and had only one child, Gerry, born when his mother was forty-two. Tragedy had struck a year later when she was diagnosed with cancer. She died soon after Gerry's first birthday.

Stricken with grief, his father had not remarried. His own health seemed to go downhill after that. He developed osteoporosis as a result of an unhealthy lifestyle; and hyper-calciuria, which led to a further deterioration in his bones. It was inevitable that he'd be confined to a wheelchair. He managed to cope for several years, and learned to fend for himself, with a carer coming in twice a week.

But it wasn't long before Gerry was summoned by the GP he shared with his father. The doctor presented him with a stark choice: either Mr Delahant senior must be admitted to a hospital or care home, or Gerry must make other arrangements.

The Delahants live in a detached, two-storied house in the west of Dublin City. Theirs is a pleasant street; the houses were built during the 1950s, and the trees are mature; there's an air of suburban refinement.

What sets the Delahant house apart from its neighbours is an enormous front window to the left of the hall door. It spoils the symmetry. It extends to ground level and has a sliding patio door. A ramp slopes gently from the doorway to the driveway, which is, I note, paved over completely.

"We had it done for my dad," Gerry tells me with some pride. "Edel and I discussed the best solution for him. We could have built a granny flat out the back but Edel wouldn't hear of it. She was very attached to my dad; she didn't want him having to come in and out like he was a persona non grata, somebody we were ashamed of."

Edel shows me the section of the house they'd had converted in order to accommodate Granddad Delahant's needs. It is extensive. It consists of a wonderfully bright front room, a kitchen and an en-suite bedroom. I notice that the doors are wider than is usual.

"Yes, we had to widen all the inner doors to give him wheelchair access," Edel says, and goes on to tell me that the kitchen and bathroom fittings had to be at a certain height.

I remark that the whole thing must have a cost a fortune.

"It wasn't cheap," she assures me. "But Granddad sold his house and we were able to build this for him. He still had a sizeable amount left in the bank. So everybody was happy."

She says the last with a wistful look. The happiness she alludes to was not always present in the house. The coming of Mr Delahant Senior, through no fault of his, was to have devastating consequences for the family.

Granddad's arrival did not cause as much disruption as Edel had expected. This was due in part to the fact that his moving in coincided with an end to a month and more of noise. The conversion was supposed to take three weeks at most but, as so often happens, circumstances beyond the builder's control delayed its completion.

The girls had almost got used to the noise of sawing, hammering, drilling, sanding and more. It isn't easy for a child to accept that her home is undergoing a dramatic change. It upsets her equilibrium. But Susie and Molly took it in their stride. By the time they got home from school each day the bulk of the work was usually over, and the workmen were careful to keep out of the main part of the house.

Gerry and Edel instructed the girls in the importance of privacy for their grandfather. His "space" was private and should no longer be considered as part of their home. They weren't to trespass and should enter it only when invited. They understood.

Granddad, for his part, was delighted. He loved Edel dearly and his grandchildren, if possible, even more. He was pleased with the freedom the house gave him. His wheelchair was motorized. He could literally drive it from his bedroom down to the corner shop to collect his morning paper without bothering anybody. And he could entertain in his front room. He moved in at the beginning of September when the evenings were still bright, and he could leave the sliding door open while he listened to the radio or read a book.

There was only one blot on the landscape: when it came to snoring, Granddad Delahant was in the champion league.

Nobody had noticed it when he lived alone, for the simple reason there was nobody to hear it. But Granddad's bedroom was immediately below nine-year-old Molly's. She awoke on the night of his arrival, not knowing what had disrupted her sleep.

She went out onto the landing. The noise was even worse there. Her bedroom was at the back of the house; those of her parents and sister were at the front. She was getting the full brunt of her grandfather's snoring. She went and woke her sister.

"What's that noise?" she asked.

"Somebody's snoring," Susie told her. "It must be Granddad."

It wasn't long before the girls roused their mother. She shook Gerry awake.

"The girls can't sleep," she said. "You'll have to do something about Granddad."

"What can I do? Hit him over the head with a hammer?"

The girls giggled.

He climbed out of bed with great reluctance. "All right, I'll see what I can do."

Which wasn't much. Gerry found his father lying on his back. The snores were deafening. He gently prodded him awake. Granddad confessed surprise that he snored. He promised he'd try to sleep on his side in future.

Edel made the children mugs of hot chocolate. Some time later, all had retired for the night again. Granddad's snoring started up once more, as loud as ever.

Things had got off to a bad start. Edel wondered if sharing her home with her father-in-law was such a good idea after all.

Next day, in the warm light of morning, when the girls were off to school and Gerry had left for the office, Edel had a friendly chat with Granddad in his kitchen. He was suitably contrite and apologized for the trouble he'd caused. Edel was as understanding as she could be. It wasn't his fault, she told him. People snore. It's a fact of life; Gerry snored at times, as did her own father.

But few snorers could "raise the roof" as Gerry's father did. In the days – and nights – that followed, the new "lodger" fast became a nuisance. He would disrupt Molly's sleep, always at roughly the same time: a little after two in the morning. She'd follow the pattern of the first night and go to wake Susie, and the girls would in turn wake their parents. By Saturday Edel was at her wits' end. They were due to do the weekly shop and she decided to use the opportunity to call a "council of war" as she put it. Granddad Delahant was back at the house, oblivious to the discussion. The four went to their favourite restaurant and takeaway. Over their meal they aired their grievances.

"The girls can't sleep, Gerry," Edel said. "They're tired every day and their schoolwork is suffering."

This was true. She was hearing concerned reports from teachers. Molly and Susie were displaying a listlessness that was new to her.

"So what can we do?" he said. "I can hardly ask Granddad to leave."

"I'm not saying he should leave. That would be cruel. Besides, it would be madness after the amount of work we put into his flat – not to mention the expense. I can't see us asking the builder to come round again and put everything back to how it was."

"I agree," Gerry said. "That would be madness."

"Can't Granddad take something?" Susie asked. "For his snoring."

"I'm sure there must be something all right," her father said. He turned to Edel. "We should look into it. There's a chemist here in the centre. We can ask what they have."

As it turned out, the pharmacist presented the Delahants with a bewildering choice of remedies. There were several nasal sprays that alleviated congestion at the back of the throat; there were herbal preparations that could be used as a steam bath before bedtime. Gerry bought them all. It didn't break the bank and it might, he thought, be the difference between war and peace in the home.

Granddad was happy to go along with the experiments. He'd become a changed man since moving in with the family. His quality of life had improved enormously, and he wasn't prepared to jeopardize that for the sake of a little matter like snoring.

But nothing worked. The snoring was as loud as ever. Tempers began to fray.

In desperation, Edel sought other alternatives. She consulted her GP, who recommended a mouth-guard that would keep Granddad's mouth shut at night so that he'd only breathe through his nose. It helped a bit. The doctor advised losing weight and getting more exercise but conceded that that might not be easy for a man in a wheelchair. Granddad's blood pressure was normal therefore not the cause of the snoring. Yet the GP warned that sleep apnoea could lie at the root of the problem. Given Granddad's age, it might be dangerous. There was a chance – a small chance, the doctor added hastily – that he could stop breathing and die in his sleep.

Another week went by before Edel hit on what she thought would be the perfect solution. She happened to be passing a bedding shop in the city centre when her eye fell on orthopaedic mattresses and pillows in the window. She went in.

The assistant was very helpful. She suggested to Edel that Granddad was probably lying on his back much of the night, a position that would cause his mouth to hang open and mean that he breathed less through the nose. She explained that it was next to impossible to get the sufferer to change to sleeping on his side. Instead, the so-called "snoring pillow" was designed to bring the head in line with the spinal column. The throat muscles are therefore no longer obstructed and the vibration that leads to snoring is lessened.

It was worth a try. The purchase of a single pillow could ensure that five people got a good night's sleep.

Granddad put the orthopaedic pillow through its paces on a Tuesday night. By that time he'd been lodging with the Delahants for twenty-two days and as many nights.

It seemed to produce some highly unusual results.

Molly was awoken at the by-now-depressingly-expected hour of two in the morning. But not on this occasion by Granddad's snoring. Molly felt someone pinch her cheek.

At first, still half asleep, she thought it must be her sister playing a silly game.

But when it happened a second time she shouted at her and opened her eyes – only to discover there was no one there.

She screamed, jumped out of bed and rushed into her parents' bedroom. Edel was already awake. From below came the sounds of snoring but seemingly less noisy than on previous nights. The orthopaedic pillow was working to some extent.

"Somebody nipped me, Mammy!" Molly whispered.

"You were dreaming."

"No, I wasn't."

At that moment there came a loud thump from downstairs. It was followed quickly by another. They heard more thumps. They seemed to be occurring at regular intervals.

"What's that, Mammy?"

"I don't know. We'll go and see, will we?"

"Should we wake Daddy up?"

"No, he has a busy day tomorrow."

Mother and daughter shut the bedroom door and went to the stairs. They were no more than halfway down when a door opened behind them. It was Susie, likewise awoken by the heavy thumping. She joined them.

The commotion appeared to be coming from behind the door to Granddad's quarters. Edel padded towards it. Uneasy but trying not to show it, she pressed down on the door handle. Gingerly, she pushed it open.

The curtains were fully drawn in the room, yet such was size of the wide window that the streetlights easily illuminated the interior. The thumps were loud and it was clear what was making them. The wider door to Granddad's kitchen was swinging back and forth.

"Stay there," Edel told the girls.

She was feeling less courageous than she pretended to be. As she drew closer to the door she could plainly see that no human agent was causing it to swing open and shut. As Edel watched, the door thumped against the spring stop mounted on the skirting in the living-room. The spring sent it returning with equal force so that it thumped against the corresponding spring set in the kitchen skirting. It was like watching some sort of game or a perpetual motion machine.

Edel plucked up more courage. She held out a hand and allowed the door to swing against it. It stopped. Cautiously, she pushed it open again and stepped into the kitchen. A feeling of relief swept over her.

The kitchen window was open. Her relief, however, was edged with disquiet. Granddad did not open windows. Well, he couldn't really, given his incapacity. Edel had no memory of opening the kitchen window during the day. Furthermore it was a calm night with no wind to speak of. Still, maybe Gerry opened it. And besides, new doors take a while to settle.

She crossed to the window and shut it gently. From behind the door at the far end came the rhythmic but somewhat muted snoring of Granddad. She was glad the noise hadn't disturbed him.

"Edel?"

It was Gerry. He'd come down the stairs in his dressing-gown. The girls ran to him.

"What's going on?" he asked.

"Nothing," she told him. "Did you hear the door banging?"

"The hall-door?"

"No, *that* one, Daddy!" Susie said, pointing at the now-closed swing door. "It was opening by itself."

"Maybe it's a ghost," Molly said. "The one that nipped my cheek."

Susie giggled at her sister. "You're silly."

"You were dreaming, sweetheart," Edel said.

"Well, if it's a ghost he'll just have to come during the day," said Gerry with a yawn. "I've a busy day tomorrow."

Gerry did indeed have a busy day following the night of the thumping door. Edel got the children off to school and returned to find that Granddad had risen and was enjoying the sunshine streaming through his patio doors. He was oblivious to anything untoward. He'd slept through the entire incident.

"You didn't by any chance open the kitchen window?" Edel asked. "Before you went to bed, that is?"

He gave her an odd look. "Now why would I do the like of that?"

Edel explained about the thumping door. "The strange thing is," she said, "there was no wind last night. It was very calm, but the door was swinging back and forth."

"Well, I didn't open any windows. There must be a draught," he suggested.

"A draught. And where would it come from?"

"What about the extractor above the cooker?" He was clutching at straws and they both knew it. Edel was testing the door, swinging it lightly to and fro. "That would be connected to the chimney so you might get a vacuum. That would pull the door open."

But Edel wasn't buying it. She'd seen what she'd seen. No draught had caused that. Considerable pressure would have been needed to swing the door open and shut with such force.

She put the kettle on for tea. Granddad was glad to hear that the "snoring pillow" was helping, if only to a small degree. They discussed other measures. He brought up the possibility of surgery. Edel told him it was too drastic a step; she'd read about complications arising from the procedure and it seemed to her that the cure might be worse than the complaint. No, they'd see how it went with the pillow; perhaps its effectiveness would increase over time. . . .

She wasn't prepared to discuss the possibility raised by young Molly. That there could be a ghost in the house.

The thumping door was only the beginning. The following night, Molly was once again roused from sleep by someone tweaking her cheek. She opened her eyes in fright and ran to her sleeping parents a second time.

"At first of course we didn't believe her," Edel says. "We put it down to a bad dream or just stress at having Granddad in the house, but then other strange things started happening and I realized there was far more to it, unfortunately."

To the consternation of all, the swinging door and the ghostly pinching were followed by a spate of very unusual occurrences, all centring on Molly.

First, her bedside lamp switched itself on – or so Molly claimed. She swore to her mother that she hadn't touched it. Next, the bulb in the lamp exploded into tiny pieces. Since both events happened during the day, Edel discounted them as no more than the children playing tricks on each other. However, a subsequent incident could not be explained away.

Edel and Gerry were awoken one night by screaming coming from Molly's bedroom.

Gerry was the first to enter her room. He switched on the main light, to be confronted by a very perplexing scene. His younger daughter was sitting on the floor, fists held under her chin, eyes wild, crying and shaking. The bed had been stripped. But instead of the bedding being on the floor, it was neatly folded on a chair in a far corner of the room. Molly's teddy – the one she always slept with – was sitting on top.

"A ghost pulled me out of bed, Mammy!" Molly cried as Edel tried to comfort her.

"I'll check on Dad," Gerry said. "God knows, maybe he was sleep-walking, but I doubt it."

Halfway down the hallway it was obvious he didn't even need to enter his father's quarters. Granddad's snoring put paid to that idea. Gerry went back upstairs.

Susie had entered the room by then. She seemed wide awake. She was less frightened than her sister, but only marginally.

"Is it a ghost, Daddy?" she asked.

"There's no such thing as ghosts," he told her.

It took a while to settle the girls again. Molly refused to sleep in her own bed, so went to Susie's room. The couple retired again. Gerry fell asleep almost immediately, but Edel lay awake for some time wondering what was going on. Molly did not make up things and she'd been truly terrified. Had she simply fallen out of bed? It had never happened before. But if she had, it still didn't explain the neatly folded bedding and the teddy. Who had done that? Billy the Teddy rarely left her arms while she slept.

So many questions and no ready answers.

Eventually Edel drifted into a fitful sleep.

A couple of hours later she was awake again. In an attempt to ease her mind she decided to check on the girls. Thankfully, they were both fast asleep. She was about to get back into bed when she thought she heard something: someone moving about downstairs. Tiptoeing back onto the landing, she stood at the top of the stair and waited.

Silence.

She took a few tentative steps down the stairs.

Still nothing.

She sighed with relief and turned. Only then did she hear it.

It was coming from the direction of the kitchen. Someone was opening and closing the cupboard doors. Edel caught her breath, fear growing. It couldn't be Granddad. He had his own kitchen. But maybe . . .

She rushed back up the stairs and shook Gerry awake. He was none too pleased at his sleep being disturbed for a second time.

"I think there's somebody in the kitchen," she whispered.

"Oh yeah, the bloody ghost again no doubt," he said getting up.

"Look, it could be a burglar."

Gerry kept a set of dumb-bells under the bed. He picked one up. "Right, one of these will sort him out."

They crept down the stairs. Outside the kitchen door they stood listening.

"I don't hear any –" Gerry began.

"Shush! Listen!"

Then they both heard it. The sound of someone pulling open a drawer and the rattle of cutlery.

Gerry burst through the door, dumb-bell raised. Edel threw the light switch. There was no sign of anybody, burglar or otherwise. The windows were closed, the glass intact.

Gerry lowered his improvised weapon. Edel gave out a cry and pointed.

Scattered on the draining-board were the entire contents of the cutlery drawer.

Moments later, the girls appeared in the doorway.

No one got any more sleep that night. Next morning they gathered around the kitchen table.

"It's Granddad," Susie said boldly. "He must have a ghost with him."

"Don't talk nonsense," Edel chided. "You can't blame your granddad for all this. Sure wasn't he fast asleep while all that racket was going on?"

"Maybe he sent the ghost up to my room," Molly suggested. She looked haggard. There'd be no school today. Edel would telephone and make excuses for the girls.

A light snoring could be heard coming from the direction of their grandfather's living quarters. Nobody wished to wake him.

"I want you to promise me something, girls," Edel said. "I want you to promise me you'll say nothing to anybody about this. Is that clear? Nobody."

"Why not?" Susie asked.

"Because people would laugh at us, that's why."

"That's silly, Mammy."

Edel grew exasperated. How was she going to explain it to her pre-teen daughters? Would she tell them about Monica, her old school friend? That was indeed a cautionary tale.

Monica had inherited a house from a maiden aunt a decade before. It was situated in an older part of Dublin. Monica's aunt had neglected to tell anybody that her house had a ghost. It was not really a matter of concern – certain visitors would remark on a strange "atmosphere"; others had seen inexplicable shadows; objects seemed to vanish for no good reason, only to reappear elsewhere in the house.

The ghostly phenomena had continued to manifest when Monica and her family were present. The children had told their friends; the friends had told their parents; the parents had told many others. Before too long the whole neighbourhood knew of "the haunted house". When Monica tried to sell it some years later she encountered great difficulties. It finally went to a couple from the Midlands, strangers to the locality, who of course knew nothing of the benighted house's history.

"It's not silly," Edel told Susie, choosing her words with care. "It's silly to talk about ghosts; that's what's silly. If your friends hear you believe in ghosts they'll think you're mad, and you wouldn't want that, would you?"

The girls assured her that it was the last thing they'd want. Edel knew from bitter experience how children can be bullied at school on the slightest pretext.

"Maybe it's a poltergeist like in the film?" Susie said suddenly.

Edel was taken aback. "A *poltergeist*? And how would you know about poltergeists, Susie?"

"We saw the movie, Mammy," Molly chipped in.

Gerry and Edel exchanged anxious looks. Was it any wonder Molly was having bad dreams?

"When did you see that?" Gerry asked. The girls had asked him to rent the DVD some time before. He'd refused, judging it to be unsuitable.

"In Gráinne's house. It was awesome!"

Edel was not pleased by the news. She considered that it made matters worse. She hadn't seen the film but knew it was fairly terrifying.

"Well, that's all made up," she said. "Poltergeists aren't really like that. They just . . . they just like to have fun. Make fools of people."

"Why would they do that, Mammy?"

The questions children ask! "I don't know, darling. Nobody knows. But you mustn't think that a poltergeist is like a monster. It isn't. In fact, it's best to ignore a poltergeist. If you ignore it, it'll go away. But you mustn't say anything about it, especially not to Gráinne. Is that clear?"

The girls agreed with some reluctance that it would probably be best to keep quiet about the mysterious goings-on in their home. Edel breathed a sigh of relief.

She also had to ensure that Granddad Delahant held his tongue. From neighbours – and the newsagent – she'd gathered that he was a bit of a gossip. She could understand that; he needed somebody to talk to during the day when nobody else was at home. But the last thing she wanted was him telling all and sundry that there was something "not right" with the house. She knocked on his door and went through to his quarters.

"Sure why would I say anything about poltergeists?" he said. "I haven't seen a thing. Haven't heard anything either."

I'm not surprised, with the racket you make every night, Edel thought. Then Granddad said something that affected her deeply.

"It wasn't a great idea, me moving in with you, was it? I've been nothing but trouble."

"But it's not your fault! It's not as if you brought the poltergeist with you, is it?"

"How do we know I didn't, Edel?"

"You're being silly."

It was the second time that morning she'd accused somebody of silliness. She told her father-in-law that he wasn't to upset himself over the incidents, left him, and returned to the main part of the house.

Back in her own kitchen she decided to distract herself by giving the place a good clean. There was nothing like housework to refocus the mind.

She'd cleared the worktop and was filling a basin when she thought she heard something. It sounded like one of the children running up the stairs. But she knew that couldn't be: they were both at school. There was no one in the main house but her.

Edel was worried now. All this was too much to be attributed to her imagination. She took off her apron and made her way slowly out of the kitchen. She was going to investigate those footsteps.

She heard nothing out of the ordinary as she climbed the stairs. It was only when she reached the landing that she heard an odd sound. A rapid knocking noise coming from Molly's room.

"Molly?" she called out, knowing there was no way the child could be there.

She pushed open the door. The knocking stopped, abruptly.

As she was surveying Molly's room from the safety of the doorway there came an audible thud from her own bedroom. As though something heavy had been dropped.

Edel felt as though she was going out or her mind. She knew that, apart from her wheelchair-bound father-in-law, she was alone in the house. She hardly dared venture into the bedroom but, summoning up her courage, she did. There was no one in the room.

Her relief was short-lived, however.

"We had this souvenir from Lourdes on top of a chest of drawers. It was a fairly big thing, showing the grotto. There were two little statues, one of Bernadette and one of Our Lady. It came in different parts, you see, so the statues fitted into their own slots in the grotto."

The statuette of the Virgin Mary was missing.

Edel crouched down to look for it. At first she couldn't find it. But something told her to look behind the bedside locker. Sure enough, the statuette lay there, broken in two.

"That was when I became truly frightened," she says. "I knew that it couldn't have fallen all by itself. You'd have to lift it out of its slot. I don't know why but when I saw the Blessed Virgin lying broken like that I was more afraid than I'd been during those nights. I just knew that this was more than a poltergeist."

She dashed from the room.

Her car was parked, as always, in the driveway.

"I didn't even know where I was going," she says. "It was stupid but I wasn't myself then. All I knew is that I wanted to be as far away from that house as I could go. I needed to be out in the open. So I took the turning for the M50. Once I was out on the open road I felt better. I felt I could think."

She drove as far as Clondalkin before pulling over onto the hard shoulder. She'd come to a decision.

"It had been at the back of my mind for days," she says. "It was the feeling that we were dealing with more than ghosts. I don't want to use the word 'evil' but all the same I felt that whatever it was, it wasn't very nice at all. I knew it was something that didn't like religion. I kept thinking of the broken statue of the Virgin Mary."

As luck would have it, Edel's impromptu car journey had taken her very close to the parish where she'd grown up. Within a minute or two of leaving the motorway she was pulling up outside the church where she'd made her First Holy Communion and been confirmed into the Faith. She knew two of the priests. Both were quite elderly by then. Father Morrison, a man in his seventies, remembered her well and welcomed her into his sitting-room.

Edel related her story. But the priest was reluctant to believe that the phenomena were more than the work of a poltergeist. Edel could not be sure if he wasn't simply trying to put her mind at rest.

"He said there'd be no harm in saying a Mass," Edel tells me. "Those were the words he used: 'no harm'. Which

I suppose was stating the obvious. He said he'd be along the following morning, if that was convenient. What could I say? It was *more* than convenient!"

But it didn't work out as arranged. Edel answered the telephone early the next day. The call was from Father Morrison's parochial house; the housekeeper explained that the priest had taken ill unexpectedly and had to cancel all his duties for that day. Nor was there another priest who could say Mass in his place. Father Morrison would do his best to call to the Delahant home the following day.

It was a blow and Edel felt it keenly. Never mind, she thought: one day more or less won't make much of a difference.

That night it was Granddad Delahant's turn to be roused by unwelcome attention. He'd been sleeping – and snoring – for three hours or more when he suddenly woke up in a panic.

He'd been lying on his back as usual. He felt a weight pressing down on him. He described it later as the sensation of something heavy pressing down on his chest. He tried to get out of bed, and failed. Even though he could move his arms and legs, the weight on his chest was so intense he could not rise.

Granddad roared out in pain and terror. Later he described having seen "a black cloud spinning very fast" above him, before vanishing. With its disappearance he was released.

Upstairs, Gerry and Edel had been awoken by Granddad's screams. Their bedroom door opened. Two very frightened girls came in. Both were speaking at once and it was hard to understand them.

Susie was saying something about her light going on and off "like a disco light" and Molly was crying. She said there was whispering in her room. Then she asked a very odd question: "Is Granddad going to die, Mammy?"

Gerry reached his father first. He switched on the light in the bedroom. Never before had he seen his father so scared.

"I know it's a cliché," he says, "but he looked as if he'd seen a ghost. Isn't that what people say? The funny thing was, Dad hadn't *seen* a ghost – he'd felt one. Or so he said. But right at that moment I was ready to believe anything."

Granddad blurted out to Gerry what he'd experienced. He didn't want to remain in the bed, in the room. Gerry helped him into his wheelchair and they went into the front room.

The house was silent except for Edel and the children, who'd gone into the kitchen. Gerry and Granddad joined them there.

"Nobody got any more sleep that night," Edel says. "How could we? I was really concerned about Granddad. What Molly had said really worried me. He was as white as a sheet. There were tears in his eyes. I told him it was all right, that the priest would be along in a few hours' time."

Father Morrison called to the Delahant house at the appointed time, twenty-four hours later. He knew by the faces of Edel and her family that he hadn't come a moment too soon.

"We looked a sight," she says. "Gerry and myself were exhausted. Susie and Molly didn't say a word. They couldn't even meet the priest's eye. Granddad could barely shake his hand. What must he have thought of us at all? When he heard about the attack on Granddad he decided that he'd say Mass in his room. So me and the girls set up a kind of altar for him in there."

The celebration of the Eucharist was uneventful – much to everybody's relief.

"I don't know why," Edel confesses, "but I genuinely expected something to happen. I suppose that comes of watching too many scary movies. But it was actually a very beautiful Mass. It was probably wishful thinking on our part but when Father Morrison left we all agreed that the house felt different. More peaceful."

And that is how the house remained – for one whole day and night.

Two days following the Mass, something else happened to Molly. She'd gone to bed at about nine in the evening. She could have a lie-in the next day, it being Saturday.

She woke up several hours later, annoyed. Her mother had given her earplugs but she refused to use them; they were uncomfortable, made as they were for adult ears.

The whispering voices, the ones she'd heard before, had returned. They were coming from the corner of the room. She put her hands over her ears, but still she heard them. Muffled voices.

"They're back again!" she told her mother. "Granddad's gonna die, isn't he?"

"Now, Molly, don't talk such nonsense."

Molly burst into tears. "But they told me, Mammy!"

"You were dreaming. Now, stop this at once."

She took the child back to her room. All was quiet.

But alas it was not to be a quiet night. When she'd got Molly settled back in bed there came a loud thud from downstairs. It was quickly followed by a second and a third.

"I couldn't believe it," Edel tells me. "It was the same thumping sound I'd heard on that first night. Like the kitchen door swinging open and closing. But by the time I went into Granddad's quarters it had stopped."

But that wasn't all that had stopped.

"I suddenly realized I was missing something," she says. "And I knew what it was. Snoring. I didn't hear any. I got a bad feeling then. Don't ask me how, but I knew something was wrong. I opened his door and looked in. He was lying as he always did: on his back. But his eyes were wide open. I knew at once he was dead."

Gerry called an ambulance but it was too late. There was no pulse, no heartbeat. They concluded that Granddad had died peacefully in his sleep. He probably hadn't heard what turned out to be the final racket made by the poltergeist: the slamming of the door. Edel thought it was significant that a door had opened and shut roughly at the time of her father-in-law's departure.

They laid him to rest the following Monday, with Father Morrison celebrating the Mass.

The poltergeist did not return.

Edel's story does not have a neat ending. Such stories seldom do, except in works of fiction. If her story had ended neatly then we might be in a position to better understand the paranormal phenomena that beset the family. As it is,

Granddad Delahant's death left behind more questions than answers.

Inevitably the first question must be: what attracted the poltergeist? We know that its appearance coincided more or less with Granddad Delahant's arrival in Edel's house. This can hardly be coincidence. Edel and Gerry are adamant that, prior to the elderly man's moving in, their home had never played host to ghostly visitants of any description. Neither had ever seen a ghost. They didn't even know anybody who'd seen – or heard – a ghost, or had had an experience of the paranormal. We must therefore conclude that Granddad's presence and the poltergeist were somehow related.

The second question that arises is: Did the girls play a part in attracting the poltergeist? If that's the case then it would certainly fit with what we know of such things. There's no doubt that Granddad's arrival created quite a bit of psychological tension in the girls. And it is generally believed that anxious, pubertal youngsters are a magnet for poltergeists. Some investigators even go so far as to suggest that the children actually "manufacture" the manifestations. The theory goes that the advent of puberty creates in certain individuals an upheaval of such magnitude that great forces are unleashed. Some believe that those forces are physical as opposed to psychic – that they can actually be measured. All of which leads neatly back to the phenomenon with which I began this case: psychokinesis or PK.

I alluded to it in *The Dark Sacrament*, the book I co-wrote in 2006. I believe a point that was examined in that book bears repeating here:

The trouble with the psychokinetic (or PK) theory is that the phenomenon has never been scientifically proven. There is, to be sure, a vast body of research, most conducted since the 1930s. This is not to say that the human body contains no energy. It does, and experiments show that our bodies can generate enough static electricity to power a light bulb. What is more, if the body is subjected to a high charge of electricity, this is sufficient to cause the same light bulb to glow when held a centimetre or two away from the body.

But this falls far short of the phenomenal amount of energy one would require to propel that same bulb through the air without the use of one's hands. Nor does the theory explain how larger objects can fly about a room or transport themselves from place to place. An energy source is needed in each case, and the first law of thermodynamics states, in brief, that the universe contains a constant amount of energy; in order to move an object, energy must be converted from one form to another. Although the human body can store about eighty watts even when in repose, the brain itself uses on average only twenty watts. Anyone who has tried to read by the light of a 25W bulb will appreciate that this is a minute amount of energy. The notion that a human brain can move objects, unaided by the rest of the body, seems absurd.

Since *The Dark Sacrament* was published the situation remains unchanged. There is no earthly reason to believe that objects can be moved by the power of the mind. If there is an *unearthly* reason, we have yet to discover it.

Until such time that we do, I for one am keeping an open mind.

The third and final question must be: Did the celebration of the Mass cause the poltergeist to leave? It is generally accepted that a poltergeist is a mindless entity and, as such, is unresponsive to prayer. It is also regarded as a "neutral" entity, neither good nor evil. Clergymen generally hold that once religious objects come under attack it is a sign that evil spirits are at work. The breaking of the statue of the Virgin Mary was the only incidence of such in this case. There were other sacred objects in the home; none was targeted.

Overall, there is little to suggest that the Delahant poltergeist was evil. It seems to have been more mischievous than anything else and a classic – though modern – case of the mysterious phenomenon known as the "noisy spirit". Whatever it was, one thing is certain: like all poltergeists it came equipped with talents that can only be called "perverse".

4

Aoife and the Mischievous Ghost

*Home is a place you grow up wanting to leave,
and grow old wanting to get back to.*

JOHN ED PEARCE

There comes a moment in every woman's life when she must choose between the devil and the deep blue sea. Aoife Kelleher's moment came on a cold March night in 1995 in a small town not far from Dublin City. The choice she made that night was to have terrifying consequences for her, and for her as yet unborn son.

To understand her quandary we must go back a few days before, when Aoife, then aged sixteen, found herself pregnant by her boyfriend Joe, the seventeen-year-old who would eventually become her husband.

On hearing the news, Aoife's father was furious. He was of the "old school" – deeply religious and a firm opponent of sex outside marriage. He wasn't having a

"Jezebel" in his house, he said. He went at once to the parish priest and returned with him in tow. Between them, they arranged for Aoife to be admitted into a convent until she'd brought the pregnancy to term. The baby would then be given up for adoption.

He had other plans for Joe. He reported him to the Gardaí and demanded that they arrest him, which they duly did. Joe was charged with the rape of a minor and taken into custody.

This was – and is – perfectly legal. In the Republic of Ireland the age of consent is seventeen; Aoife was therefore underage. Joe's parents were appalled when they learned of his predicament. His father posted bail. All agreed that it was unlikely that the case would ever come to trial and, if it did, a judge would probably show leniency. That was not certain however.

Joe was released from custody on a Friday. It was arranged that Aoife's father would drive her to the convent on the Monday morning. The young lovers met clandestinely on Saturday and hatched a plan. They would elope: to England. Aoife had made the decision that was to have frightening consequences.

I meet Aoife in a Dublin hotel in 2009. She assures me she no longer resembles the callow young girl she was in 1995. Certainly there can be little physical resemblance. She's in her late twenties but looks older; there are lines in her face that should not be there. She's a mother of four, a fact she proudly proves by showing me the pictures she carries about in her handbag. Two girls and two boys. The older boy is thirteen, she tells me, already at secondary school.

She called him Clifford, after a young man she and Joe befriended in London and who helped them get on their feet.

Clifford junior, I learn, was the reason for their elopement. She speaks about him with great tenderness.

"I nearly lost him," she says. "If my dad had had his way he'd have been put up for adoption. I might never have seen him again. If I think about all the happiness he brought me and Joe . . . well, it's almost unthinkable that it might never have been."

Aoife still speaks with more than a trace of an English accent even though she returned to Ireland five years ago. It was an emotional time for her. She'd received news of the death of her father. His passing had paved the way for a family reconciliation.

"My mam had always kept in touch with me," she says. "Unbeknownst to my dad. She'd phone me when he was out and let me know what was going on. To be honest with you, there weren't many tears shed when he died. He gave everybody a hard time, including my mam. He'd had a rough childhood, you see, so I suppose you can't blame him too much for the way he turned out. All the same . . ."

All the same, her father's obduracy had given Aoife more grief than was decent. It had split the family. He steadfastly refused to withdraw the charge against Joe, even though Joe's parents – the Kellehers – pleaded with him, adding their voices to those of Aoife's mother and other family members.

In the end, Joe and Aoife returned for the funeral and stayed on for a couple of days. There were arrangements to be made. Mr Kelleher had engaged a solicitor to investigate what could be done to resolve his son's predicament. A settlement was arrived at. A meeting took place in a judge's private chambers, where it was decided that the interests of the young family would not be served by punishing the father for a youthful indiscretion. He had, after all, "made good" the damage done by marrying the girl he'd made pregnant.

But the legal wrangle was not the worst of the hardships that Joe and Aoife had encountered. She gives me an account of their early life in London, during which they struggled to make ends meet. With a baby on the way and little or no money coming in, life had been tough for the young couple.

I wonder about their "elopement". Aoife laughs bitterly.

"It was classic," she says. "All that was missing was the ladder up to the window. I sneaked a suitcase out of the box room in the afternoon and stuffed it with my things. Mam and Dad and the others were watching telly that evening so I could slip out the back with the case. I hid it in the backyard and went back to watch telly with them. They didn't suspect a thing."

Aoife went to her room at her usual time and waited until the hour she'd appointed with Joe. He'd persuaded his older brother to drive them to Dublin so they could catch the ferry from Dún Laoghaire. At three o'clock Aoife dressed and crept downstairs. Joe and his brother were waiting for her at the back gate. They set off some minutes later. Aoife knew that, it being Saturday, her parents would have a lie-in. She'd be well on her way before they even knew she was gone.

All went according to plan. In 1995, six years before the attack on the World Trade Center and fully a decade before the 7/7 bombing of London, security was lax on the Irish Sea ferry routes, and had been since the IRA ceasefire of 1994. Britain no longer mistrusted her Irish neighbour. Aoife bought two tickets using her passport as ID. She gave the name of her fellow passenger as that of her brother. There were no questions asked, as Joe had expected.

The ferry docked in Wales before noon on Sunday. By mid-afternoon the couple were approaching London by train. They knew where they were going.

"Joe has an aunt in North London," Aoife explains. "She has a family so we couldn't stay with her for too long. But she agreed to put us up for a few days when she heard what happened. We were dog-tired when we arrived. I could have slept for a week. But the important thing was that we were free. We were in a big, anonymous city. No one but Joe's aunt knew where we were, and she wasn't going to tell anybody."

There were practical problems to contend with. Not least was the matter of education. Joe had been in his final year of secondary school, had been preparing to sit his Leaving Certificate. He wished to study engineering at university or, failing that, to enrol at a technical college. Their flight from Ireland had scuppered those plans.

By the same token, Aoife could not complete her own schooling. This would have been difficult in any case, owing to the pregnancy, but her father had assured her she could carry on where she'd left off when the baby was given up for adoption.

A job, or jobs, would have to be found. Joe had no savings; Aoife had left home with little more than enough to buy the ferry tickets. Neither had ever worked before, apart from taking summer jobs. They'd paid no national insurance and were registered nowhere. They had to face facts: they were on a par with illegal immigrants and would have to accept work in the "black" economy. No papers, no questions asked. It would be hard, possibly dirty, and certainly badly paid.

And so it turned out. While they were lodging with his aunt, Joe scoured the newspaper classifieds for an employer who offered casual work. But the jobs on offer turned out to be little more than slave labour: back-breaking work for a pitifully low wage. Yet he was earning something at least. His aunt refused to accept any money for their keep. She also gave them their meals so Joe could save a little. He wandered from one dead-end job to another before finding work that suited him – and work that he could do without interference from the authorities. A car mechanic in the neighbourhood needed an "apprentice" and jack-of-all-trades. Joe was good with his hands and liked to tinker with machinery. He took to the work with ease.

Matters were otherwise for Aoife. In the beginning she had no difficulty in finding temporary work. There were plenty of opportunities, provided a girl wasn't too demanding about salary and working conditions. The important thing was that she was adding to their savings, all the time being acutely conscious of the fact that they'd need money when the baby came. They could not call upon social services; having the authorities involved would lead to awkward questions being asked and perhaps checks being made in Ireland.

Joe's aunt had made clear that the young couple could not remain under her roof for longer than was necessary. She was a kind woman and, had she had her way, they could have postponed their departure until "you get properly on your feet", as she put it. But her husband was less keen to have Joe and Aoife in his home. Eight weeks following their arrival in London, Joe's aunt informed them that they were no longer welcome.

She had, however, been working behind the scenes on their behalf, sounding out her friends and acquaintances with regard to accommodation. She seemed to have found the ideal place. It was, she said, "no palace". It was a run-down, three-storied house in a quiet cul-de-sac not far from her own home. It was scheduled for redevelopment within a year or two – depending on whether the developer could raise the necessary finance. In the meantime he was letting it out at bargain rates. There was Abdul and Sarita Ramadja, a couple of Indian ethnicity, living on the ground floor with their five children and a grandparent; the upper floors were shared by groups of friends.

The basement area, a throwback to a time when servants would cook and perform other domestic duties "below stairs", had become vacant. Joe and Aoife could move in at any time. He'd be even closer to the garage.

It promised to be the perfect solution.

"It's very damp," Aoife said, looking about her. "I don't know if that's healthy."

In the way of things, the basement flat had appeared different when they'd viewed it the previous week. Seen now in daylight, the cracks were beginning to show. Literally in some cases. It was easily seen that the building hadn't been maintained but allowed to fall into disrepair. Aoife hated it. Yet it was their own, and anything was better than continuing to impose on Joe's aunt and her family.

Aoife describes it as being quite spacious. There was one main room, which evidently had been the kitchen at one time but was now partitioned off to allow for a small sitting-room. The big old AGA range was still there and seemed to be in good working order. It was filthy though, as was the rest of the flat. Aoife would have her hands full trying to make the place habitable while Joe was working in the garage.

The ceilings were all quite low, as was to be expected in a basement. That alone had a depressing effect on Aoife. To add to it, the walls had been done in a mustard-coloured emulsion, and were peeling and stained in places. Joe promised to paint them white at the first opportunity.

Light was another matter. There were only two small windows set almost immediately under the ceiling. One admitted light into the kitchen, the other into the sitting-room. But the room they'd allotted as their bedroom had no window at all. Nor had the bathroom and toilet; both were accessed via the bedroom.

"So actually you can tell your mates you have an en-suite bathroom," she joked to Joe. "They'll think we're very posh."

In fact, it was the presence of the "mates" that made the flat tolerable. On moving in, Joe and Aoife had met a young man in the hallway, who'd welcomed them and introduced them to the people with whom he shared the first floor. There were five of them, aged between eighteen and twenty-two: three girls and two boys. Each had his or her own room and shared a communal kitchen and living-room. They'd immediately invited the young couple to "dinner", which consisted of pizza and copious cans of lager. A good time was had by all.

It was the last time Aoife would drink alcohol before the birth of their child. By now she was five months pregnant and already showing. She was working part-time in a bakery; that would also have to end soon, she told their new friends.

"Do you know where you're going to have the baby?" asked Miriam, a pretty twenty-year-old Glaswegian who worked as a dental assistant. "I mean, which hospital?"

Aoife already had one lined up. She was going to pretend she was on her way home to Ireland when the labour pains started. They must never forget that a cloud hung over them.

Miriam very kindly offered to help out when the time came. She was a kind person, warm and generous. She did, however, have a very unusual hobby. She had a fascination for all things occult.

And she liked nothing better than to dabble with a Ouija board.

"It should by rights be called an Oujda board," Miriam told the group clustered about the table. "You probably never heard of the place but me and Tommy trekked there two summers ago. It's in Morocco, by the way. Great place, lots of students."

Aoife and Joe had been in the basement flat for a little over a week. The place was looking better: the walls were white, they'd cleaned it thoroughly, and Joe's aunt had "donated" some pieces of furniture, curtains and other odds and ends. It was a home.

They were returning the hospitality shown to them by the young occupants of the first floor. Three responded to Aoife's invitation to dine with them: Miriam and the two young men, Tommy (her boyfriend) and Clifford, a native Londoner. Clifford had proved to be more than neighbourly: he'd helped Joe with the painting and decorating and had asked for nothing in return. Aoife had improved on the pizza dinner by preparing a home-cooked meal. By way of returning the compliment, Miriam had offered to fetch her Ouija board and "read your future" as she put it.

"I don't mind telling you I had my doubts," Aoife says. "My granny never had a good word to say about the Ouija board. She always used to say it brought 'bad luck on a house'. Of course I laughed at her . . . but all the same I told Miriam that I wasn't too keen on the idea. Joe had had a few beers – I was cold sober – and he said, 'Don't be silly. It'll be a bit of craic.'"

And so the dinner table had been cleared to make space for Miriam's board. It turned out to be an unusual specimen; she'd made it herself and was particularly proud of it.

"I didn't like the look of the thing," Aoife says. "There was the usual alphabet and numbers, and the words 'yes', 'no', 'hello' and 'goodbye'. But she'd also painted strange pictures of angels and demons, and all sorts of weird-looking creatures – like something you'd see in *Lord of the Rings*. She'd put a glaze over it so it was like glass. Very professionally done."

"They say it was invented in ancient China," Miriam went on, warming to her subject. "The Celts had one too, by the way. But it was only in the 1800s that an American inventor designed his own version. He called it Oujda but it soon became known as Ouija, because people thought it meant 'yes' in French and German. He sold it to Parker, who trademarked the name. Basically it's the same as this one."

She drew from her handbag a small object. It was made of Perspex.

"This is the pointer," she said. "I bought this. Too hard to make yourself. But it's very good. What you do is put your finger on it and wait for it to move."

"I know," Joe said. "I've seen the movies."

"And they usually end up with someone being killed," Aoife said.

Miriam had laughed. "That's all made up. Nothing like that ever happens in real life."

Aoife had believed her. Joe switched off the lights and they lit a couple of candles. It was after eleven and the street outside was largely in darkness. The Ramadja family on the ground floor were early risers and had already retired for the night. A quiet had descended on the house.

"Okay," Miriam said when all five had rested a forefinger on the pointer, "now we have to summon the spirits."

"I didn't like the sound of that one bit," Aoife tells me, "but I kept quiet. It was all very innocent anyway. Most of us had a lot to drink and we were in a playful mood. When Miriam talked about 'spirits' somebody made a weak joke about Scotch whisky and that was the extent of it."

The session began innocently enough. Miriam asked over and over if there was "anybody there". Aoife giggled at the serious way she was asking the question. The seriousness

106

seemed out of place with the light-hearted dinner they'd enjoyed together. But Miriam was not amused. She glanced reproachfully at Aoife, who fell silent.

The pointer moved.

"I thought that somebody was acting the eejit," Aoife says. "You know how people are. We all had a finger on that thing so any one of us could have pushed it. But Joe swore to me later that he hadn't pushed it. He said that it just seemed to move all by itself, and that's what I felt too."

"We have a visitor," Miriam announced. She raised her head towards the low, freshly painted ceiling. "Is there somebody?"

The pointer shot straight to the "yes" on the board.

"Who's messing?" Joe said with a laugh. "Who moved that?"

Everybody denied having exerted any pressure on the pointer.

"This is how it works," Miriam told him. Looking at the ceiling again she said, "Who are you? Please identify yourself."

To Aoife's astonishment the pointer went from letter to letter, spelling out what seemed to be a foreign name.

N-O-M-E-N   N-E-S-C-I-O

"Miriam looked it up later and it turned out to be Latin," Aoife says. "It means something like 'I don't know the name' or 'Anonymous'. She'd never heard it before and that night we all thought it was somebody's real name."

The "game" continued. The unseen visitor responded quickly and without hesitation to a number of questions put to the Ouija board. It didn't seem to mind who asked the questions, or how trivial they were. Somebody asked whether Nomen Nescio could predict that week's lottery results. The pointer went to the "yes". But when asked for the winning numbers it spelled out the words "not for you".

Then, abruptly, it spelled out Aoife's name.

"I didn't know what to think," she says. "Nobody had asked anything. It just seemed to be moving of its own accord. I have to say I began to get a bit nervous then. Joe and the others had been drinking all the time but I was cold sober. They all found it a great lark but I didn't. Still, I didn't want to spoil the evening so I thought I'd go along with the craic. I said something like, 'Yes, I'm here'."

The pointer spelled out A-S-K.

Aoife played along. She asked the first thing that came into her head: the sex of the baby that was growing inside her. The answer came at once.

B-O-Y

Well, she thought, I'm impressed but it's hardly rocket science. A fifty-fifty chance that the prediction was correct. All the same, the board's reply was to influence her thinking about the baby from that evening on. She would refer to it as "he" and think of it as a baby boy. She even got Joe into the habit of talking about "our son".

The pointer moved again. Once more it spelled out the letters A-S-K.

"Somebody else now," Aoife said. "Let somebody else have a go."

"No," Miriam said, "I think our Mr Nescio means you again. I think he's taken a fancy to you." She grinned at Joe. "Better watch it, you."

"Okay," said Aoife. She thought for several moments then said: "Will we go back to Ireland?"

The pointer moved immediately to the "yes".

"When?"

N-O-T S-O-O-N

She hadn't expected this. But, she thought, it's not necessarily a bad thing. She was getting used to London. It had more to offer than the stuffiness of her hometown. She'd made new friends and was enjoying a sense of independence she felt would have been impossible in her old life. Yet she was intrigued. She wished to know more. She asked a third question.

"When will we go back?"

The answer shocked Aoife. It was the last thing she'd expected. Up until that point the game had been fun. She'd half-believed in the veracity of the Ouija board. It hadn't really told her anything of importance, anything that she could not have guessed – or worked out for herself. Now it spelled out:

W-H-E-N H-E D-I-E-S

She yanked her hand away from the pointer in disgust.

"That's it! I'm not playing any more."

She stood up from the table. Four faces turned to look at her. Even though no one was sober, all could see that she was deadly serious. The evening was over.

"I'm sorry," Aoife said. "I've gone and spoiled it now."

Joe was on his feet and comforting her. "Don't worry about it, love." He glanced at his watch. "It's late anyhow. We'll call it a night."

Miriam was a little disappointed and said so. Never mind, Aoife said, she and Joe would organize another Ouija session and invite them down again.

They never did. That single session had been enough to unleash strange forces in the basement flat.

It began harmlessly enough, in keeping with the manner in which such things usually unfold. Three days had elapsed since the dinner in the basement.

Aoife and Joe had spoken about the odd – and certainly disturbing – response she'd received to her final question. Mention of death is never pleasant. Even more unsettling is when one doesn't know whose death is at issue. Aoife, now seventeen, had never even seen a dead person let alone experienced the death of someone close to her.

Joe did his level best to persuade her that the Ouija board was all nonsense and that she should pay it no heed. In response she patted her belly.

"See this?" she said. "Before Friday night I hadn't a clue if I was carrying a boy or a girl. But now I know it's a boy. I *know*, Joe! I know it more than anything. Miriam's board was right about this, and it was right when it said that somebody is going to die. Some fella's going to die. That's the only way you and me are ever going home again."

Nothing he could say would change her mind. On Tuesday morning he set off for work at ten to eight, his usual time. He could walk to the garage now instead of taking the bus. That way they could put by even more money. Every little helped.

The morning was cold and overcast, a typical October morning. Aoife still had the lights on in the kitchen. She

110

busied herself by tidying away the breakfast things. She could hear Mrs Ramadja upstairs, remonstrating with her children, going through the daily routine of getting them ready for school. Aoife had made friends with Sarita by then. She was a very outgoing person, in her twenties and highly educated. She'd expressed her delight on learning of Aoife's pregnancy and had very kindly offered to help in any way she could when the baby was born. She even told Aoife that her mother had worked as a midwife in India, and if she'd prefer a home-birth rather than go to the hospital then she need only ask. Aoife told her she'd think about it.

While she listened to the sometimes loud snatches of children's conversation from upstairs, Aoife's thoughts turned to her own child. She knew what she was going to call him: Clifford. Joe had gone along with the idea at once. They liked their new neighbour very much and thought he'd be honoured to share his name with their son. Aoife spoke about having him as a godfather. It would be nice. . . .

"Quick, quick. Never say die."

"They grow up so fast, don't they?"

Aoife had stopped what she was doing on hearing the first voice. She turned, listening. The voices came again.

"Quick, quick. Never say die."

"They grow up so fast, don't they?"

They seemed to be coming from the sitting-room. Two people: a man and a woman. They sounded elderly. They spoke with English accents, possibly London. She pushed open the connecting door.

There was nobody in the room. The chairs and table were as they'd left them the night before, as were the soft seats. The table – the one on which Miriam had conducted the Ouija session – still had the magazine Aoife had been reading and two tea mugs she'd forgotten to tidy up.

"Quick, quick. Never say die."

"They grow up so fast, don't they?"

She spun round in fright. The voices had come from the kitchen. It was impossible. Was somebody playing a trick on her?

"I thought about hidden microphones and speakers," she says. "You know: you can hide a little speaker behind a cushion or something and scare people with it. But then I asked myself who'd be playing practical jokes on me. Joe? No way. And I couldn't see Clifford or the rest doing something like that. Besides, how would they have got in? They hadn't been in our flat since the Friday."

"Quick, quick. Never say die."

"They grow up so fast, don't they?"

Aoife rushed back into the kitchen, expecting to see something out of the ordinary there. The voices had stopped as soon as she went through the door. She looked about her, half-expecting to locate a hidden speaker, or some other means by which the voices had been produced. They'd sounded so lifelike, exactly as if a man and woman had been holding a conversation. She'd heard them distinctly and the words they'd used. Words that made no sense.

On an impulse she went into the sitting-room again. The voices stopped abruptly. But as Aoife stood looking about her in mystification, she heard them again – coming this time from the kitchen.

She'd had enough. She hurried out into the hallway, put on her coat, grabbed her handbag and door-keys and left the flat.

She was on edge. She needed fresh air. The basement was a little claustrophobic at the best of times. Now it was threatening into the bargain.

Aoife mounted the steps that led up onto street level. Once there, she looked up at the other floors. She considered going and ringing somebody's bell. But at that hour there'd be nobody home except Sarita Ramadja's mother. Her English was poor and Aoife thought better of disturbing her.

So she spent that morning walking about the area, not knowing what to do or where to go. Joe would be coming home for his lunch at a little after one. At ten to one she braved it back indoors. The flat was eerily quiet. Aoife switched on the radio and turned up the volume – her defence mechanism. By the time Joe came through the door, she had the kettle on and the lunch prepared. She'd recovered somewhat. She felt better now that she was no longer by herself in the basement.

"Joe," she said, "I think we have ghosts."

Joe was convinced that Aoife was seeing and hearing things: hallucinating. He even went so far as to speak to his boss's wife about pregnancy and its possible effects on a woman. She told him he was being silly, that pregnancy was "the most natural thing in the world" and it was highly unlikely to lead to delusions. Or forgetfulness. She'd given birth to seven children and was something of an expert. She suggested that Aoife might be on her own too often and that perhaps she needed a companion while Joe was at work.

In fact, Aoife had reached the same conclusion independently of Joe. She was still on edge the day after the incident with the voices. She couldn't concentrate, kept looking behind her and imagined she was hearing noises that shouldn't have been there. When she'd finished the breakfast dishes and tidied up, she went and rang the Ramadjas' doorbell. Sarita's mother invited her in at once, sat her down and made tea.

A half-hour passed pleasantly. Aoife found that she could converse reasonably well with Mrs Ramadja as long as the topic did not stray too far from the everyday. Children, school, the neighbourhood . . .

Then Aoife heard the unmistakable sound of Joe's work-boots on the steps to the basement. Puzzled, she looked at the clock on the mantelpiece.

"What is the matter, dear?"

"It's Joe," Aoife told her. "He's come home early."

"You must go to him," said Mrs Ramadja.

Aoife was intrigued to note that the floor insulation, despite the carpet, was poor. She could plainly follow Joe's footsteps as he tramped about downstairs. She wondered if they'd made too much noise the week before. She excused herself and let herself out.

She'd locked the door to the flat, as she always did. She was fumbling in her bag for the keys when it dawned on her that there was no need: Joe would have already opened the door.

But the door was locked. Most odd. Why, she asked herself, would he lock the door behind him? Bewildered, she fished the keys out of her bag and let herself in.

"Joe?" she called out.

There was no response. She heard his boots on the tiled floor of the bathroom. She went through into the sitting-room, still calling his name. The footfalls ceased.

Joe was nowhere to be seen.

Was he playing tricks on her? But why would he do such a thing? He'd been very sympathetic when she told him of her experiences the previous day. She had the feeling he didn't believe her, but that was no excuse for teasing her. Besides, Joe wasn't like that at all.

Gripped by a sudden fear, she fled the flat, not even stopping to lock the door. She spent the remainder of the morning with Mrs Ramadja.

"It sounds to me like a poltergeist," Miriam said.

"Which *you* brought in, you and your bloody Ouija board!"

"Och, keep a calm sooch," Miriam said. "You don't know what you're saying, Aoife. It's got nothing to do with the board. I've been using the talking-board for years and it's never brought anything but good into a person's life."

Miriam had dropped by that evening to express her gratitude for the nice evening. She'd been perturbed by Aoife's behaviour when the board had mentioned death. The last thing she wanted was to frighten her young housemate, and said so.

"So how do you account for it?" Aoife asked.

"The poltergeist? It could be any number of things." She jerked a thumb at the ceiling. "Sarita's daughter Padmal is eleven now. She's probably going through puberty. That could cause it, you know. It's a well-known fact that poltergeists tend to latch onto girls going through puberty."

"Really?"

"Aye. I'm not saying it's true, mind, but that's what they say. Did you ever hear of the Enfield poltergeist?"

"Enfield?" Aoife repeated in alarm. "Sure that's where Joe works! I didn't–"

"No, that's not what I'm saying at all. This was a long while ago. In nineteen seventy-seven, I think. There was a family living in Enfield who were plagued by a poltergeist. They had an eleven-year-old daughter by the name of Janet, and the poltergeist seemed to be targeting her. It shook her bed up and down, that sort of thing. And she heard voices as well – just like you did."

"Hmm. So why doesn't it torment the Ramadjas? Why is it bothering *me*?"

Miriam shrugged. "Who knows? And maybe it's tormenting them as well and they're keeping quiet about it. Most people would – if they've any sense."

"Thanks, Miriam."

"Och, I don't mean *you*, Aoife. And you know you can confide in me about such things. Please do. I won't laugh or think the worst of you. I take this kind of thing seriously."

Which was just as well because Joe still doubted her. She didn't blame him for that. After all, she was the sole witness to the mysterious activity. She almost hoped that something similar would occur while he was present in the flat, if only to persuade him that she wasn't losing her mind.

But she was going to have to wait for that eventuality. In the meantime Joe went about his business, leaving her alone in the flat. On occasions she'd go and pay a visit to Mrs Ramadja. It took her out of herself. She also visited a friend she'd made while working at the bakery on the girl's day off and passed a pleasant few hours discussing work colleagues, family and babies.

It was when Aoife returned home that day, at about five o'clock, that the poltergeist made its presence known again. No sooner had she stepped into the kitchen than she heard them: the strange voices. One male, the other female, coming from behind the door to the sitting-room.

"Quick, quick. Never say die."

"They grow up so fast, don't they?"

"I was stopped in my tracks," she tells me. "I hadn't heard or seen anything spooky for over a week. I thought whatever it was had decided to leave me in peace. When I heard those voices again I knew at once it wasn't natural. It couldn't have been."

Then all of a sudden the radio in the kitchen switched itself on, blasting out rock music, something Aoife dislikes.

"I got it turned off and unplugged it at the wall," she says. "Then the weirdest thing happened. It came on again all by itself. I nearly died because I knew there were no batteries in it. I was going mad. I wanted to go upstairs to the Ramadjas, to Sarita and her mother. But just as I was mounting the stairs, Joe came home. I showed him the radio and he tried to turn it off too. It was only then that he believed me."

In the days and weeks that followed, the poltergeist activity came and went, ebbed and flowed. At times it was little more than lights flickering or the occasional thump or creak – minor matters that would irritate rather than frighten Aoife. At other times she'd hear the mysterious voices again, sometimes calling her name. Worse was when the entity pretended to be Joe, as it had done when she'd been visiting Mrs Ramadja. It would mimic his footsteps. She'd be busy doing something and hurry automatically into another room, swearing he was there.

"They like to create mischief," Miriam told her. "They're sometimes called 'mischievous ghosts'. Some people say they're spirits that haven't grown up, sort of pre-teen ghosts you might say. They like to fool around. But basically they're harmless."

Aoife had thought about this. She could, however, see a flaw in the argument.

"You remember when we were asking the Ouija board stuff and that strange name came up?"

"Nomen Nescio?"

"Yes. That didn't sound like a ten- or twelve-year-old to me."

"And it wasn't," Miriam agreed. "It may not even have anything to do with my board at all."

"Except that all this weird stuff came in after that night."

"Och, yes, that's true. I feel bad about that, love. I really do."

Miriam neglected to mention that the Ouija tends to attract the less reputable type of entity. Such spirits are called variously "lower spirits", "elementals" and "lower astral beings". Rarely, if ever, does a board attract an entity of worth. It is as though such spirits shun the Ouija, regarding it as being little more than a plaything – and a dangerous one at that . . .

The activity took on a new and more frightening aspect a day after her heart-to-heart talk with Miriam. During the afternoon Aoife heard the usual footsteps and noises from all quarters of the flat. It had become so much a part of her day that she described it as "background music". It no longer scared her in any way. She'd call out to the poltergeist –

"Don't bother me, you stupid ghost!" – and even make jokes along the lines of, "Have you no home to go to?"

This is by no means unusual behaviour. It very often is the case that individuals who are exposed to prolonged poltergeist activity will become quite accustomed to it after a time. Once they've overcome their initial fear – and providing the poltergeist does no more than create mischief – the victims will usually take all the bumps and thumps in their stride. Other, more serious, occurrences can have a devastating effect on a house's occupants when repeated over a long period of time. In the 1990s a Catholic priest was called to a house in Omagh, County Tyrone, which had been disturbed by such activity for more than two decades. The family would hear a child wailing, heavy footsteps would tramp across the first floor, furniture would be moved about at all hours, and fixtures would shake. In desperation the family abandoned the first floor entirely, and lived, ate and slept downstairs.

In the case of the Omagh haunting the cause was finally established. Apparently a child had been cruelly abused and murdered in the house a long time before the family moved in.

"Jesus, Mary and Joseph!" Aoife cried out.

She'd awoken suddenly in the middle of the night, to find the bed rocking from side to side. Her cry woke Joe. The bed continued to rock violently. Joe grabbed her hand and they dashed from the room.

"We're getting out of here *now*," he said.

"But where can we go?"

"Anywhere. There's always something open in London, love, no matter what time it is. We'll find an all-night chipper or something. It doesn't matter. Anything's better than staying in this madhouse."

They dressed in haste and fled. Sure enough, within a ten-minute taxi ride from the flat they found an all-night café as Joe had predicted. They remained there until it grew light, drinking cups of tea and feeling sorry for themselves – and even sorrier for their unborn child.

"We'll have to get help," she told him later that day. "Maybe we should call in a priest to say a Mass and bless the flat."

But Miriam cautioned against it.

"It might get upset if you do that," she said. "You might make it worse."

"But what can we *do*?" Aoife wailed. "It's driving me mad."

"It'll most likely go away all by itself," Miriam said. "They're very unpredictable. And maybe the baby will drive it away. That sometimes happens too. You'll be giving the baby all your attention and the spirit won't like that. It'll try to get attention elsewhere."

"I'd never forgive myself if anything happened to my baby," Aoife said.

"Don't worry. If the worst comes to the worst you can always leave." She looked about at the dingy interior, made only marginally better by the application of fresh paint. "There are more places to rent, you know. This is London after all."

It was a cold and dank evening in December. Aoife had calculated that she was due to give birth the following day or the day after. They'd planned it down to the last detail.

As soon as her labour pains began Joe would take three days off work; he'd have liked to take more but his boss told him he couldn't be missed.

They had a minicab on standby. The driver lived just around the corner and had informed Joe that he had no other customers that day. He was in semiretirement and was busy with some overdue DIY. The hospital was no more than a two-minute drive away; five at the most if there was congestion.

When they went to bed that night at about half past ten there was no sign yet of labour pains. All was going well. The entity had left them alone for four whole days and nights. Aoife actually considered that it might have left them alone for good.

Her dream began quite innocuously. When she recalled it later she realized that most of the images thrown up by her subconscious mind centred on babies and childbirth. No surprises there. She dreamed of a garden she'd known in childhood. It was teeming with children of all ages, from newborn babes to toddlers to six- and seven-year-olds. They were playing.

"They grow up so fast, don't they?" a voice suddenly said. It seemed to Aoife that it came from directly behind her. In her dream she turned round in mild bemusement. There was nobody.

The scene switched abruptly in the way of dreams. The children were replaced by a hospital ward, one that was as vast as a cathedral, with a ceiling as tall as the sky, the whole being illuminated by unnaturally white light. There were men and women in white coats milling about, with nurses wheeling gurneys that seemed to be shoulder-high.

Aoife heard baby laughter interspersed with screams as from women in pain. Faces came at her from nowhere; people called her name. She saw Joe walking past her and called out to him. He ignored her and continued walking. She followed him, still calling his name.

Her point of view changed again. Now she found herself lying on a bed in the same gigantic hospital ward. The walls were altering from white to yellow to orange and back again. Men and women in white uniform were bending over her.

"It won't come," somebody by her bedside said. "It refuses."

She saw a man's face leaning close to hers, filling her field of vision. A white surgical mask covered the lower part of his face.

In her dream Aoife was in labour – and a very painful labour it was too. She was pushing with all her might but seemed to be making no headway at all. Her baby was refusing to come into the world.

"I thought I was dying," she says. "It was so vivid. I know I'd gone over it all in my head before and got all sorts of advice from people who'd given birth. I knew more or less what to expect. But this was horrendous. I kept thinking: it's either me or the baby. One of us is going to die."

Aoife woke up screeching.

She saw a bright, white ceiling and a face leaning over her – and thought she hadn't escaped the horrid nightmare after all. But it was Joe's face, and it wore a look of great concern.

"What's the matter, love?" he said, cradling her head in his arms. "A bad dream, was it?"

That was when she felt her first labour pain.

Within minutes she was dressed and all set to go, her overnight bag already packed. The minicab driver had responded to Joe's urgent call and was waiting up on the street. In double quick time Joe was helping her through the door of the maternity hospital.

The baby – a boy – was born a little over two hours later. When Aoife held him in her arms every vestige of her dreadful dream was forgotten. It had all been worth it. Clifford was the most beautiful little thing she'd ever seen, and she wept with joy.

"I felt a bit nervous bringing Clifford back home with us," Aoife tells me. "I was genuinely afraid for him, afraid that the . . . thing would do something to harm him. But I knew it was only for a week. We'd found another flat by then."

Aoife believes that the ghost must have known of their plans. She believes it because that night it unleashed the full fury of its displeasure or, in her own words, "all hell broke loose". The entity seems to have reserved all its force for this concerted attack, as though it was a grim sort of "going-away" present.

There are precedents for this sort of behaviour. The Proctor family of Willington Mill in Northumberland, England, endured seventeen years of poltergeist activity in the nineteenth century. The manifestations took many and varied forms, and not all were frightening: once, the appearance of a monkey both startled and delighted the children, who played with the animal before it disappeared as mysteriously as it came. However, when the Proctors could stand it no more and were in the throes of leaving the house, the poltergeist redoubled its efforts throughout the final night. The Proctors heard "boxes apparently being dragged with heavy thuds down the now carpetless stairs, non-human footsteps stumped on the floors . . . and impossible furniture . . . dragged hither and thither by inscrutable agency; in short, a pantomimic or spiritualistic repetition of all the noises incident to a household flitting".

It occurred to the Proctors as they listened in dread to the hullabaloo made by the ghostly "removals men" that the poltergeist was planning on joining them in their new home and was noisily doing its own packing. As it turned out, their fears were unfounded.

Now the poltergeist in the basement flat in north London was doing something similar: it was going through its entire "repertoire" of tricks, as though it wished to take one parting shot at Joe, Aoife and their baby.

First, it attacked the bed. Aoife awoke to find Joe clinging on to her as the bottom of the bed was lifted up and down. They were almost flung out onto the floor. Joe was cursing and swearing to beat the band. The baby was wailing pitifully.

There was no need to turn on the lights – the poltergeist had taken care of that. Lights throughout the room and elsewhere in the flat were rapidly turning themselves on and off.

The voices were back as well, repeating their "quick, quick" entreaties. For Aoife it was a rerun of her terrible nightmare but played out now in the real world. There was nothing else for it. They were leaving.

They took a taxi to Joe's aunt's place. She was none too pleased to be awoken in early morning. Joe's explanations about paranormal manifestations fell on deaf ears. All the same, it was clear to her that the young couple – for whatever reason – were in fear of something in their home. There was also little Clifford to consider.

They moved into their new flat the following day. It was recently built and close to where Joe's aunt lived. They would be the first tenants.

The place was mercifully devoid of unearthly spirits of any description.

Several years passed. Life changed for Aoife and Joe. Three more children were born to them. Joe found more lucrative work and their standard of living improved. Theirs was no easy life, however; there were now six mouths to feed. They needed security.

Moreover, both were homesick. They'd been little more than children when they left Ireland. London had been good to them yet had robbed them of a part of their lives they should better have spent among their "own kind": the teenagers they'd known in the past, who were now grown up like themselves, with families of their own.

In 2001 Aoife received an urgent phone call. It was her mother. Her father had dropped dead of a heart-attack that morning. Would Aoife like to come home?

A tearful reunion took place two days later, the day her father was laid to rest. They'd left the children in the care of friends in order to attend the funeral. Aoife promised her mother that she'd see her grandchildren before too long.

Her mother had plans of her own. She urged Aoife and Joe to come and live with her, in the house that she was "rattling around in", now that Aoife's brothers had left and her father was gone. It was an offer they found hard to turn down.

Joe's parents were anxious that he should complete his education and he enrolled in UCD to study engineering, his life-long ambition. He graduated and found a fine job, one that enabled him to put a deposit on a house in the suburbs. Aoife's mother went with them. In that same month, the couple married. It had long been Aoife's wish and was made possible at last.

Life is good now for all concerned.

"We went back to London last year," Aoife tells me. "Just the two of us, Joe and me. We stayed with his aunt. We looked up Clifford and Miriam too – we'd kept in touch all that time."

I ask about the house with the infamous basement, whether they were still living there and if any more poltergeist activity had taken place.

Aoife shakes her head.

"They tore the house down," she says with what seems to me like grim satisfaction. "It was due for demolition anyway. Only the landlord's planning permission came through about two years earlier than he expected it to. They all had to go: the Ramadjas and everybody else. He only gave them two weeks' notice so it was rough.

"I asked Joe to take me there. I just wanted to see what was in its place. He didn't want to at first but I persuaded him. We took a bus and deliberately got out one stop too soon. I wanted to get a feel for the place, you see. Well, I hardly recognized the street when we turned into it. Most of the old houses were gone and new ones in their place. There was a block of flats where ours was. Six stories. Nice flats. I wouldn't have minded at all living in one of them."

I ask the question that's uppermost in my mind.

"Yes," Aoife replies without hesitation. "We went in. The front door was wide open and there were kids playing there and two mothers chatting. It was a Saturday. I expect you're wondering if I felt anything. Well, yes, I suppose I did. But I really think it was more my imagination than anything else. I went over to the women and asked them how to get to the basement; I didn't see any stairs. I wondered if I'd feel anything down there. And you'll never guess what they told me."

She pauses for several moments as though choosing her words carefully.

"They said the landlord had had the stairs blocked up a few months after the place was built. A fire had broken out down there. Nobody knew how it got started but the fire brigade got there in the nick of time. They declared it a health hazard, too dangerous. So the landlord got the builder in to cement up the entrance to the stairs. The women pointed it out to me. You could just about see where it had been."

Does Aoife believe the fire was connected to her experiences? She shrugs.

"I think it left when we left," she says. "Miriam said that nobody reported seeing or hearing anything. Two guys moved in there after us and they never had any bother. So do I think the fire was connected? No, I'd say it was just a coincidence. And if it wasn't then it's over for good now. No basement, no people. And what's the use in being a poltergeist if you don't have any people to torment?"

5

The Haunting of Aisling, aged Eight

To perceive a "haunting" one needs, as a general rule, to be slightly psychic; it is for this reason that children . . . suffer severely from such interferences . . .

DION FORTUNE

In 2004 I was engaged in researching my book on exorcism in modern Ireland. I found it a fascinating – if somewhat unsettling – subject. One of the most endearing cases involved "Lucy", a charming little girl of nine, the middle child of a family living in rural Ireland.

She resembled most girls of her age in all but one respect: she saw ghosts. In fact she saw a great many of them, all on her parents' farm. They appeared to her in the house, upstairs and down. Lucy even saw a young man out in the yard. He was laid out as if in death, on a bier, bathed in a golden light.

When I came to write the book I stated that there was nothing sinister about Lucy's apparitions. This remains my conviction. Sometimes the appearance of a ghost may have sinister undertones; mostly it has not.

In the introduction to her book, *Ghost in the Mirror: Real Cases of Spirit Encounters*, Leslie Rule suggests that many more children than we think see ghosts but "the witnesses simply don't *remember* their spirit encounters."

Few people remember the details of early childhood. As they age, they forget the ghosts they have met. . . . For the innocents among us are privy to things that most of us cannot sense. . . . Kids lose the ability to see, partly because they are taught by adults "not to make up stories".

It turned out that Lucy's home had been built on the site of an army barracks, one that had played an active role in recruitment during World War One. The Church of Ireland minister who investigated the phenomena concluded that the apparitions were the ghosts of individuals who'd lived and died there around that time. There was, for instance, the ghost of a soldier who was missing an arm, presumably lost in combat. Harder to explain was the appearance of a little girl, who would eventually vanish through the wall halfway up the stairs. Or mysterious lights that Lucy saw entering the kitchen and hovering about the heads of her brother and sister as they were having dinner.

Yet Lucy's experiences, I was to discover, are by no means uncommon in Irish children. Granted, the other children I spoke to had seen nothing like the sheer volume and variety of paranormal events Lucy had witnessed. Why this should be I cannot say. The location may have played an important role. There is also the possibility that Lucy possesses a "gift", a mysterious faculty absent in most children.

In recent decades much has been made of the existence of such psychic youngsters. The interest can be traced back to Nancy Ann Tappe, an American parapsychologist. In the 1960s she coined the term "indigo children" to describe the phenomenon, explaining that such children possessed an "aura" of that colour, and had telepathic powers. A whole industry grew up around her beliefs, no doubt due to their appeal to parents who liked to think that their children were somehow more psychically gifted than others. Some even insisted that we were witnessing a new phase in our evolution. Although belief in indigo children continued into our century, no supporting evidence has ever been presented.

We are usually quick to dismiss as fantasy – or, worse, invention – ghost sightings by young children. Children, by their very nature, live in a world of make-believe. Yet occasionally we are forced to examine the data more closely, especially when a child's supposed fantasy does not fit the customary pattern.

Occasionally we have to conclude that something remarkable is going on.

No one can say for certain when Aisling began to receive her "communications" from the unknown. Aisling believes she was about five at the time but is, understandably, vague about this. Nor can her parents, Mick and Treasa Burke, put a date on it. Each recalls Aisling saying something about "friends" and "messages" from time to time, but admit that they paid little heed. Aisling is the youngest of four. Two have already flown the parental nest, leaving her and her brother Jack, who is four years older than she.

Like Lucy, Aisling is a bubbly little girl, interested in essentially the same things that engage her school-friends and neighbouring children. She loves clothes, has her own mobile phone and laptop, adores *Hannah Montana* and can't get enough of Westlife.

She also communicates with the dead.

Treasa Burke is unable to say when the communication began. She runs her own small business – as does her husband. This gives her more freedom than most women who are part of the workforce. She can decide her own hours, within reason. This fact allows her to take time off when necessary, and to spend more time with her family when business is slow.

She's forty-five, a year younger than her husband Mick. They live in a large, three-storey house not far from Kilkenny. Treasa's beauty salon is in town; Mick works as a freelance consultant with a software company. It often happens that the two are away from home at the same time; equally often, both will be there for the children. This was the case on 8 December 2006, six days after Aisling's birthday. She'd turned eight.

It was a Friday afternoon, close to five o'clock. It had begun to grow dark an hour before, and Treasa had the lights on. Jack had finished his homework very quickly – a little *too* quickly, his mother thought – and was upstairs in his room. But he was a quiet boy, gave no "trouble", and Treasa indulged him.

Aisling was, if anything, the exact opposite. She was gregarious from a very early age. She loved company, and parties. Most days, the Burke house would play host to an assortment of her friends and Jack would take himself diplomatically "off side".

On that particular Friday, Aisling had brought two classmates, Holly and Lauren, home with her. They'd do their homework together at the kitchen table. That, at least, was the theory and Treasa had gone along with it. As it was, the kitchen was noisy with little-girl chatter and not much homework had been completed.

As usual Aisling was the centre of attention. She was explaining to Holly how she'd go about answering a tricky maths question. They were noisily voicing their disagreement.

"Hush, girls," Treasa admonished. "Fighting won't get you anywhere. And if you don't hurry up you'll be late for your tea." She set glasses of orange juice down on the table.

"No!" Aisling exclaimed.

Treasa turned to her daughter.

"I *beg* your pardon, young lady?" She wasn't used to backchat from her children, not even from Aisling.

"No, go 'way!" the girl cried. She looked angry. "Go 'way."

It was then Treasa noticed that Aisling wasn't looking her way at all. Her eyes seemed to be fixed on the kitchen window.

"Who are you talking to, Aisling?" she asked carefully.

"Him. The little man."

"What little man?" Treasa went to the window. She hadn't drawn the curtains yet. The security light was powerful; she liked the way it illuminated the back garden and was

133

reflected in the glass of the conservatory. She'd never thought of the lit garden as in any way spooky; its shadows and ambiance appealed to the romantic in her.

But there was plainly no one at the window, she saw now. The garden was likewise empty of visitors. Treasa drew the curtains.

"There's no man there, Aisling. Stop making up stories."

"I'm not, Mammy. There *was* a little man. I *saw* him."

Treasa said no more about it until that evening. She'd tucked Aisling into bed and finished the story they'd started a few nights before. She thought it was time to broach the subject that had been niggling her.

"This man, Aisling . . . the one you saw outside the window. What–"

"No," the child interrupted, "he wasn't outside, Mammy. He was in the kitchen. He's always in the kitchen."

Treasa was suddenly nervous. Yet she had no good reason to be, she assured herself. Aisling had an unusually vivid imagination. It wasn't the first time she'd made up imaginary friends. All the same, Treasa didn't like the sound of this. She was also recalling Aisling's words at the kitchen table.

"Tell me about this man," she said. "What did he want?"

"Don't know."

"Is he an old man?"

Aisling shook her head.

"As old as Daddy then?" Treasa said.

"He's sort of between Daddy and Grandda."

Treasa digested this. Mick's father was in his mid-sixties. So Aisling's imaginary friend would be about fifty.

"And what does he look like?"

"He's a bit blurry but he's small . . . about the height of me. And he's got a beard."

The mother had to smile. Her daughter was describing a character out of a fantasy film they'd watched together the day after her birthday. The DVD had been one of her birthday presents. The mystery was being resolved.

"So he's a dwarf then, is he? He's not a hobbit?"

"I think he must be a dwarf, yeah, 'cause hobbits don't have beards."

"I didn't think so. How is he dressed?"

"He doesn't wear any clothes, Mammy."

"What!"

Treasa felt a chill stealing over her. She did not like the sound of this. She was prepared to tolerate her eight-year-old making up stories about imaginary friends, but this was going too far. She studied her daughter, curled up in her bed with her favourite soft toys on either side of her, and her face lit by the soft pink glow of her Disney Princess bedside lamp. *Something* had put that image into her head, she decided. Children do not invent naked men.

"Are you saying he doesn't wear anything at all, dear?" she asked carefully.

"Only a necklace and a skirt thing, but from here to here," said Aisling, pointing from her chest to her waist. "He's all white."

Treasa wasn't sure if this new revelation made matters better or worse. She had to know more.

"What sort of a necklace, Aisling?"

"I dunno. It's kind of long . . . with pointy things on it."

"And the skirt. What's it like?"

135

Aisling screwed up her little face deep in thought. "It's short and I think it's got pointy things on it, too."

Treasa smiled and sat down on the bed. "Well, he's a well-coordinated dwarf, I'll give him that. Now listen to me, sweetheart," she said a little more sternly, "I don't mind you making up stories, all right? But you shouldn't make up stories like this, you hear me? They're not nice. Did you say anything to anyone else about this?"

"Only Holly and Lauren."

"And what did they say?"

"They said I was stupid."

"Well, there you are, Aisling. That's what you get when you make up stories. Do you want everybody making fun of you?"

The child shrugged and raised her blue eyes to the ceiling. "I suppose not. . . ."

"Good. Now off to sleep with you and forget about dwarfs in the kitchen, all right?"

"All right, Mammy."

But it wasn't all right, as Treasa discovered next morning. Mick had left for the shop to buy the paper and to drop Jack off at his friend's house. They'd be going to football practice together later on. Aisling was helping her mother with the washing up. There wasn't much; they seldom ate a big breakfast on Saturdays, preferring to save their appetite for lunchtime.

Treasa was reaching into a cupboard for a fresh tea-towel when she noticed her daughter had stopped what she was doing. She seemed to be staring intently at something in the corner of the kitchen. There was nothing there apart from a cheese plant, which, Treasa noted, needed watering and repotting.

"Aisling?"

The girl turned. She had a guilty look; her cheeks had reddened.

"Is it that little man again?"

Aisling nodded. Her mother went to her. There was something about the child's demeanour that dispelled any irritation she might have been feeling.

"I had the impression," Treasa would say later, "that Aisling was torn between telling me the truth and ignoring what she was seeing. She knew I'd be angry with her if she talked about the little man again. I could sense her struggle. It can't have been easy for her."

Treasa went to her daughter, grasped her by the shoulders, and turned her around again to face the cheese plant. She could feel the child trembling slightly.

"Is he still there?"

Aisling nodded vigorously.

"What's he want?"

"Don't know."

"Is he saying anything?"

Aisling shook her head. "He's just sad, Mammy."

Treasa was baffled. She could think of no good reason why the child would defy her and insist she was still seeing him. She decided to probe further.

"How do you know he's sad?" she asked.

"'Cos he's doing *this*." Aisling struck a pose, head tilted to one side, hands held up in front of her in an attitude of supplication.

"Is he still wearing the skirt?"

Aisling nodded.

"And the necklace?"

"Yeah, but I see it better this time. It's like the one Daddy got in America with the claws on it."

Treasa knew at once what Aisling was alluding to. Mick had returned from a trip to California the previous year with a Navajo necklace. It was a bit too gaudy for Treasa's liking: all turquoise and bear claws. She'd worn it once just to please him. She wondered what it was about the necklace that was fuelling Aisling's imagination. She still refused to accept the possibility that the girl was actually seeing a figure that remained invisible to her or anybody else.

"Right," Treasa said carefully. "Just ask him to go away."

Aisling turned to face her. "It's all right, Mammy. He's gone away now anyhow."

Treasa was disturbed for the remainder of the weekend. When Monday morning came she'd almost decided not to go to work. But she changed her mind. What good would it do to sit at home brooding?

The salon wasn't busy that morning. That was unfortunate because Treasa had hoped that pressure of work might distract her from her worries. They had not lessened. Her greatest concern was that there was something very wrong with Aisling. Children did not start seeing things for no apparent reason. She'd almost considered taking Aisling to see the doctor. She simply did not know whom to turn to.

Her second appointment was an old friend: Kathleen Johnston. They'd known each other since childhood. Kathleen was almost the first customer through the door when Treasa opened her beauty salon, five years before. They were close;

Treasa felt she could confide in her, and did so as soon as they were alone. She was giving Kathleen her fortnightly manicure.

"It's certainly weird," Kathleen said. "Did she come out with this sort of thing before?"

"Oh, a few times. You know how kids are with their imaginary friends."

"I do indeed."

"But that all stopped when Aisling was about six or so. And now this. I don't know what to make of it."

"Has Jack noticed anything?" Kathleen asked.

Treasa didn't like the way she said it. "What do you mean?"

"I mean: has he been seeing this 'dwarf' as well?"

Treasa stopped what she was doing.

"No, but then I didn't ask him. Aisling seeing things like this leprechaun is enough!"

"I thought you said it was a dwarf."

"Dwarfs, leprechauns, fairies, banshees! Sure it's all in the mind, Kathleen. Kids make these things up. They'll see something on the telly or a DVD and they're away."

"Away with the fairies, yes. Would you like me to have a word with a friend of mine?"

"What sort of friend might that be?"

Kathleen hesitated before replying.

"Well, I suppose you could call her a medium."

"What!"

"A clairvoyant. She has a gift, Treasa. She can see things."

"Oh, yes, that's all I need! Isn't it bad enough having my youngest seeing things without roping in a grown-up who sees things as well."

But Kathleen's words had aroused Treasa's interest. She was no stranger to clairvoyants – or "fortune-tellers" as she liked to think of them. She'd visited several when in her teens. It had all been done in a spirit of fun: a group of teenage girls having a laugh, finding out which of their number would be the first to fall in love, get engaged, marry, the number of children. That sort of thing. Treasa had entered into the spirit of things.

Hearing Kathleen making the suggestion with all seriousness caused Treasa to go over those early memories from her teens. One fortune-teller had told her she'd marry a rich foreigner; another told her she wouldn't marry at all. A third was convinced she'd marry her boyfriend of the time – a young man who went on to become a priest. Treasa smiled at the absurdity of it all.

"I don't believe in fortune-tellers," she said. "It's all a lot of hokum."

"I'm not talking about somebody reading your palm now," Kathleen said. "I'm not talking about somebody telling your future. This is about the present, not the future. Would you not give it a try?"

Treasa shrugged. "Tell you what, if I start seeing this little man myself, God forbid, I just might call on her."

Alas, as is sometimes the way in these matters, that flippant remark would come back to haunt her. It was a couple of nights later. She didn't actually see the "little man", but believes she heard him.

Mick and the children had already gone to bed. Treasa was downstairs tidying up. On her way out of the kitchen she thought she heard something – what could have been a moaning sound. It seemed to be coming from behind the door to the utility room. She assumed immediately it was their little terrier dog. Mick always put him out before going to bed. But maybe he'd forgotten – which would have been a first.

As she approached the door the moaning stopped.

"Bounce!" she called out. "Are you in there?"

She expected the dog to bark, and it did, a couple of times. But from outside the kitchen window, from the direction of his kennel.

Then the moaning started up again. No, it definitely wasn't the dog. It sounded like someone gasping for air. She thought of the strange pleading pose Aisling had struck when asked what her ghost man was doing. Treasa backed away from the door, too afraid to open it.

She went up to bed, but didn't mention anything to Mick.

"I lay awake for most of that night," she says. "I knew what I heard and I sensed that there was something to Aisling's story. That's when I decided to take Kathleen up on her offer."

According to Treasa, the medium was known only by her first name: Sheila. She worked from home: a nondescript house on the southern outskirts of Kilkenny and close to the Waterford road. She received the friends at a little after seven in the evening.

Treasa had been prepared to take Aisling along but Kathleen dissuaded her.

"Better to have a chat with her first," she said. "Tell her a bit about Aisling. It's better for you as well. You can decide for yourself if you want her to see Aisling."

Sheila was perhaps in her late sixties, early seventies. She ushered her guests into the front room and had them sit on a comfortable old sofa. Treasa had a quick glance about the room. She guessed it was where Sheila held her "séances" – she disliked the word but could think of no other. The room was very ordinary, she thought. A little like Sheila herself.

"I'd expected an old hippy in a floral smock," Treasa tells me with a wry smile, "or, God forbid, a kaftan! You know the sort of thing: jade beads and hoop earrings. Instead she turned out to be a smartly dressed lady and the only unusual thing about her, as far as I could see, was a pair of butterfly-framed glasses on a gold chain."

The room did smell of incense, however, and there were oriental prints and ornaments. They were not overdone, though, and Treasa thought the room was very tastefully appointed.

Sheila put them at their ease at once with a tray of tea and cakes.

"So tell me about little Aisling," she said. "I understand she's eight."

Treasa gave the medium a brief rundown on her daughter. Asked if she had many friends, she replied she had, that Aisling was a very popular child. Everybody loved her.

"I'm asking this," Sheila said, "because sometimes a mother will come to me with a little girl or boy who claims to have an invisible friend. Nine times out of ten the child is lonely, doesn't have anyone to talk to or play with. I suppose they turn in on themselves when that's the case."

Treasa was surprised to hear the medium use that sort of language. It seemed to her to be more suited to a counsellor or care worker.

"I've studied psychology," Sheila said with a smile. "I know it's an unusual combination: psychology and spiritualism. But I see no reason why the two can't complement one another. After all, they both deal with things we can't see. If I were to ask you what colour fear is, would you be able to tell me? No, of course not. But we recognize that fear exists, don't we?"

Treasa was warming to the elderly lady. She was most certainly nothing like what she'd expected a medium to be. Treasa is a sensible woman, not given to superstition, and was pleased with the way the conversation was going.

"Is there any reason, do you think," Sheila went on, "why Aisling would make up stories about a non-existent person?"

"No. She used to – when she was much younger. But she grew out of that."

"Where were you living then? When she was younger. Was it the same house?"

"No, we only moved into this one in March." She paused. "Do you think it's got something to do with the house?"

"Well, I couldn't say until I pay you a visit."

Sheila enquired about the house. Was there, she wondered, anything unusual about it? Treasa told her that it had been in her husband's family for several generations. It was built in the eighteenth century but destroyed by fire in 1906. The owners rebuilt it using the original foundations.

"Do you happen to know who the owners were?" Sheila asked.

Treasa nodded. "Their name was McCormick. The family were legal people. The house itself belonged to a judge, who died in about 1920. That's when the house was sold to Mick's great-grandfather. He passed it on to his son, who left it to Mick in his will."

"The fire," Sheila said. "Do you know anything about it? How it started?"

"As far as I know there was a thunderstorm and one of the outhouses got struck by lightning. Before anybody could do anything, it spread to the house."

"Was anybody . . . er . . . ?"

"Injured? No. Nothing like that."

"When can I come and see you?" Sheila asked. "And Aisling too of course."

"You don't want me to bring her here?"

"No, I think it might be better if I went to see her. And the house. Yes, under the circumstances I do feel that would be the thing to do."

Treasa had had a difficult time of it. She'd had to explain to Aisling that they'd have a special visitor the following evening: a Saturday.

"Who's that?" Aisling asked.

"She's a friend. She's a nice old lady. You'll like her. She's interested in dwarfs."

Aisling's eyes opened wide.

"Really? Has she seen one?"

"Oh, plenty! You two should have a lot to talk about."

Sheila showed up on the dot of seven. She was dressed more casually – Treasa guessed it was to put Aisling more at ease – and was carrying a large shopping bag.

Mick and the children were watching television in the front room so Treasa thought it best to have a chat with the visitor elsewhere.

"Why not the kitchen?" Sheila said without hesitation.

"Are you sure?"

"Of course. Lead the way."

Treasa had noted Sheila's behaviour from the moment she'd entered the house. The medium had stood for several seconds on the threshold before stepping into the hall. Now, as she was led down the hallway, she paused several times, glancing all about her as if searching for something. Outside the kitchen door she stopped. She wore a puzzled look.

"Is there something the matter?"

"That's just it," Sheila said. "There doesn't seem to be anything the matter. Usually when I come into a house that's reputed to be haunted I detect a presence at once. Not here. There's nothing."

Treasa freely admits that she felt very foolish at that moment. Foolish because she'd placed so much credence in her daughter's stories, and foolish because, on account of those stories, she'd been persuaded to invite a medium into her home.

A medium. She'd had a hard time explaining that to Mick.

"Are you out of your mind, love?" he'd said. "A medium! We'll be a laughing-stock if anyone hears about this."

"Well, we won't tell anyone, will we?" Treasa had responded. "I need to do this for my peace of mind. You can't begrudge me that, can you? And I'm thinking of Aisling as well."

He'd given in and had made one stipulation: he wasn't to be involved. That was fine by Treasa. She'd no wish to have him spoil everything by making fun of Sheila – as she suspected he would.

She opened the kitchen door.

"Oh, dear," Sheila said.

She'd stopped abruptly. Now she followed Treasa into the kitchen and shut the door behind her.

"What is it?" Treasa asked nervously. "What do you see?"

"I see nothing. But that's not so unusual. My gift is stronger on the clairsentient level than clairvoyant. I sense things, feel presences. And there's one here."

Treasa remained silent as the medium began to walk slowly about the room. The blinds and curtains were drawn. The kitchen was lit only by the spots above the worktop and hob, and a floor lamp in one corner. Sheila went carefully to the worktop and ran a hand along it. She inched along its length, keeping her hand on its surface.

She came to the sink and stopped. She cocked an ear as if listening for dripping water, a leak perhaps. Treasa knew there was none; they'd had the place replumbed only that summer, when the new kitchen was installed.

The medium then went to the cheese plant and stood for a few moments. She placed her hands on the wall directly behind it, the one that separated the utility room from the kitchen, and began feeling along its surface with the palms of her hands.

"I'm getting a presence here," she said. "It's confined to this area. Would this be where Aisling usually sees him?"

"Well . . . yes, it is," Treasa said, a little astonished. One part of her was prepared to believe that this stranger was telling the truth; another part was reminding her that she'd informed Sheila that the ghostly dwarf was confined to the kitchen. As far as she could recall she hadn't mentioned *where* exactly in the kitchen.

"Is it . . ." She hesitated. "Is it good or bad?"

"You mean: is it malevolent? No, I don't think so. But it's too early to say." She laid a hand gently on Treasa's forearm. "I'll have a little word with Aisling now."

It was the moment Treasa had been dreading. She found the girl curled up on the sofa beside her brother. Mike smiled in encouragement as mother and daughter left the room together.

Much to Treasa's delight she found that Sheila had a great rapport with children. She shook the little girl's hand and joked with her. It was obvious that Aisling was warming to the sweet old lady with "the funny glasses" as she'd call them later.

But there was work to be done.

"Now, your little man, he usually appears over there by the cheese plant?" Sheila asked.

Aisling nodded.

"Is he there now?"

"No."

"And when you do see him, Aisling, what does he look like?"

"He's little and he has a beard."

"And what does he have on?"

"A necklace and a little skirt."

"Like a kilt. I see. What's he wearing on his head?"

"Nothing."

"And on his feet?"

"He doesn't *have* any feet."

"Really?"

147

"I can't see any."

This was news to Treasa. After hearing from Aisling about the skirt, she hadn't thought to enquire further. She could see that Sheila was used to asking certain questions.

"Does he have knees then?"

"Yes, his knees are on the floor."

"I understand," Sheila said, and Treasa wished she could share that understanding. "Now just one last question. You're doing very well. Do you think he knows you're there?"

Aisling nodded.

"Ah . . . and how can you tell that, Aisling?"

"'Cos he moves his head like he's looking at me."

"Good girl. You're a very clever girl, Aisling." The medium smiled. She beckoned to Treasa to join them. "Now, you and me and your mummy are going to send your little man up to heaven again. He got lost, you see, and that's why he's sad, and he wants us to help him find his way again. D'you think you can help me do that?"

Aisling nodded.

Sheila opened her big bag. Treasa now saw the reason for its size. The medium drew out what looked like a large multi-coloured blanket. She spread it on the floor before the cheese plant. Next she put a candle in a holder, lit it and placed it in the middle.

"Are we gonna have a picnic?" Aisling asked, looking excitedly at her mum.

"Well, a kind of picnic," Sheila smiled. "But this one's a bit different because we pray for your little man first. And then afterwards we'll have ourselves some sweets, all right?"

The trio sat on the rug, held hands and closed their eyes while Sheila led them through a simple meditation. She asked Aisling and her mother to imagine an angel coming down from the sky and taking the little man up to heaven. She then asked God to bless the house and keep everyone safe.

"There," she said when mother and daughter had opened their eyes again.

"Is he back in heaven now?" Aisling asked.

"Yes, he is, dear. He's happy now and you won't be seeing him again."

"It was lovely the way she dealt with Aisling," Treasa says. "I was a bit on edge having her be part of something I wasn't really sure about myself. But I could see that she won her over right away. And looking back, I know it was good for Aisling to believe that her dwarf had gone up to heaven."

Did Sheila's work end there?

"Oh, no," Treasa tells me. "I thought so too. But after she finished with Aisling, Sheila said she needed to perform a cleansing ritual in the kitchen. She said I didn't have to be part of it if I didn't want to. So I left her to it and waited in the hallway."

I ask her if anything untoward occurred, whether she felt or heard anything.

"Well, the lights did flicker on a couple of occasions, but that could have been a power surge or anything – we do get them sometimes. And I heard her speaking. And this may sound strange, but it sounded like she was having a conversation with someone."

Not a prayer or incantation then?

"No, that's just it," Treasa says. "That's why I mention it. To me it sounded like someone was being spoken to, but I really couldn't make out what was being said, or if it was even English."

Whatever it was, it took a lot out of the medium. Treasa reports that, having finished the ritual, she emerged from the kitchen looking quite weary. She assured Treasa that she'd released their strange visitor and he wouldn't be bothering little Aisling again.

Not ever.

Two aspects of Aisling's story intrigue me. One: her ghost wasn't wearing very much and what he was wearing was most unusual. Two: his feet were invisible. In fact, as Sheila discovered from Aisling, his lower legs were invisible. From this I conclude that there was some truth in it. But children make things up and Aisling was no different.

I'm at the Burke house. Mick has taken the children out for the afternoon and Treasa is playing host. She tells me that there have been no further visits by Aisling's little friend since Sheila performed her ritual, nor has there been anything else that one might consider paranormal. We discuss the mysterious dwarf. Treasa relates the medium's theory.

According to Sheila the "dwarf" was most probably a so-called bog man. The bodies have been found in peat bogs in Ireland and elsewhere in Europe. They're very ancient, but because they were found in bogs they were very well preserved.

I tell Treasa that I see a difficulty here: the Burke house is nowhere near a bog.

"That's true," she readily concedes. "But Sheila said that Aisling's dwarf was most likely a sacrificial victim, as were the bog men they found. She was also intrigued about the necklace the child described. It sounded to her like something a primitive tribesman would wear, and not as decoration. She came to the conclusion that he'd been strangled with it, as part of the sacrifice.

The inference is highly plausible. Many such corpses show evidence of ritual killing. We can but guess at their purpose. Were they attempts to improve the harvest, to appease the gods? There might have been any number of reasons. Often the victims were sacrificed and buried on the boundary separating two baronies or kingdoms. It's possible that if we were to study old maps of the area we'd find that the Burke house was built on just such a border.

Treasa agrees that this makes some sort of sense. I wonder about the missing legs. Were they amputated as part of the ritual? I ask whether Sheila had an explanation.

"She said that in all likelihood the ghost was following a different ground-plan," Treasa explains. "She had the idea that the kitchen floor of our house is two feet or so higher than the level of the land a few thousand years ago. So if a ghost was walking on *that* then his legs would appear be cut off to the knee."

This rings a bell with me. I tell her about a British ghost sighting I came across some time ago. It concerned an apprentice plumber named Harry Martingale, who was working in the cellars of the Treasurer's House in the city of York. While standing on a ladder he witnessed a procession of Roman soldiers with dark complexions. They emerged from one wall and marched across the room, where they vanished through the opposite wall. Martingale also heard what sounded like a trumpet. He was astonished to see that the soldiers appeared to be marching on their knees. Only later did he realize that they were marching on the original Roman road that lay beneath the cellar floor.

Treasa tells me that I've touched on a matter that has bothered her for a long time. It concerns the appearance of ghosts. She explains her misgiving.

"I know a lot of people claim to have seen a ghost," she says. "Nearly everybody seemed certain that their ghost was wearing clothes. That was what I found so different about Aisling's story: her ghost was almost naked. But Sheila's explanation about the ritual murder meant that this bog man would have been stripped before being killed. Now my question is this. We see ghosts because they were once living creatures. But clothes and shoes aren't alive. So how come they survive death as well?"

It's an interesting question. I give Treasa a potted account of the beliefs of various primitive peoples. I tell her about the ancient Egyptians and their belief in what they called the *ka*. It seems to have been a body that "lived" within the flesh-and-blood body. It was composed of a fine material, finer than the molecules that make up the human body. At death it was released, to travel to some realm or other beyond our world.

"You'll see it pictured on old Egyptian carvings," I tell her. "It's usually depicted as a being with wings, in more or less the way we imagine angels to be."

Over time, other peoples adopted the idea and gave the *ka* other names. In our time it's known variously as the "astral body", the "ethereal body" or the "body of light". Some people claim to have released this astral body when undergoing a near-death experience. Given that much of our clothing is derived from organic materials – wool, cotton, leather, etc – it doesn't require a leap of faith to see why our astral bodies should not also be clothed in materials appropriate to the "fineness" of those bodies.

Yet another intriguing aspect of this story is how closely it relates to the "residual hauntings" as perceived by young Lucy, the child I mentioned at the beginning of the case. Experts on the paranormal would not place Aisling's experience in that category; they'd consider it to be an instance of "entity haunting".

As we have seen, the residual haunting can be likened to a piece of film that's shown over and over again. It's just a moving image, nothing more. It doesn't actually connect in any way with the person who sees it. It doesn't speak, nor does it seem to know that it's being observed.

Some say that such hauntings occur at the site of unusually traumatic events. A person might have witnessed a gruesome murder or the like. The images were so terrible that they became imprinted on the locale itself.

The entity haunting can also occur at a place where great violence or tragedy was played out. The difference is that such a spirit can interact with the living. Little Aisling said that the man followed her movements, indicating that he was aware of her. She said also that he was "blurry" and that's a telling description. Such spirits tend to be indistinct, but they make up for that by giving out a strong presence. This is absent in a residual haunting.

It's worth mentioning here a theory that's gained support in recent times. It concerns the blurring or fading of ghosts. Some argue that ghosts are little more than a form of energy, and one moreover whose lifespan is limited. There are well-documented cases of ancient ghosts which disappear over time, almost as though their energy is being depleted. Old records will describe the appearance of a ghost as being scarcely distinguishable from the appearance of a living person. Colours are vibrant. Yet as the years pass, the colours will fade, growing lighter and lighter until they become pale and translucent. Not long after, the ghost disappears, never to be sighted again.

I have to ask the final question, the one that's been troubling me. I know it's been troubling Treasa as well.

"Did Sheila say anything about the ghost coming back? Did she think there was a possibility that it might?"

Treasa shakes her head with great determination.

"No. Sheila said she could almost guarantee that it wouldn't be seen again. She said she'd been called in to help with this sort of thing several times. Each time, the spirit didn't know it was dead."

Treasa tells me that she'd like to think the blessing gave the spirit peace to continue its journey – that she'd like to believe that anyhow.

As do I. It's a reassuring thought.

6

The Night the Veil was Rent

We are predisposed to see order, pattern, and meaning in the world, and we find randomness, chaos, and meaninglessness unsatisfying. Human nature abhors a lack of predictability and the absence of meaning. As a consequence, we tend to "see" order where there is none, and we spot meaningful patterns where only the vagaries of chance are operating.

THOMAS GILOVICH, *How We Know What Isn't So*

The summer of 1998 was an eventful one for Ellen Fitzsimmons. She graduated from college and got engaged to Richard, her long-time boyfriend. They decided that before the summer was over they'd have their own home. It would have to be a rental. Richard's job was as yet not well paid (that would come later) and Ellen had no income at all. They put their heads together and decided that a

155

place in the country would be ideal. It would be less expensive than a flat or house in a town or city.

Their assumption proved to be correct. The little house they found was all that Ellen could have hoped for. It was not far from her parents' home in Tuam, but sufficiently distant from the hustle and bustle of Galway City, where she and Richard had lived for more than a year. They'd longed for the quiet of the countryside.

The house had been built as a "granny annex". It was a small extension to a farmhouse, whose owners, the Hannigans, were away much of the time and wanted a comfortable, self-contained dwelling for their elderly mother. When Ellen and Richard found the little house via an estate agent it had lain vacant for more than a year – ever since the mother died. Ellen felt that the house was perfect. She immediately christened it the *tigín*, or little house.

"The *tigín* was everything I wanted," she says. "It was small but had two floors. There was a living-room, which gave on to a small dining area, open plan. The kitchen was at the end. It was connected by an archway. There were no connecting doors, which I liked. You could make tea or coffee in the kitchen and carry it through to the living-room without having to open and close doors."

In fact the kitchen had two doors. One led out to the garden; the other was connected to the farmhouse next door.

"That door was always locked from our side," Ellen says. "Mrs Brennan, the woman who rented us the house, said they kept it unlocked when her mother was alive. She and her brother, John Hannigan, could keep and eye on her, make sure she was all right. The door was made of thin pine. It was the sort of interior door you find in many houses. If Mrs Brennan was next door she could hear her mum moving around. But it didn't disturb us or anything."

The *tigín* was tastefully decorated. It was quite unlike anything Ellen had seen before. Everywhere she looked she saw paintings and little pieces of sculpture. It turned out that Mrs Brennan's mother had been something of an artist. She'd loved to paint and sculpt.

"I know very little about art," Ellen says, "but the stuff I saw wasn't bad at all. You could tell it wasn't done by a professional but it was very good and you could see that the old woman had good taste. She'd had the whole place done in blues and greens. She was a great lover of candles too, because there were so many different kinds of holders. Over the mantelpiece downstairs was the most wonderful sculpture of an angel. I'd never seen anything like it. It took pride of place. And I remember thinking that where other women like my mother would have a religious picture or a crucifix in that spot, this woman had an angel and that was lovely. Just this lovely white angel with gold wings watching over you. No blood or sadness, just this lovely, uplifting image."

A small, narrow staircase led off the living-room. At the top of the stairs was another open-plan arrangement. There was a bathroom to the right of the stairs, and a long and narrow bedroom took up the rest of the space.

The whole of the upstairs floor followed the tasteful colour scheme that Ellen had so admired below. The walls were the same shade of muted sea green and the furniture had been painted in a matt blue. There were three bookcases. One was set against the stair-rail; a taller one stood to one side of the window; a third was on the "bedroom" side of the banister, neatly enclosing the sleeping quarters. A ceiling-high built-in wardrobe ran the length of the bedroom, from the stair to the wide window against which the head of the bed was set. Like the rooms in the rest of the *tigín* it had blue, floral-pattern curtains.

Ellen inspected the bookshelves. The old lady seemed to have been an avid reader. There were many books on art, and a great many with spiritual themes, mostly the sort of self-help and self-awareness books made popular in the seventies and eighties, mainly by American authors, the like of Dale Carnegie and Louise L Hay.

There were several large canvases on the walls. They were clearly the granny's own work but all were unsigned. They continued the themes Ellen had seen below: studies in oil of her children and grandchildren, as well as portraits of women from the past. The most striking picture was of what Ellen took to be Eve in the Garden of Eden. It hung facing the bed. It was well executed but there was something eerie about it: the eyes were black. Not just the pupils; the eyes themselves were entirely black. Ellen resolved to remove the painting as soon as possible.

The bathroom was eerie as well. On the one hand it was bright and cheerful, owing to the size of the window, which ran almost from floor to ceiling. Much of the wall space was taken up by a mural, a little crudely done but having as its theme the ocean and sea creatures: fishes, anemones, and here and there a mermaid. But the eeriness was due to the presence of a woman's personal effects. There was a partly used jar of bath salts and two bottles of perfume. There was even a sponge and a shower cap. It was as if the house's occupant had gone out for an hour or two and was due to return soon.

Or, thought Ellen, it was a shrine to the departed.

"It was all a bit unsettling," she confesses. "I knew they belonged to the old lady because they looked a bit ancient. I didn't like to say anything to Mrs Brennan because she was a nice lady, but I couldn't understand how she could just leave all her mother's intimate things like that. I know if it was *my* mother I'd have packed them all away. There was even a dressing-gown on a coat-stand."

Mrs Brennan, however, made no move to pack anything away. She told Ellen and Richard that she was "leaving you to it" and returning to her own home in Dublin. She said that the family used the farmhouse as a "base". By this she meant that from time to time one or more of the Brennans or the Hannigans might stop by for a few days at a time. She assured the couple they wouldn't be disturbed and that they'd have the place to themselves.

Ellen and Richard settled in within a day or two. The *tigín* continued to be an enchanting place. There was the garden for a start.

It extended on two sides. The living-room window looked out on the part of the garden that ran alongside the road, it being enclosed by a pretty privet hedge. The other portion extended beyond the front door and could also be reached from the kitchen. It caught the sun from early morning and they could throw open the kitchen door, allowing the brightness in for hours at a stretch.

"You could tell that the garden had been cared for by somebody with green fingers," Ellen says, "and who loved to be surrounded by flowers and plants. The hedge ran from the gate and made a right angle with the side of the *tigín*. There was a lawn with white gravel that curved out to the gate and an ornamental fountain in the middle of one part of the lawn. But the rockery was the nicest thing of all. It was done with big white marble stones and we had all sorts of wild flowers growing there. The colours were beautiful. We had bees and butterflies in the garden from early morning to evening."

Best of all, whoever had designed the *tigín* had built a veranda that ran along the two sides facing the garden. It was the old-fashioned kind, with boards painted white and two wrought-iron benches to match. Each bench had blue and green cushions, seemingly permanent fixtures. They were dry to the touch; it hadn't rained in a while and the veranda gave shelter in any case.

Having moved their belongings in, Ellen and Richard set about making some space for themselves.

"We didn't want to throw anything out of course," Ellen says. "It wasn't our place. So I put the bathroom stuff into a cupboard under the sink. I found the bathroom stuff a bit off-putting I have to say." She makes a face. "Well, what woman wouldn't? There was a wardrobe full of her clothes and things as well, but that was okay because two wardrobes had been left free for us anyway."

After stowing away everything and unpacking, the couple finally felt that the place was theirs at last. They uncorked a bottle of white wine and took it outside to the veranda.

The sun was just going down beyond the privet hedge. The air was still warm with the heat of the day. The flowers in the rockery were closing up for the night. They watched as a flock of starlings passed overhead; they heard the bleating of sheep in neighbouring fields. It was idyllic. They felt they were home at last.

Yet, despite all that tranquillity and beauty, Ellen felt ill at ease. There was something "not right" about the place.

They went to bed some hours later, their first night in the bedroom that had once belonged to a deceased pensioner. Ellen had made the bed with their own sheets, pillow-cases and duvet. When Richard switched out the light they could well have been in bed in their old flat.

With one notable exception. Even though the light in the room was dim to the point of darkness, Ellen could clearly make out the detail in a large painting that hung on the wall facing the bed: *Eve in the Garden*. The black eyes seemed to stand out from the rest of the face. They seemed to be staring straight into hers.

She threw back the duvet and climbed out.

"What's up?" Richard asked moments later. He'd assumed she was paying a visit to the bathroom.

"Taking this down," she said. "This painting."

He was wide awake and switching on the bedside lamp. He sat up, puzzled. Ellen was stowing the canvas to one side. He saw that she'd turned it round so that it faced the wall.

"I couldn't sleep with that thing," she told him, returning to bed. "It was staring at me. Ugh!"

"Eyes do that," he said. "When they're painted looking straight at you they seem to follow you around the room."

"It doesn't *have* any eyes!" she snapped.

"Sorry for living," he said, and lay back down again.

Ellen awoke not long after. It seemed to her that no more than an hour had passed. She was uncertain but sensed that something had roused her. Something in another part of the *tigín*.

She heard footsteps. She was fully awake now, staring at the ceiling and her heart thudding in her chest. The footsteps were coming from the other side of the built-in wardrobe. At least, she thought they were.

But it was hard to say. Ellen was still unused to her new surroundings. The acoustics, she decided, might be deceptive. The footsteps might not be footsteps at all. For all she knew, they could be made by a farm animal shifting about in a byre.

She thought about the Brennans. To the best of her knowledge none of the family had come to the farmhouse that day, or that evening. She'd have heard a car drawing up and it was highly unlikely that somebody had arrived on foot, or even by bicycle.

She heard somebody moving about downstairs.

She panicked, sat up and shook Richard awake.

"What is it *now*?" he demanded.

"There's someone in the house," she whispered.

"Yeah, you and me. Go back to sleep."

"Don't you hear it?"

"What am I supposed to hear?"

"I heard footsteps," she continued in a lowered voice. "I thought they were from next door but there's nobody there. Then I heard something downstairs."

162

"You want me to go and look?"

"Would you?"

"If it means I can get back to sleep," said Richard sourly, climbing out of bed, "then I don't mind going and having a look."

She waited nervously until he'd returned. He'd been gone no more than two minutes – the *tigín* had very few places to investigate.

"Nothing?" she asked.

"Nothing. I think you imagined it. You're not used to the place, Ellen. New places have that effect on people. Especially after dark. Now can I get some sleep?"

Ellen was the first to wake the following morning. Richard was slumbering quietly next to her. She liked the way he slept. He was as quiet in sleep as he was when awake. She slipped out from under the duvet and padded towards the bathroom, glancing as she passed it at the canvas propped against the wall where she'd placed it the previous night. No more black-eyed Eves to disturb her.

But once over the threshold of the bathroom something *did* disturb her. A strong, sweet aroma hung in the air. It was a sickly scent she didn't recognize. She looked about her. Maybe it was coming from outside, or from next door.

Her eyes locked on something by the mirror. A jar of bath salts. She recognized it. She was certain she'd put it away the day before, along with the other "intimate" things that shouldn't have been there. It was back again on the shelf.

Feeling rather uneasy and too afraid to touch it, she leaned over and sniffed. Mystery solved. "Essence of

163

Sweet Almond" she read on the label. Well, it solved the mystery of the scent, but how had the jar got back onto the shelf?

Nervous now, she shook Richard awake. He wasn't pleased and told her so.

"Go into the bathroom," was all she said.

He complied. Seconds later he emerged wearing a puzzled expression.

"Smells a bit funny," he said. "Is that all that's bothering you?"

"Did you not see what's on the shelf?"

He ducked into the bathroom again, and came out moments later.

"A jar of something. So what? You're not saying you woke me up for–"

"Oh, for God's sake Richard! I put all her stuff away yesterday, including that jar. So who took it out again? It sure as hell wasn't me."

He laughed. "Maybe the ghost you heard last night."

"Look, it's *not* funny!"

"Well, maybe it was me, then," he said. "Maybe I was looking for something and took it out accidentally."

Ellen knew he was only trying to humour her, and let it go for the time being. She went back to the bathroom and made sure he witnessed her returning the jar to the cupboard.

"Right," she said, "if it happens again, we'll know."

Ellen need not have worried: the bath salts remained in the cupboard that night. She felt a bit more relaxed the next day.

In the afternoon they visited friends in Galway City. They discussed the *tigín*, telling their friends how lovely it was and how fortunate they were to have found it. Ellen was careful not to mention anything about her weird experiences and invited their friends to visit at their earliest opportunity. They left later in the evening.

A surprise lay in store for them on their return. The beautiful sculpted angel above the mantelpiece, the one Ellen had admired so much, lay shattered on the floor.

She went over and picked up the broken pieces.

"God, how did *that* happen?"

"Well, whatever was holding it must have come loose," said Richard. He checked the nail in the wall. "But the nail's still here."

The angel had split into three pieces; the wings had separated from the main body of the statue. Ellen turned the torso over. She saw that the loop of cord, which suspended the angel from the nail, was still intact.

"So how do you explain that?" she said to Richard. "The cord isn't broken and the nail's still in the wall."

He examined it. "That's funny, right enough."

"Christ, Richard, that's not 'funny'; it's mad! First the bath salts, now this. There's something not right about this place."

"Oh, for heaven's sake, you're always jumping to conclusions."

"So *you* explain how it happened then."

"Vibration."

"What?"

"Vibration. A truck going past out on the road could have done that. I've seen it happen before." He saw Ellen's disbelief. "Look, I remember it happening at my uncle's on a few occasions. He lived near a railway. The rumble of a passing train could have the plates jumping off the table."

"Yeah, right."

"I swear! So stop always thinking the worst. There's always a logical explanation for everything, believe me."

Ellen, reluctantly, gave him the benefit of the doubt. They made a quick snack, watched some television and retired for the night.

Nothing disturbed their slumbers. Ellen had to use the bathroom once. She confesses to having been a little nervous but no more than that.

She awoke with the bright sunlight blooming in the windows and the notes of songbirds in the trees. She yawned, stretched, and opened her eyes.

Another pair of eyes was regarding her from the wall opposite the end of the bed. The eyes were black.

Eve in the Garden was hanging on the wall again.

"Richard!"

He was a little disturbed to be woken, but when he saw the picture he understood immediately.

"How did *that* get there? I thought you took it down."

"I did. You saw me taking it down. I didn't put it back up."

"I didn't either."

Ellen was already on her feet, pulling on her bathrobe.

"Where are you going?" he asked.

"I don't know. Out."

He found her sitting on one of the benches on the veranda. She was staring fixedly at the rockery. He joined her.

"What's going on, Richard? This is ridiculous."

"I know," was all he could say.

"What are we going to do? I'm not staying here."

He put an arm around her shoulders.

"You're being silly, Ellen. You can't let a little thing like this upset you."

"'Little thing'! What do you mean, 'little thing'? This is serious. Somebody doesn't want us here. And I think I know who that somebody is."

"You mean Mrs Brennan's mother, don't you? She's dead, Ellen."

"That may be. But she's the one that's doing this. I know she is."

They went in and had breakfast. It was Monday and Richard had to leave for work in Galway. Ellen would be alone in the house until 6.30 p.m. or later. He offered to take her with him so that she could spend the day in the city, but she declined. She'd be all right, she told him. She had him open the padlock on the garden shed. She'd decided to busy herself in the garden. It was less oppressive there.

She was jumpy the whole day. She'd wanted to do some things in the *tigín* but found she couldn't. In order to take her mind off the strange occurrences she fetched the lawn-mower, put some oil on its working parts, and set about trimming the lawns. It took her a while. She found a pair of garden shears as well, and carefully cut back the grass in and around the rockery.

The day could not have been more pleasant. She only wished she was better able to appreciate it but the events of the previous days were nagging at her. She tried to reason them away but could not. She'd seen what she'd seen and it made no sense.

Ellen took a break at midday and went inside to make herself lunch. She'd left the kitchen door wide open and it was bright and airy. Yet she found herself casting darting glances at the door that connected it with the Brennan farmhouse. She found herself imagining all sorts of secrets that lay beyond it. It was unsettling.

She carried a small table and chair out to the garden. She ate her lunch in the sun, surrounded by the scent of newly cut grass, and the hum of bees among the flowers in the rockery. The day was exactly as she'd hoped her days in her new surroundings would be. She was beginning to resent rather than fear the mysterious intruder that seemed intent on spoiling it all for her.

A week passed and nothing untoward happened in the *tigín*. Ellen had put the incidents of the bath salts, the angel and the painting behind her. She was enjoying herself at last, as was Richard. He would look forward to coming home at the end of his working day, to have his evening meal served in the garden. The summer was proving to be one of the finest in years. He joked about *The Good Life*.

Ellen had taken to gardening. She spent most of her day tending the flowers, weeding the rockery and the hedges. She'd found an old bird table and would set out breadcrumbs, to watch the birds feasting. They grew to trust her and that made her happy. She didn't miss the city at all; she felt she belonged in the countryside. She even found herself wondering whether the Brennans might be persuaded to sell the *tigín* if Richard could stump up a deposit. She was sure her parents would chip in.

But Ellen's peace of mind was shattered towards the end of their second week. Richard awoke in the middle of the night to find her sitting up and sobbing. She was distraught.

"What is it?" he cried. "What's the matter, love?"

"I had a horrible dream. It was horrible, Richard."

He switched on the bedside lamp. Ellen was shaking. He'd never seen her so upset. Something was very, very wrong.

"Let's go downstairs," he said.

He made her a cup of tea and took it to her in the living-room, where she was curled up on a couch. He draped a throw about her shoulders.

"Nance came to me in the dream," she told him. "She said she was murdered."

"Nance? Who's Nance?"

"Mrs Brennan's mother. They killed her, Richard! She told me."

In the days that followed, Richard began to believe that Ellen was losing her mind. Or, if that were not the case, then she was certainly losing her grip on reality.

That night, the night of the dream, as she sat on the couch in the living-room, she'd recounted in great detail what had occurred. Her dream, she said, was one of the most unusual she'd ever had. Scarcely had she fallen asleep but she began to dream in the most lucid way.

As she lay in the bed she saw a figure appear from the stairwell. It crossed in front of the door to the bathroom and she could see it clearly in the faint light from the far window. It was an elderly woman. There was little about her that was out of the ordinary. She was rather plain in appearance and wore what looked like a bulky cardigan over an ankle-length dress.

She approached the bed where Ellen lay next to the sleeping Richard. As she drew closer she raised a finger to her lips. She did not speak but Ellen heard her voice as though it came from inside her own head.

"We've never met," she told Ellen, "but I used to live here. This was my home. I am Nance."

"She told me she'd died in the house but hadn't died a natural death," Ellen says. "She said she was glad we'd moved in and that I reminded her of herself in her young days. Then she said something about 'them' trying to come in, and not to worry: she'd protect us from 'them'."

The last thing Ellen remembers the old lady saying was something about the rockery. That was when she woke up.

Downstairs, as they spoke long into the night, Richard did his best to convince her that it had all been a dream. An unusually vivid dream, but a dream nonetheless. He did not believe in ghosts. And even less in ghosts that came to people in dreams in order to disclose dark secrets. Eventually he persuaded Ellen that she'd feel better if she got some rest. They went back to bed.

He woke up the next morning – a Sunday – to find himself alone in the bed. There was neither sight nor sound of Ellen. Intrigued, and not a little wary, he dressed and made his way downstairs. There was no sign of her anywhere in the *tigín*.

He heard sounds from outside, noises he could not at once identify. The front door stood ajar. He stepped out onto the veranda.

"What the–"

Where once had been a beautiful, well-tended rockery was a scene of devastation. The white stones had been upturned and rolled away in all directions, leaving trails of

170

soil on the lawn. Flowers had been torn out by the roots and strewn far and wide.

It wasn't hard to find the culprit. She was standing amid the destruction with her back to him, digging in the earth with a spade.

"Christ Almighty, Ellen! What are you doing?"

She gave no sign that she'd even heard him. He left the veranda.

"Ellen, what's going on?"

Still she ignored him. Richard came up behind her and grasped her arm, preventing her from continuing with her furious digging. He jerked her around to face him. Her face was expressionless. It was like looking at a sleepwalker.

"Ellen, put the spade down."

In the end he had to prise it from her hands. She hadn't said a word the whole time. Taking her gently by the hand, he led her to the bench on the veranda and sat her down. Her shoes had trailed dirt from the ruined rockery, marring the white boards. But that was of no concern to Richard at that moment. He was terribly anxious.

"I honestly thought Ellen had lost her mind," he tells me. "That she'd flipped. I was thinking about that night and what she'd said about the dream. I knew it had upset her but I didn't think she'd take it as bad as she seemed to be taking it. I couldn't take my eyes off the rockery, and neither could see. She still hadn't said a word, just kept staring at it. I knew the work she'd put into it. I was thinking that any moment she'd come to her senses and see what she'd done. But she didn't – at least that's the impression I had."

Eventually, after much coaxing from Richard, Ellen broke her silence.

"She said something about the rockery, Richard. Maybe she wants me to find something."

"It was only a *dream*, love."

"No!" She was adamant. She'd grown suddenly agitated. Richard was convinced he'd have to restrain her to prevent her returning to her frenetic digging.

"Calm down," he said. "We'll talk about it, okay?"

"We have to help her!"

"Fair enough, Ellen. But this isn't the way to do it. Look, let's go inside. You sit down and I'll make us breakfast, all right?"

He managed to persuade her to come indoors. They ate breakfast together in the living-room and Ellen seemed to have reverted to her old self again. He saw, however, that she still had a haunted look. He wondered if it might be a good idea to take her to see her doctor, perhaps have her put on a course of antidepressants. He was disturbed by the change in her personality. She'd always been a very sensible person; it was why he was attracted to her in the first place. He knew she scoffed at such things as ghosts and the paranormal. As far as he knew she'd stopped being a practising Catholic when still at secondary school. He wasn't sure she even believed in God, never mind the afterlife and all things connected with it.

"If it makes you feel any better," he said, "we can make inquiries. Find out how Mrs Brennan's mother died. How do you feel about that?"

She seemed mollified and that came as a great relief to Richard. But no sooner had he made the suggestion than he began to question the wisdom of it. Where would they start? He didn't know when the woman had died. All he knew was that the *tigín* had stood vacant for about a year. That meant nothing of course. Granted, there was the matter of the abandoned personal items. It seemed likely that she'd left in a hurry. Richard didn't know too much about such things yet he reasoned that if an elderly woman was taken to, say, an old folk's home towards the end of her days then she would more than likely wish to take her clothes and personal effects with her. All things pointed to the woman having left hurriedly.

Or, he thought, having been *dispatched* hurriedly.

As luck would have it, Richard didn't have to wait too long before embarking on his investigation. He was tidying up the garden shed around midday. It occurred to him that he hadn't told Ellen where he'd put the key to the padlock so how could she have got in to fetch the spade? Or at least he'd no recollection of telling her. He'd helped Ellen repair some of the damage she'd done to the rockery and was putting away the spade and other implements when he heard a car draw up in the adjoining yard. He shut the door to the shed and went to see who it was.

The visitor was a young man of about nineteen or twenty. He recalled Mrs Brennan having said that family members used the farmhouse from time to time, whenever they needed a place to stay in the area. This, Richard decided, might be such a case.

"Hello!" he called out.

The young stranger introduced himself as Jack Hannigan. He was the son of one of Mrs Brennan's brothers, and had returned from England, where he was at university. Richard invited him around to the *tigín*.

Jack didn't even glance at the rockery or the soil-strewn grass as he accompanied Richard into the little house. Richard guessed that gardens were low on his list of priorities. He recalled his own student days; they'd been spent in a series of rooms and flats that had nothing more than a money plant or a window-box. He couldn't even remember so much as watering a plant.

Jack Brennan accepted a beer gladly and Ellen, after some hesitation, joined the men in the living-room.

"So you like Gran's place then, do you?" Jack asked.

"We do," said Richard. "It's very quiet. That's what we like about it. Did she live here long?"

"I'd say about ten years. She loved it here. We hardly ever knew she was at home, she was so quiet. She'd spend most of her time painting." He looked about him. "I see you've left her stuff hanging."

Ellen and Richard exchanged meaningful looks. Each was wondering who was going to broach the awkward subject, the reason why Richard had invited Jack in the first place. To Richard's surprise, it was Ellen who took the initiative.

"Did she die here?" she asked. "Your granny?"

Richard looked at her sharply. But Jack only shook his head without much emotion.

"No," he said. "Not here, no. She was visiting an old friend in Tuam. In the nursing home. My aunt dropped her off there. Why do you ask?"

"Oh, it's just that we thought it was a bit strange that she left her stuff behind. Now I understand."

It appeared to Richard that Jack was a little reluctant to talk about it. At the same time he didn't want Ellen asking any more questions either. He knew she was still very upset, even if she was outwardly calmer now. The last thing he wanted was to arouse Jack's suspicions. The whole matter was getting out of hand as far as he was concerned.

He thought back on Ellen's unusual dream. He wondered if there might be something in it after all. But if there was any investigating to be done it was better if it was done calmly.

He thanked Jack for the information and they left the *tigín* together. Out in the garden he confided to the young man that Ellen was feeling a bit uneasy in the house. She was superstitious, he said, and like so many people felt uncomfortable in the presence of death. They joked about it as Richard knew that Ellen was out of earshot. But he had to know two things.

"Do you happen to know who the old friend was?" Richard asked as casually as he could. "It's just that Ellen was interested in your gran's paintings. I think she was curious as to where she got her inspiration."

"Aye. Kitty Mulvany. They used to be neighbours."

"And she's in the nursing home, is she?"

"I think so. It's the Greendale, just south of Tuam."

Richard thanked Jack, said goodbye, and returned indoors. Ellen was nowhere to be seen but he heard her moving about upstairs. He called out to her.

"I think you better come up here, Richard."

He found her sitting on the bed. There were papers spread out on the duvet. He saw that one of the wardrobe doors was open. It was the section that contained the old lady's clothing and shoes. Richard saw that a drawer was open.

He sat down next to Ellen. She was studying a number of old handwritten letters.

"They're hers," she said.

"I don't know if you should be reading those, Ellen. They're –"

"Look!" She was holding a letter up so he could see it better. Her hand trembled slightly. "Look at the name."

"Nance Hannigan?"

"Yes, *Nance*! Richard, how did I know her name? Mrs Brennan didn't mention it. She only spoke about her mother. How could I have known?"

"Her paintings? Her books?"

"She didn't sign any of her paintings, Richard! And I didn't even open any of her books. So I couldn't have known."

"I'm sure there's a logical explanation, love."

"Is there?"

"Maybe you heard the name. Maybe –"

"Wouldn't I remember if I had? I mean, it's a very unusual name, isn't it? I never heard it before. What would it be the short for? Nancy? Frances? I don't know. But I know I didn't hear it until last night."

He patted her wrist. "I believe you."

"So what are we going to do, Richard?"

He looked at the clock on the bedside locker. It was a little after two.

"Well," he said, "if it'll put your mind at ease, we'll go to Tuam."

The nursing home proved to be only a fifteen-minute drive away. A mile or two south of Tuam they found a small sign pointing the way. Presently they were turning in at the gate and approaching the big house.

There was nothing remarkable about Greendale Nursing Home. It resembled several such places that Ellen had visited over the years, usually in her mother's company. It was a plain, grey building that might have been built in Victorian times or earlier. But it stood in parkland that was well kept, its lawns beautifully tended. As they drove slowly up the drive they could see tables set out in front of the building and large umbrellas to give shade. A number of elderly people were seated, some in animated conversation, others alone with rugs over their knees.

"We're looking for Mrs Kitty Mulvany," Richard told the young woman in reception.

"I'm afraid Mrs Mulvany is no longer with us. Are you a relative?"

Richard tried hard not to show his disappointment. "You mean she's . . . eh . . . "

"She died about three months ago, yes."

"Oh dear."

"I'm sorry. Is there any way I can help?"

"There is actually," he said. "We were hoping she could tell us a little about a friend of hers: a Mrs Hannigan. We're renting her old cottage and we found some private papers of hers. We were wondering what to do with them." Richard knew as he said it that it was a very flimsy story, but couldn't think of a more convincing one.

"Nance Hannigan?"

"That's right."

"I'm afraid Nance is–"

"Yes, I know. I understand she passed away here as well. You see–"

"No, she died at home. She only ever visited here. She was never a resident."

"Oh, I thought she–"

"Have you spoken to Nance's family?" The receptionist looked puzzled. "Surely you should be talking to Mrs Brennan about–"

"Yes, of course," said Ellen. "Maybe that's the best thing to do."

The couple left the nursing home bewildered. Why, they wondered, had young Jack lied about the circumstances surrounding his grandmother's death?

That evening the phone rang. Ellen answered it. It was Mrs Brennan.

"What's going on?" she demanded. "Why were you asking about my mother?"

Ellen was taken off guard, but recovered quickly.

"Er, your nephew Jack was talking about her. We were just making conversation, that's all."

"I'm not talking about Jack!" Mrs Brennan snapped. "I'm talking about your visit to the nursing home. They got in touch with me. What business had you in going there?"

Ellen had had enough. She didn't like the woman's tone at all.

"Mrs Brennan," she said as calmly as she could, "we went to see Kitty Mulvany. We didn't know she'd died. And what Richard and I do on a Sunday is really no business of yours."

There was a silence on the other end of the line. After a few moments Mrs Brennan's voice returned.

"Well, you can pack your bags tomorrow," she said. "I want you out of there. Is that clear? I'm getting in touch with my solicitor right this minute."

And she hung up.

"What was *that* all about?" Richard said.

"The bitch is evicting us."

"*What!* She can't do that."

Ellen laughed shortly. "You don't think so? Landlords can get away with murder in this country. Hmm, maybe that's the wrong thing to say. But if madam wants us out you can be sure madam has something to hide."

Richard was looking at her queerly. "Well, maybe," he said.

On their final night, and for the second time in a row, Ellen's sleep was disrupted by an unsettling dream. Again, Richard awoke to find her sobbing beside him.

"She came again," she said. "Nance. She was definitely murdered, Richard."

"Look, you were only dreaming. Anyhow, we'll be out of here tomorrow – and not before time."

Ellen's agitated state told him it would be a while before they could sleep again. He suggested they go downstairs for a while. He was concerned for her mental health. And she still hadn't explained what had led to her destruction of the rockery. Perhaps now was as good a time as any to ask her about it – but gently.

"What came over you yesterday morning?" he asked when she'd regained her composure. "At the rockery. It was like you were a different person. Or you were walking in

179

your sleep? I didn't want to upset you by harping on about it but maybe you want to talk about it now."

She nodded. "I didn't want to talk about it, but I suppose I should."

The story came out, and it mystified Richard more than ever. Ellen had woken early the previous morning, the Sunday, with the remnants of a second dream in her consciousness. She couldn't remember any of it, she told him, but felt the presence of Nance Hannigan in the bedroom. The old woman was urging her to go outside.

She confessed that the first she knew of her destruction of the rockery was when he'd come out of the house and stopped her. The previous hours were a blank for her.

"It was as if," she told him, "it happened to another person."

"You were sleepwalking, love," he said. "It happens. Mostly people do it at night. But it can happen during the day as well."

"I don't think so, Richard. There was more to this. Nance was trying to tell me something. She kept saying something about the rockery."

"Well, maybe she liked the way you were tending to it."

"No, I don't think so."

"Look, you dreamed it all up yourself, love. Literally. And there's no point in dwelling on it any more. She can annoy the next unfortunates who move in here."

Richard phoned the office, told them he wasn't feeling well and would be taking the day off. It had been a second night of disrupted sleep and arguments. Besides, they had to get their things together in anticipation of Mrs Brennan's impending arrival.

At around three in the afternoon they heard her car pull into the yard. She stepped out as Richard was opening the front door. The rockery caught her eye. He saw her shake her head and bite her lip.

"You better come in," he said.

There were no pleasantries. Mrs Brennan was in no mood for them. The couple surmised that she'd driven from Dublin, and she confirmed it.

"I spoke to Ellen yesterday," she told Richard, "and I believe I made my position clear." She was looking steadily about the living-room and beyond. "I'm sorry but you seem to have overstepped the mark as far as my mother is concerned. You'd no right to pry into our family's affairs. What business was it of yours?"

"None, I suppose," Richard began but she cut him short.

"How would you feel if I was to do the same with you and your family? I don't even know you. No, I want you to leave."

She opened her bag and drew out some banknotes.

"Here. I'm returning the month's rent you paid, minus the week you've been here."

"What about our deposit?" Ellen said weakly.

Mrs Brennan nodded grimly. "I'm holding on to that." She reached into her bag again and drew out her copy of the lease Richard had signed. She turned to the second page. "You're in breach of the contract, as you well know. You agreed to maintain the property in the state you found it in. Which you didn't. I've seen the garden; you destroyed it. And my mother was so proud of her garden. How could you do such a thing? What possessed you?"

What possessed you? It was a question that would return to haunt Ellen in the days and weeks to come. And it haunts her still.

To this day she has no rational explanation for her behaviour on that Sunday morning. The couple moved out of the *tigín* later that day and returned to Galway. Friends had offered to put them up until they got on their feet.

Eventually they found another flat in the city. It was on the second floor, and of course had no garden. Ellen didn't mind. She'd had enough of gardens.

They never returned to the vicinity of the Hannigan farmhouse and the *tigín*. They heard later on that the Hannigans had let it out to an elderly widow, who by all accounts had settled in very well.

If old Nance had objected to the new tenant, she gave no sign.

Ellen's story ends there. It ends, as do so many cases involving the paranormal, leaving unanswered questions. It's probably fair to say that they will never be answered.

Ellen remains convinced that the occurrences in the *tigín* defy explanation. Aside from her curious dreams there's the matter of the jar of bath salts that made its way back to its original place on the shelf. The painting of Eve that mysteriously returned to its hook on the wall. And the plaster angel that fell from the wall, even though the nail remained in place and the string was unbroken.

What really took place in the *tigín*? In the final analysis we're left with a number of possibilities.

One: Ellen was suffering from delusions, as manifested in the dreams. The movement of the jar of bath salts could be put down to plain forgetfulness, but the broken angel could not. Did she break it herself to convince Richard? It seems unlikely. Family and friends of the couple will vouch for her absolute honesty and level-headedness. I have no reason to doubt them. I believe I'm a good judge of character and Ellen strikes me as being a very reliable witness, and one, moreover, who is not given to exaggeration.

There is also the matter of motive. There is no good reason why she should lie about her experience. She had nothing to gain, and much to lose. Real names do not appear in *Ireland's Haunted Women* therefore attention-seekers would have drawn a short straw.

Two: An unknown entity was pulling the wool over Ellen's eyes. Some would consider this to be a likely possibility.

A poltergeist is sometimes called a "mischievous ghost". However, the great psychoanalyst CG Jung applied the word "malicious" to the tricks and sometimes destructive activity that such entities engage in. He wrote that certain paranormal phenomena

remind us of the trickster. These are the phenomena connected with poltergeists . . . The malicious tricks played by the poltergeist are as well known as the low level of his intelligence and the fatuity of his "communications".

This explanation does not fit the bill. The entity that visited Ellen seems to have possessed much more than a "low level" of intelligence. This was more than a prankster from "the other side" at work. It seems to suggest a well-thought-out scheme or campaign, one designed to place a wedge between the Hannigan family and their new tenants. It also succeeded – for a time at least.

If we accept this last as the best explanation for what went on in the little house then the implications are frightening. This was no mindless intelligence but one which was coldly calculating. It knew enough about the late Nance Hannigan to be able to impersonate her, and to convince a bright young college graduate that it was the genuine article.

But to what purpose? I doubt we will ever know the answer, just as so much remains hidden to us. It's hard to see what was achieved by this deception. Certainly it was of no benefit to either Ellen or Richard, and the Hannigan family – Mrs Brennan in particular – suffered unduly because of it. There can be no question of wrongdoing on the woman's part; on seeing the wrecked garden she was simply annoyed – and reacted as anybody would on finding their mother's property damaged.

One comes across many incidences of ghosts appearing to the living for noble or worthwhile reasons. Often the purpose of the visitation is to right an ancient wrong, or to reveal the whereabouts of the mortal remains of the visitant. But in the case of the late Nance Hannigan no such purpose was served.

The third, and final, explanation is that Nance Hannigan could not accept that she'd passed on. Having been thrust into the spirit world she was unprepared for such a transition and simply couldn't let go of her material existence. On seeing others encroach on her territory, she concocted the story of her murder in order to drive the couple away. She was intent on making mischief. If that was the case then she succeeded very well.

Her plan worked to perfection.

7

The Unquiet Spirit of Hazel Quinn

The goblins of her fancy lurked in every shadow about her, reaching out their cold, fleshless hands to grasp the terrified small girl who had called them into being.

LUCY MAUD MONTGOMERY, *Anne of Green Gables*

All were agreed that the accident should never have happened. And all in the quiet suburb of Letterkenny, County Donegal, expressed their dismay that a young family should be so cruelly left without a mother.

Hazel Quinn was only thirty-six when she died. Her killer was perhaps fifteen or sixteen, far too young to have been driving a car. That was the conclusion of the only person to witness the accident at close hand: a man walking his dog on the opposite side of the street. It was a little after eleven o'clock on a balmy summer's evening in 1997.

Hazel was returning home from a night out with some women friends. She'd meet them every other Thursday, go

186

for an enjoyable meal, catching up on gossip and renewing acquaintances. Her husband Peter didn't mind at all: he enjoyed his own "lads' night out" twice a month.

The car driven by the youthful joy-rider struck Hazel just after she'd stepped off the pavement. In the ordinary run of things she'd have looked to the right before crossing, but two of her girlfriends had honked their car horns simultaneously as they departed in the opposite direction, thereby distracting her and masking the sound of the car that collided with her. The joy-rider sped on. Hazel died in the ambulance on the way to the hospital.

She left behind three children: Maeve, aged fourteen, Conor, twelve, and Mikayla, who'd just turned seven.

There are a great many photographs of Hazel in the Quinn home. Peter has several albums showing his wife together with him and the children; framed pictures of her hang in every room and stand on every mantelpiece and dresser. She must have been stunning in life: tall and curvaceous with shoulder-length black hair that she invariably wore tied in a ponytail. Her eyes are dark and large; she has the complexion of a Spaniard or an Italian.

The children, on the other hand, take after their father: all three are strawberry blond and blue-eyed. Peter shows me a snapshot taken in 1997, three months after the tragedy. The children seem tall for their ages; Maeve could pass for an eighteen-year-old. She gazes into the camera with a look of maturity beyond her years. This is no accident; following the death of her mother she took over the care of her younger siblings, almost becoming a surrogate mother to them. She kept the family together, Peter insists, and it's clear he's tremendously proud of her.

For of course it was no easy time for any of them. Maeve had gone for the summer to a Gaeltacht in Donegal. Her studies were cut short at once when news reached her that her mother was dead. An uncle came to collect her.

It was a grim group of relatives that gathered that morning in the Quinn home, the morning following Hazel's death. It's a beautiful, four-bedroomed detached house on the eastern edge of Letterkenny. It stands in its own grounds, overlooking Lough Swilly. Even in winter it's impressive. The Quinns bought it in 1995 when Peter was appointed assistant manager of a bank in the town centre. It was where he met Hazel; she'd been working in the same office. They married in 1990 after a whirlwind courtship.

Those who knew them well say they were among the most devoted couples they'd ever met. They seemed to have so much in common; each had grown up in a rural area close to Letterkenny; both had graduated in Economics and Finance from University College Dublin, though at different times. It was the bank that brought them together. They were bright and destined for great things. Hazel had vowed to return to the workplace when the children had finished school; she and Peter had planned on setting up a consultancy together.

A moment's madness on the part of a teenaged tearaway was to put paid to those plans and alter the course of their lives.

The ghost made its first appearance to seven-year-old Mikayla, the youngest child. And it broke the first "rule" of a haunting: it appeared to her in daylight.

As we have seen, there are, roughly speaking, three types of ghost. The first is far and away the most common: the so-called residual haunting.

The experts are largely in agreement that no actual intelligence lies behind this phenomenon. It is little more than a sort of psychic hologram, a "loop" or sequence that is replayed over and over again. It resembles more than anything a 3D movie. It's "projected" onto a locality and does not interact with those who witness it. No one knows what causes the residual haunting, even though theories abound.

The poltergeist is a horse of a different colour. There seems little doubt that intelligence – or consciousness – is involved. The poltergeist appears to be very aware of its surroundings and, more to the point, of those it targets. Yet it seems to have no purpose other than to torment, hence its often-used nickname: the "mischievous spirit". Some say, however, that the poltergeist will "turn nasty" on occasion, that an entity with evil intent will take the place of the poltergeist and create havoc in the home. It's for this reason, they insist, that poltergeist activity should be nipped in the bud whenever possible.

The third type of ghost is that known as the "restless dead". It combines characteristics we associate with both residual hauntings and poltergeist activity. It's visible, will sometimes speak and even touch. Most importantly it will interact with the percipient, often seeking to impose its will on the living. In short, this is a phantom with a purpose.

The ghost appeared on a warm afternoon towards the end of August, seven weeks following Hazel Quinn's death. Mikayla was out cycling with her best friend Joanna.

The two were virtually inseparable. They sat together in class, went to and from school together, alternated doing their homework together at one another's houses. Strangers took them for twin sisters. Small wonder: they tended to dress alike and wear their hair the same way.

The friends had made a tour of the park near where they lived and were homeward bound. Mikayla would, as usual, take her leave of her friend at Joanna's place and cycle home to her own. She turned onto the street that led to her house. She was used to this, and knew to get up extra speed in preparation for the incline.

She pulled the bike up short – and nearly fell from the saddle.

Standing by a wall a few doors up was a woman who looked uncannily like her mother.

Mikayla didn't know whether to shout for joy or scream in fear. Her mother had returned from the dead. She stared at the apparition. There was nothing ghostlike about the woman. In the clear light of the evening sun she looked as solid and as real as any person of flesh and blood. Moreover, she was wearing a beige trench coat, a garment her mother always favoured; it was almost her trademark. She was also carrying a brown handbag, one Mikayla recognized as well. There could be no doubt in the girl's mind: she was looking at her mother.

She continued to stare at the figure, hardly daring to breathe. She wanted somebody to come along, someone she knew. She wanted to be able to grasp them by the arm and say: "Look! Do you see her? That's my mammy."

But nobody came. The street was deserted; there was no traffic, no pedestrians. It was only Mikayla and the ghost.

All of a sudden the spectral woman raised a hand. She waved to Mikayla. She was wearing a smile that spoke to the child of great happiness. Then she began to fade. Within perhaps fifteen seconds she was gone without a trace, leaving the little girl staring at a garden wall.

Mikayla ran with her bike and leaped onto it. She pedalled as fast as she could, heart racing, and didn't slow until she'd turned in at the gate leading to her home. Moments later she burst into the kitchen. She found her brother Conor there, still in his school uniform and making himself a sandwich.

"I saw Mammy!" she blurted out.

Fourteen-year-old Maeve came home a half-hour later, to find her young siblings having a stand-up row in the living-room. Little Mikayla was in floods of tears.

"Did you hit your sister?" Maeve demanded, grabbing Conor.

"No, I didn't! Lemme go! She was telling lies about Mammy."

Maeve rounded on Mikayla. "Is that true?"

"No, it isn't!" cried a blubbering Mikayla. "I saw Mammy when I came home from school. I swear I did."

And she told Maeve what it was she'd seen.

"Listen to me, Mikayla," her sister said. "Don't you say a word about this to Daddy, you hear me? He'll–"

"But I *did* see her! Why doesn't anybody believe me?"

"Just don't. Do you understand? I'll be very cross with you if you do. And so will Daddy."

Maeve took control, as she'd done since her mother's death. She was doing a very good job of keeping the family on an even keel. She was a sensible girl, always had been.

She'd had a lot of fast growing up to do in the past couple of months. But the younger children looked up to her and trusted her. She made them feel safe, something they had not felt since the accident.

When Peter Quinn came home early that evening he found his three children busy with their homework. No one had mentioned ghosts.

Conor Quinn, aged twelve, sat up in bed the following night. He'd awakened from the latest in a spate of horrid nightmares he'd been having since his mother's death. Not surprisingly, speeding cars and traffic accidents were involved, and sometimes he'd wake up screaming.

This time, however, his awakening had been gradual and not in the least bit frightening. He'd opened his eyes and glanced automatically at his bedside clock to check the time – you never knew with the dark mornings; it might even be close to getting-up time.

He'd sat up in bed because he thought he saw something moving past his window. He looked again. There was somebody there. Somebody with long hair.

"Maeve, is that you?" He had no idea why she'd entered his room; she never did.

It wasn't Maeve, however. This person's hair was tied in a ponytail. Now Conor could see that she was dressed in the light-coloured coat that Mikayla had described and was carrying the same handbag.

It was his mother.

Later, when telling Maeve about it, Conor was sure that his initial reaction was not one of fear. It was more perplexity bordering on incredulity – although needless to say he didn't use those words. He says that one of his first thoughts was that he must be experiencing what Mikayla had earlier. His second thought was that he was sorry to have called her a liar.

The woman had her face turned away from him.

"Mammy?"

At the sound of the boy's voice, her head slowly turned. It was Hazel Quinn. She smiled serenely at her young son – the light in Conor's bedroom was strong enough to show that.

For reasons he cannot explain he burst out crying. It was probably a case of the sadness within him welling up at that moment. As the only boy in the family he'd perhaps have felt that he had to put a brave face on it when he lost his mother. But he was only a child and the loss was devastating. Now he broke down completely and began to wail.

That was how his father found him.

Conor hadn't heard him coming into the room. The first he knew of it was when he felt strong arms grip and hug him.

"Bad dream, son?"

Conor shook his head and continued to sob. He pointed. "Mammy's here."

Peter looked about him, half-expecting to see something out of the ordinary. He wasn't at all surprised to find nobody there. Dreams can appear terribly real to a twelve-year-old.

"Would you like to sleep in my bed?" Peter asked gently.

Conor shook his head vehemently. He was too old for that. "I'm fine, Dad. But I really did see Mammy. She was here. Mikayla saw her as well."

"*What!*"

"Today. After school. I'm not supposed to tell you."

"Well, I'm glad you did. Tell me more."

When Conor finished his account of his sister's strange experience Peter didn't know what to believe. Conor assured him that the figure Mikayla saw tallied with the apparition in his bedroom. It was definitely their mother.

Peter did his utmost to reassure his son, told him not to worry and returned to his own room. It took him a while to get back to sleep, brooding as he did on what he'd heard. Children tended to make up stories – that was a given. And he knew that his own children were not averse to storytelling.

Yet the more he thought about Conor's story, and the boy's account of Mikayla's "vision" in the street, the less he felt inclined to doubt that there was something in it. Conor had been genuinely upset; it was out of character.

He waited until the following day, when they'd had the evening meal. The dishes had been put away and the children were engaged in their usual activities: completing extra homework, watching television or listening to music. Mikayla was doing the latter, in her room. Peter knocked politely – as he always did. On receiving no answer – as always – he pushed open the door, to find Mikayla sitting on her bed and tapping her stockinged feet to a tinny rhythm coming over her earphones. She looked up in surprise and switched off her Walkman. He sat down on the bed.

"Now don't take this the wrong way, love," he said gently. "Conor didn't tell me of his own accord. I had to twist his arm, you see."

194

She laughed.

"It's about you seeing your mammy yesterday . . . "

Her reaction caught him off guard. He'd expected her to grow angry and complain about her brother "squealing on me", as she invariably did. Instead she burst into tears – in almost the exact same way Conor had done the previous night.

Touched, Peter did what he could to console her. It was at that point, he would say later, that he understood that his children had been hiding their real feelings from him – and from the world at large. He'd spoken to their teachers and received excellent reports. All three seemed to have taken their mother's death better than could have been expected. Peter had heard nothing but praise for his offspring, and for Mikayla in particular. It was thought that the youngest would have felt the loss most keenly. She'd surprised everyone.

Now Peter realized that Mikayla's courage had been a sham. As he did his best to comfort her, he fancied he could sense some of the heart-tearing grief she must have suffered. A deep chasm had been left in the little girl's life, and it was a chasm that would probably never be filled.

"Do you want to talk about it?" he asked.

She shook her head vigorously.

"It's okay, Mikayla. I won't laugh at you. Did you really see Mammy?"

She nodded.

"What did she look like?"

"Like Mammy."

"No, I mean: was she happy – or sad?"

"I think she was happy. She smiled and waved at me. Then she went away again."

Mikayla was confirming what Conor had already told him. He pressed her for more information: anything that would shed more light on the event. But the child assured him that the experience had been brief.

He told her that he loved her. That her dead mammy loved her too and that was why she'd appeared. He hadn't the heart to tell the child that he didn't believe in such things. It was not that he suspected her of making up stories, more that he thought that the "apparition" was the result of an over-active imagination – of trying to come to terms with an unendurable loss.

It made some sort of sense. The one child sees what she believes is the ghost of her dead mother. Her brother sees something similar a few hours later. To Peter's analytical mind it was a clear instance of one imagination influencing another.

All the same, having to console two grieving children in less than a day was far from pleasant. Their stories had also re-opened wounds that had but recently healed – after a fashion. Peter was still devastated by Hazel's untimely death. If he were honest with himself, he hadn't really come to terms with it. He saw very clearly that his children were the true victims in all of this.

They say that good things come in threes. Whatever the truth of that, Maeve Quinn was the third member of the family to receive a ghostly visit from her mother, and she certainly considered it to be a good thing.

She'd been very dubious on hearing of Mikayla's sighting; she'd sided with her brother and decided that the girl was making it up. "Looking for attention" was the expression she'd used.

When Conor professed to having seen his mother as well, Maeve very unkindly considered it to be no more than a case of him playing the "copycat" – his own way of seeking attention. Maeve did not believe in ghosts. She was a very devout girl, a weekly communicant and a member of the Legion of Mary. Her RE teachers and priests frowned on anything paranormal, and that was good enough for Maeve.

The day following Conor's "visitation" was a Saturday, hence washday. Maeve had taken over this duty and had even set a time for it: ten in the morning. Once the washing was done she could allow it to dry for the rest of the day, even hang it outside, weather permitting.

But this particular Saturday morning was overcast and bleak, with a cold wind blowing in off Lough Swilly. Maeve collected the laundry basket from each of the two bathrooms and brought them out to the utility room. It was at the rear of the house, overlooking the garden and conservatory.

She filled the machine and switched it on. But as she was bending over to select the correct programme, something in the conservatory caught her eye. She straightened.

There was a figure standing there. And it wasn't her father. It was her *mother*.

We do not know what went through the girl's head at that moment. Nevertheless we can imagine that it was a seminal moment for her. At once, her doubts were swept aside; she went from being a sceptic to a believer. Her siblings had not been fibbing, as she'd supposed.

The woman who had been Hazel Quinn in life was dressed as Maeve's brother and sister had described her: the same coat and handbag. She'd remained standing on the one spot in the middle of the conservatory, no more than five metres from where Maeve stood. She didn't move, merely stood smiling at the girl.

Overcome with emotion, Maeve rushed out of the utility room and through the kitchen. But in the few seconds it took her to reach the conservatory her mother had vanished.

Maeve was dumbfounded. She stood looking up through the glass at the grey, melancholy sky, willing her mother to return, totally happy at having seen her again and desperately sad that she hadn't been able to reach her in time. But alas, she could not summon her back, no matter how hard she willed it or walked about the conservatory praying for it to happen again.

Feeling terribly cheated, she cupped her face in her hands and began to cry.

As chance would have it, Peter Quinn was in the kitchen during those moments, looking out at the garden through the sliding patio door. He'd been debating whether to wash the car. From that vantage point he had an excellent view of the conservatory. He was bemused to see his elder daughter stumbling about with her hands pressed to her cheeks. She stopped; she seemed to be peering at something. He couldn't see her face from that angle, or read her expression. But he was concerned. There was something wrong.

"I couldn't understand it," he would say later. "It was so out of character for Maeve. She seemed out of sorts. Normally she'd be all go on a Saturday morning – unlike the others. She'd be doing the washing and other stuff. You didn't dare get in her way. Now she looked like some kind of lost soul. I knew right away that something was up."

Peter went into the conservatory. He found Maeve standing there with an expression of bewilderment. He saw that she'd been weeping.

"I saw Mammy," she said. She pointed. "Right there. Daddy, she's alive!"

Peter was at a loss. He'd been concerned about Maeve more than her younger siblings. He knew how it felt to be fourteen, to be undergoing such momentous changes, going from childhood to maturity. It wasn't easy. He'd wished so often that Hazel had been around to guide her. On the other hand he was disconcerted to hear her words, coming as they did so hard on the heels of the wild stories Conor and Mikayla were telling. He'd given Maeve credit for more sense. He went to her and took her hand.

"Mammy's dead, sweetheart," he said. "You know that."

"But I *saw* her, Daddy! She was right there. She was smiling. I can't believe you didn't see her."

"I didn't see her because there was nothing to see, Maeve. Now will you stop this nonsense? I don't want you upsetting the others."

Her reaction surprised him. She pulled her hand roughly out of his. She was fuming with anger.

"I'm telling you I saw her, Daddy! If you don't believe me, that's *your* problem." She turned on her heel, then added tearfully: "Mammy wants to get in touch with us. That's what this is all about. She's telling us that she still loves us, that she cares about us – even if you don't."

And with that Maeve fled back into the house.

Two days later she took Mikayla to one side. Their father and brother were safely out of earshot.

"I'm sorry," she said. "I really thought you were telling lies when you said you saw Mammy. I just want to tell you that I saw her as well."

The news astonished Mikayla. She'd half-believed her brother when he'd spoken of his own experience; she suspected he was trying to go one better, which he frequently did – with Maeve as well as Mikayla.

"Did you tell Daddy?"

"Yes," Maeve said. "He must have seen her too because he could see right into the conservatory. But he didn't believe me."

"Maybe it's like fairies," Mikayla said. "Grown-ups can't see them but kids can."

"Don't be stupid."

It was the wrong thing to say and Maeve regretted it at once. But the damage had been done; her sister stormed off in a huff. All the same, the little exchange had brought the two together. Maeve no longer doubted that they – and Conor too – had seen something that was completely wonderful. She also wondered why her father denied seeing what had been as clear as anything in the conservatory that day. Mammy was trying to tell them something.

But she still had no idea what it could be. Nobody had.

"I want you to come to my cousin's birthday party," Joanna announced to her best friend as they cycled home from school.

The evenings were "drawing in" as they say in the vicinity. August had given way to September, and even at four in the afternoon dusk was settling over Lough Swilly and environs.

"Sophie? But she didn't invite me," Mikayla said.

"That's okay. She said I could bring anybody I liked. And I sort of like *you*."

The girls giggled. Mikayla agreed that it was "cool". She hadn't been to a birthday party in a long time. Memories of her own party were overshadowed by what had occurred that night not two weeks later on a street in Letterkenny.

Joanna's cousin Sophie lived on her parents' farm, a good twenty miles to the northwest of the town. It was arranged that Joanna's mother would drive the girls there, would keep her sister-in-law company while the party was in progress, and drive them home again.

Mikayla had made the journey several times before. Each time, Joanna's mother had done the driving. She was a careful driver. She always made sure the girls travelled in the back and that their seat-belts were securely fastened.

The day of the party arrived. Joanna's mother drove the short distance to the Quinn house and rang the doorbell at the appointed time: two fifteen in the afternoon.

"Mikayla!" Peter Quinn called out. "Joanna's here."

Up in her room Mikayla was brushing her hair in the mirror. She'd already dressed up, and even had Maeve do her nails for her with shiny purple glitter varnish.

"Coming!" she shouted, glancing out of the window.

She was about to say something else but the words died in her throat. Her mother was standing down in the yard, gazing up at her.

Mikayla blinked. No, she hadn't imagined it. It was Hazel Quinn, dressed exactly as before, her hair worn in the familiar ponytail. The girl didn't know whether to be happy or sad. Once again she was overcome with emotion.

"Mikaaayyyyla!" It was Joanna in the hallway downstairs, sounding impatient. "Hurry up or we'll miss all the ice cream."

But on this occasion her mother wasn't smiling. She wore a sad expression and was slowly shaking her head from side to side. The message was unambiguous.

Don't go to the party.

The apparition faded. Two minutes later Mikayla was seen coming slowly down the stairs. Peter looked up in alarm on noting her pallor. She appeared most unwell. Joanna and her mother stared.

"What's the matter, love?" Peter said. "Are you all right?"

"Feel sick."

"She doesn't look well at all," Joanna's mother said. "Is it your tummy, Mikayla?"

"Yeah. I can't come to the party."

She'd reached the bottom of the stairs. The three saw her turn and look back the way she'd come.

"It's okay," her father said gently. "If you're not well, you're not well. Nobody's making you go to the old party." He led her to the door to the living-room. "Just you lie down for a minute, love. I'll get you an aspirin."

He apologized to Joanna and her mother and wished them well with the party. They departed from the Quinn house at about two thirty.

Six hours later the phone rang. It was the police.

Joanna's mother knew the route like the back of her hand. As well she might; she'd grown up on the farm. It had passed to her eldest brother a decade before.

It wasn't a particularly dangerous route, mainly because a car could not get up much speed because of the

202

narrowness of the road and the frequent bends. Nevertheless there was one spot that had seen a number of accidents in the past. It was a crossroads, the junction of two roads of equal importance. Visibility there was bad. Even at night, when motorists were using headlights, it was difficult to see a car approaching from another direction.

The policemen who were first on the scene had pieced together as best they could what had happened sometime after 8 p.m. The car in which Joanna was travelling was halfway across the intersection when it was struck by a car approaching from the right. It had been driven at some speed. The other driver had lost control on seeing the car blocking his way. He'd swerved to avoid it but ended up colliding with the rear passenger door.

Mother and daughter had been thrown wildly about the car's interior. The car had ended up in a ditch. Joanna suffered severe concussion and fractures to her right leg and ribcage. Her mother broke an arm.

Summing up at a later stage, a Garda spokesman voiced the opinion that it was fortunate for Joanna that she'd been sitting on the left and not directly behind her mother. Had that been the case, he said, the accident would have probably cost her her life.

The man was not to know that that very seat was sometimes occupied by a little girl named Mikayla Quinn. She invariably sat there when accompanying her best friend Joanna on one of their many outings together.

Nor was he to know that, a few short hours before the accident, Mikayla had been dissuaded from joining her friend and going to her cousin's birthday party.

If he'd known the circumstances surrounding the girl's reluctance to make the journey he'd most certainly have disbelieved her.

Joanna's mother was declared out of danger within two hours of being treated for her injuries. Joanna herself was less fortunate. It was touch and go whether she was going to pull through. Since the accident, she'd failed to regain consciousness. The doctors had done all they could; now it was up to the little patient's own determination to survive.

Mikayla kept a vigil at her friend's bedside when the hospital staff permitted it. At other times she waited outside with Joanna's mother and her sister Maeve. She was inconsolable. She'd cried so many tears that they'd all but dried up.

But Joanna came out of her coma forty-eight hours following her operation. Mikayla was present when the girl opened her eyes. A miracle had happened; she'd survived against the odds. The friends hugged each other as hard as Joanna's injuries would allow.

The girl made a good recovery. Four months after the accident she could walk again without the aid of crutches. A light scarring to her right leg and ribcage was all that remained of the damage. A month after that, she was joining Mikayla to cycle to and from school.

The Quinn story came to my attention by an unusually circuitous route. Mikayla (aged twenty-one at the time of writing) told her story to an American friend, who told it in turn to a mutual friend. I shall call him George. He has an avid interest both in science and the paranormal, and likes to approach each haunting he comes across with an open mind.

He concedes that the Quinn case is intriguing. Nevertheless he's wary and advises caution when drawing conclusions.

"You're dealing with children," he says. "And children are notorious for having unreliable recall. It's not that they make things up (they do that too!) but that the memory of an event from childhood will change over time. It will be added to by the memories of others, in this case Mikayla's brother and sister. You'll rarely hear the story told exactly the same every time. And that's important to remember."

He is, in essence, saying that a memory of a paranormal occurrence will alter to fit the facts. Lucid but wholly bogus memories can easily be induced by a few cues or idle conversation. A child's memory can be contaminated relatively easily, whether by accident or design. False memories can be implanted in minds that have not reached maturity. Even adults are not immune to what psychiatrists call false-memory syndrome.

"I come across this all the time," George says. "For example, I spoke with a woman who claimed to have predicted the 9/11 attack on the World Trade Center. She said it was shown to her in a dream. The problem was that her dream was way too detailed, and the chronology of events closely followed the real thing. Dreams aren't like that. They're vague at best; they obey their own inner logic. It's only when we wake up that we realize how illogical the dream sequence was."

In the Quinn case, he reminds me that the sole "evidence" we have for the appearance of the ghost is the word of three children who, at the time, were still highly traumatized by their mother's death and consequently susceptible to suggestion.

In short, George remains convinced that the ghost was little more than a product of the children's imagination. He suggests that they "manufactured" their own ghost. He cites another case, one I recall having come across several years ago. It concerns an experiment conducted in the 1970s by the Toronto Society of Psychical Research. It is well documented. The group set out to create a fictitious person, whom they called "Philip". He would be given an entire history – or life-story if you wish.

They did it under the guidance of Dr George Owen and his wife Iris, who specialized in cases of poltergeist activity. Dr Owen was a member of the Department for Preventative Medicine and Biostatistics at the University of Toronto. The Owens were interested in testing a theory that predicted that manifestations could be produced by harnessing the power of the "group mind" of participants. Was it possible, they asked themselves, that by concentrating on the fake ghost – Philip – he could be induced to make contact?

The important thing was that this fake biography would be full of historical errors. It was agreed that he would be a seventeenth-century Englishman. They supplied the group with the following bogus information.

Philip was an aristocratic Englishman living in the middle 1600s at the time of Oliver Cromwell. He had been a supporter of the king and was a Catholic. He was married to a beautiful but cold and frigid wife, Dorothea, the daughter of a neighbouring nobleman. One day, when out riding on the boundaries of his estates, Philip came across a gypsy encampment and saw there a beautiful dark-eyed, raven-haired gypsy girl, Margo, and fell instantly in love with her.

He brought her back secretly to live in the gatehouse near the stables of Diddington Manor – his family home. For some time he kept his love-nest secret, but eventually Dorothea, realizing he was keeping someone else there, found Margo, and accused her of witchcraft and of stealing her husband. Philip was too scared of losing his reputation and his possessions to protest at the trial of Margo, and she was convicted of witchcraft and burned at the stake. Philip subsequently was stricken with remorse that he had not tried to defend Margo and used to pace the battlements of Diddington in despair. Finally one morning his body was found at the foot of the battlements where he had cast himself in a fit of agony and remorse.

Philip the fake ghost actually made contact, although only after several months of fruitless attempts. The group had hoped to experience a ghostly manifestation. Instead Philip began to communicate via a series of exchanges that took the form of table-rapping. When questioned about his past, the ghost supplied answers that conformed exactly to his fake biography.

It's a compelling argument: that a ghost can be invented out of thin air, as it were. And I can see how it could come about that three impressionable children could concoct one. They were, after all, as George reminds me, severely traumatized by the sudden death of their mother. Unlike children who lose a parent to a prolonged illness, the Quinns were given no opportunity of preparing for the tragedy. My own mother died very suddenly when I was in my teens. For months afterwards I kept imagining I was seeing her in the street, in towns and cities. I suppose it's the psyche's way of compensating for such a dreadful and unexpected loss. I can well understand how little Mikayla could invent an "invisible friend" to replace the best friend who'd been taken from her without warning.

At the same time I'm sceptical. While the story of "Philip" is interesting – indeed astonishing – it seems to me that it pales beside that of Hazel Quinn. Philip was little more than a series of raps on a table; Hazel walked, moved and interacted with her children. Plainly her "reality" was of a different order.

But for a ghostly manifestation to be considered authentic, it must be repeatable and to be seen (or heard) by a variety of people. I wonder if it's enough that only three *children* communed with the ghost of Hazel Quinn.

Lastly, it's generally believed that this third type of ghost, the phenomenon that interacts with the living, appears for a purpose. It's very tempting to conclude that Hazel Quinn's intention was to dissuade her youngest child from joining her friend on a car journey that would in all likelihood have proved fatal. She herself had died as a result of a collision; she would surely have wished to spare her daughter a similar fate – if that were at all within her power.

If we choose to believe this second hypothesis then a whole vista of possibilities opens up. The most exciting of these possibilities is of course the notion that the human personality can – and does – survive death. That a mother's love for her children can transcend the laws of the physical universe, enabling her spirit to interact with the consciousness of those she has left behind.

That belief is shared by many: by people of all creeds and cultures.

The hypothesis has another startling implication: that time is relative, just as Einstein said it was, and as modern thinkers like the physicist Stephen Hawking corroborate. For those scientists, time is inextricably linked with the speed of light. The theory states that the closer we approach the speed of light the more slowly time will be seen to elapse. If true, then intergalactic travel will be possible; an astronaut will be able to journey to distant stars within his or her own lifetime.

But time for the spirit of Hazel Quinn was also relative. Somehow her consciousness was capable of journeying to a dark evening in September, seeing a road accident that would occur that particular evening, and warning her young daughter about the danger of travelling in that car. This seems to suggest that time is no more than a human construct: that it doesn't really exist, that events are not confined to past, present and future, but exist in a dimension which we cannot perceive with our five senses.

The Christian faith acknowledges the existence of spirit beings, often known as angels. Much is made of the so-called guardian angel, an entity that is said to accompany a human being throughout life, to protect that person when danger threatens. A difficulty, however, lies in knowing the nature of a spirit that claims to be a protector. Scripture warns that evil spirits may pretend to be what they are not. In 1 John 4:1 we learn that Christ cautioned his disciples against such imposters: "Beloved, believe not every spirit, but test the spirits whether they are of God, because many false prophets are gone out into the world."

In the final analysis, then, we might consider the intriguing possibility that the entity that appeared to the Quinn children was *not* the ghost of their dead mother. Rather, it was little Mikayla's very own guardian angel, coming to her in a guise it knew the child could relate to.

It was also important to convince Mikayla of the ghost's authenticity. It seems that the entity chose to make two further appearances in order to achieve this. Conor had to be satisfied that his little sister wasn't making it up – something he refused to believe before seeing the ghost for himself. Convincing Maeve was going to be more difficult, but there too the entity was successful. Having thus established its credentials, the guardian angel could warn Mikayla of impending danger.

According to Peter Quinn the "ghost" made no further appearances. Mikayla got on with her life, as did the other children. Both Maeve and Conor are married with families of their own. Mikayla is at university, studying Economics.

Further intervention by the guardian angel has not been necessary – but it's surely a comfort for the Quinns to know it's available, if and when required.

8

The Dead Girl who Sought Revenge

The phenomena with which we are concerned are so peculiar, and so unlike those visible and tangible facts which ordinary language is designed to deal with, that the right theory of them is bound to seem nonsense when first propounded.

PROFESSOR HH PRÍCE
(addressing the Society for Psychical Research in 1939)

Kelly Mitchelson was excited. She was nineteen years old and had just returned from the holiday of a lifetime.

It was not so much a holiday as an extended stay: she'd spent seven months in Sydney, Australia, as part of her gap year. She'd had a wonderful time, an unforgettable time. She'd worked as a barmaid and "general dogsbody" in an Irish pub. The pay was poor but the tips were lavish. So good that she hadn't needed to access the money her father had deposited in her bank account before she left her native County Tyrone.

Kelly had made many friends in Sydney; there was a certain young Australian who'd begged her to return at the first opportunity and resume what he called their "love affair". It was a youthful fantasy as far as she was concerned – a holiday romance – and she was old enough to know that holiday romances have a tendency to turn sour.

Besides, Kelly had more important matters to detain her. It was August 2001 and she'd left the family home for the second time. This move, however, was to be of a more permanent nature. She'd taken a student flat close to Queens University Belfast. All being well, the apartment would be her home for the next three years. She was scheduled to begin twin studies that coming October: Law and Psychology.

The apartment was spacious. In fact, Kelly's new home was far and away the most luxurious student accommodation enjoyed by any of her peers. For Kelly was a spoiled girl, and always had been. The only child of wealthy farmers, she'd had every advantage possible. Shopping trips to Dublin, London and Paris, expensive holidays in the United States, skiing trips to Switzerland. She passed her driving test when she was barely eighteen and her father had bought her a new car on her return from Australia.

In short: Kelly Mitchelson was the envy of her friends.

The apartment was situated in a street called after a place in Israel; the area in question is known to the people of Belfast as the Holyland. The name dates back to the nineteenth century and to a certain Sir Robert McConnell, a devout Christian and one-time mayor of Belfast. He was a regular traveller in the Middle East, where he and a friend would visit those places mentioned in the Bible. He set up a building firm that developed the area around the university. When it came to naming the new streets, McConnell drew on his travels in Palestine.

The Holyland is a lively district at the best of times, and Kelly, an extrovert young woman, loved it. She invited her mother to visit and stay for a weekend. Mrs Mitchelson accompanied her daughter on a shopping spree. The furnishings in the flat had seen better days and some bright, cheerful fabrics were called for. The ladies spent Saturday afternoon happily picking out new curtains, rugs and throws – items that were more to Kelly's liking.

On Saturday night Kelly slept in the smaller of the two bedrooms, giving her mother the use of the larger one, the one Kelly would be using as her own. Next morning, the two met in the open-plan kitchen-cum-living-room. Mrs Mitchelson was looking distinctly haggard.

"What's the matter?" Kelly asked. "Did my neighbours keep you awake?"

It was an understandable question to ask. Student nightlife in the Holyland is notorious for its exuberance.

"It's not that," her mother said. She sat down wearily. "Just couldn't sleep."

"That's not like you, Mum – you could sleep on a clothesline," Kelly said, handing her mother a coffee. "But come to think of it, the colour scheme in that room would depress anyone. It'll be a great change when I have the new curtains up. And cover up that horrible carpet. It's like something out of Soviet Russia."

Mrs Mitchelson smiled weakly. "Maybe it's me. Not used to sleeping in different surroundings, I suppose." She was looking about the kitchen. "You know, you don't have a single, solitary holy picture in this place."

"Och, Mum! We're in the twenty-first century now."

"No matter," her mother said. "I'll give you a picture when you're home. You can put it in that big bedroom over your bed."

"If you say so, Mum."

They said no more about it. In the afternoon they set to work unpacking Kelly's purchases and redecorating. By the time they'd finished, the flat was as Kelly wanted it; she'd put her personal stamp on the place. A week later she'd be starting at the university. She looked forward to returning to her new home. She and her mother drove back to the farm in County Tyrone that evening.

It was the first Sunday in September and Kelly was in high spirits. Her course would be commencing the next day and she was spending her first night in the flat.

She let herself in around 8 p.m. and went straight through to the main bedroom to unpack her travel-bag. But just as she was about to place the bag on her bed, she noticed something unusual. The bedcover was no longer neatly smoothed down the way she'd left it. It was creased, as though someone had been lying on the bed. Kelly thought back to the weekend before, when her mother had slept in the room, or rather *tried* to sleep. Mystery solved; her mum must have had a lie-down before leaving that day.

Reassured, she straightened the coverlet and unpacked her things. She began singing to herself to try and lighten the atmosphere. For she was becoming increasingly aware of something she hadn't noticed before: there was an atmosphere about the place.

The word "atmosphere" crops up very often when ghosts are being discussed. What is meant is the general mood that pervades a haunted place. It seems to take two forms: the atmosphere will be present at all times, or it will manifest prior to the appearance of the ghost. Professor HH Price, the distinguished Oxford scholar I quoted at the beginning of this case, used his famous 1939 address to the Society for Psychical Research to introduce his "psychic ether" theory of hauntings. He hypothesized that "a certain level of mind may be capable of creating a mental image that has a degree of persistence in the psychic ether." This mental construct may also have the ability to affect others telepathically. People speak of experiencing an atmosphere of depression at the site of a suicide; others tell of feeling threatened or fearful at the scene of a murder.

It is this second that Kelly was experiencing during that first week in September. She tells me this after I've ordered coffee for us. I've met her in the lobby of a quiet hotel near Queen's University. There are very few students here; it's not that sort of place.

Kelly is very calm. She seems to me to be an eminently sensible young woman. She graduated with distinction in her Law study. She tells me that she dropped the Psychology course; she found the two to be slightly conflicting. She speaks very distinctly and with measured words. I can tell she'll be successful when she begins practising law.

"I checked the window in the bedroom because I thought perhaps I'd left it open and someone had got in," she says. "You know how it is: you always look for rational explanations first. But it was shut tight, like all the other windows."

Didn't she want to call her mother?

"Well, you know, I did think about it and then I thought: well, what if she says she didn't lie down? That would have freaked me out. So I decided it was best not to know."

Kelly chose not to sleep in the bedroom that night. The next day would be her first at Queen's and she couldn't risk being tired. She needed rest and the big room was making her feel uneasy. She hung the holy picture her mother had given her – an image of "some saint or other" – above the bed, closed the door on the main bedroom and retired to the spare.

"I slept well," she says. "In fact, that first week was great. But you know, I couldn't bring myself to sleep in the big room. I was just uneasy. Every morning I'd creep in and check if the bedcover was creased. It wasn't, but I was still nervous about sleeping there. My fiancé, Brian, was coming to see me that weekend and I decided I'd wait till then."

The young couple went out for dinner on the Friday evening. Kelly wished to show Brian around her new neighbourhood. She also hints that she wished to show him off to her fellow students; apparently Brian is very attractive. They joined a group of revellers in a pub near the university, had a few drinks and laughs, and returned to Kelly's apartment shortly before two in the morning. They retired to the main bedroom. It would be Kelly's first time to sleep there. She didn't feel afraid because Brian was with her.

But Brian didn't have the best of nights from all accounts. He had a frightening dream – or imagined he'd had one. A woman had appeared at the end of the bed. A youngish woman with long, dark hair. Even though the room was in darkness he could see enough from the streetlight to make out her face. There was something not right about it. He couldn't decide *what* exactly. Some kind of disfigurement.

In his dream Brian told her to go away, but she wouldn't budge. Then quite bizarrely he found himself outside his body. He was gazing down upon three figures caught in a frozen tableau: Kelly sleeping soundly, he himself sitting up in the bed shouting mutely – and the strange woman, standing at the foot of the bed and glaring at him.

He felt threatened and very frightened by the figure. The waves of hostility coming from her were intensifying by the second. He had to get away, and fast.

He attempted to clamber out of bed, but to his horror found that his legs refused to obey him.

"It was as if Brian had done something awful to this person," Kelly tells me. "And if you knew Brian then you'd know that was out of the question. He's such a kind, loving sort of guy. He'd be the last person you'd expect to do harm to somebody else – especially to a woman. But this is what he was getting."

Brian cannot say how long his disturbing and unusual dream lasted. But strangely, when he did wake up, he found himself in the position he'd occupied in the dream: sitting up in bed. The sweat was pouring off him.

Much to his relief, he saw that there was no phantom woman at the foot of the bed. The rest of the bedroom seemed normal too. He could make out the furniture,

Kelly's dressing-table mirror, even identify the prints hanging on the walls.

He switched on the light next to him. Kelly woke up at once.

"What's the matter?" she asked.

He couldn't confide in her – not then. He felt she'd ridicule him, or tell him he'd been dreaming, that the presence was part of a nightmare that had somehow carried over into the waking state.

This happens more often than we might think. The American researcher Christine Higgins, writing in *Clinical Psychiatry News*, tells us that the

area of the brain that is important for many executive functions, such as context representation, information processing, and working memory, is the dorsolateral prefrontal cortex (DLPFC). Brain imaging data have shown that this "reasoning" area of the cortex is specifically deactivated during rapid eye movement (REM) sleep, while the rest of the cortex is highly active. It is widely recognized that dreaming occurs most frequently during the REM phase of sleep. The selective silencing of the DLPFC during REM may be the reason our illogical dreams are accepted by our sleeping brains as perfectly rational. Upon waking, this area is slowly reactivated, allowing you to once again make the distinction between fantasy and reality.

The question arises: could Brian's DLPFC have continued to be silenced minutes after he awoke from sleep? It is entirely possible. He couldn't recall having had a nightmare but that means very little; neuroscientific research shows time and again that a subject can forget that he was dreaming, even though the monitoring of his REM activity indicates that he was.

"I asked Brian if he'd been having a nightmare," Kelly says, "but he was adamant he was not. I thought perhaps he was and that he didn't remember. He seemed satisfied with that. So we went to sleep again, and that was that."

But the following night Brian once again awoke in Kelly's bed with the feeling of being menaced. If anything, it seemed more real than the previous night. This time, however, he allowed Kelly to sleep on without disturbing her. He crept out of bed and went to sleep in the other bedroom.

Whatever it was that had disturbed him for the second time, it did not follow him there.

"He told me about it over breakfast on Sunday," Kelly says. "He was a bit worried. He's normally such a Steady Eddie. He'd hate people to think he was becoming a bit weird. I told him it was okay. I said maybe he'd had too much to drink. Which of course was the wrong thing to say. Brian took it thick and he was still a bit cool towards me when he left for home that evening."

So Kelly was left alone in the apartment. She couldn't help feeling that there was something peculiar happening. First her mother had had a fitful night, then Brian. It was easy to dismiss her mother's misgivings about sleeping in the bedroom. Her mother is, in Kelly's words, "from the old school", and was brought up in a part of Tyrone where ancient religious beliefs and superstitions linger to this day. Kelly can recall a succession of visitors to the family farm:

elderly women who would speak in hushed tones about neighbours who'd attracted "bad luck" by saying the wrong things or neglecting their prayers. Even though Mrs Mitchelson drives a modern convertible and lunches with her lady friends in expensive restaurants, she's only one generation removed from the "old ways".

So much for her mother; Kelly's boyfriend is a different matter. He's young, bright – and completely secular. He believes in "nothing", as he's told her countless times. He epitomizes a brash, new generation of Irishmen.

Yet both were insistent that there was something not right in Kelly's bedroom.

The first week at university passed in an exciting blur. Kelly was so caught up in finding her feet amid a hubbub of course information, new teachers and getting to know her fellow students, that all thoughts of the unsettling bedroom were forgotten – or, rather, put from her mind. She had more important concerns.

She hadn't yet slept in the main bedroom by herself, but intended to, once she'd purchased a set of linings for the curtains. She needed darkness to sleep properly and the streetlight directly outside the bedroom window was distracting.

It was Friday evening and Kelly, with the first week of term behind her, was looking forward to the weekend. She'd planned to go home on the Friday evening, but decided against it. She was tired and rang her mother to say she'd see her the next morning.

After watching television for a couple of hours, she went to bed early: at around half past ten. Yet despite her tiredness Kelly was to have a rather restless night. Not long after falling asleep she found herself awake again.

"I had the impression that something had prodded me in the back," she says. "It was weird. I was lying on my side and something poked me. But I wasn't that scared. I just thought I was dreaming and went back to sleep."

Not for long.

"I always make sure that all the doors are shut before going to bed," Kelly continues. "It comes from living in the country I suppose. I woke up a second time because I thought I heard one of the doors in the corridor being opened."

She sat up in bed, suddenly alert. Was it her imagination? Had she been dreaming? There was only one way to find out. She threw back the bedcovers and went to investigate. She stepped out into the hallway.

As she'd expected, all three doors – those to the kitchen, bathroom and the big bedroom – were closed. Kelly concluded that someone in an adjoining flat had disrupted her sleep. Thus reassured, she returned to bed.

Sleep, however, would not come. She tried to calm herself with some deep-breathing exercises, but her mind kept returning to the door. What if she heard it again? What if she were prodded again, just as she was getting off to sleep? Perhaps it was true that Brian had seen some kind of phantom woman that night. Why would he invent something like that? Kelly's thoughts were churning like laundry on a slow spin. In the darkness of night, all that seemed rational and sane in the light of day was getting fogged up with doubt. There was only one sure-fire remedy, one she'd tried and tested often: music. A good blast of U2 in her ears.

She reached into the bedside locker for her personal stereo. It wasn't there. Then she remembered: it was on the dressing-table in the other bedroom. She'd left it there the morning before when changing handbags.

She'd have to go in there and get it.

She climbed out of bed again. From the travel clock on the locker she saw that it was going on for 3.50. Just as well she wasn't going to lectures next day. . . .

In the hallway she threw the light switch, yawned and stretched out a hand to open the door to the main bedroom.

Something occurred then – something that almost frightened the life out of her.

As her hand was reaching for the doorknob, the door swung open all by itself.

"It was as if someone was in the room and had pulled it open to let me in," she says.

I wonder if a draught couldn't have simply blown the door open. It was an old building after all. Perhaps the catch was worn.

Kelly shakes her head vehemently. "No, absolutely not. The door opened by itself. I know what I saw. I was scared witless."

She dashed back to her own room and slammed the door behind her. At first light she rang her mother to say she'd be home early.

"I decided not to tell her anything because I didn't want her to worry, so I just said I'd woken too early and would get away before the rush-hour traffic."

There wasn't much traffic at that early hour of the morning – which was probably a good thing. Kelly was exhausted from her near-sleepless night. But she knew the route well. A little distance out of the city she would join the M2 motorway and head north along the M22, which would take her westwards towards Derry.

The day was fine, if a little overcast. As she motored along she tried not to think about the strange goings-on of the previous night. She inserted a CD in the player and sang along to it to try and distract herself.

But barely twenty minutes into her journey she became conscious of a subtle change. It was so gradual that she hardly registered it at first. She was looking to her right as a row of large, white wind turbines appeared on the horizon, the early morning sun glancing off their twirling vanes. As she returned her attention to the road she noted a change in the atmosphere in the interior of the car.

"It wasn't anything I could put my finger on," she says. "In fact, I didn't find much out of the ordinary. Not at first. I thought that maybe the road was having a mesmerizing effect on me. I have that sometimes when I'm driving for a long time on a straight stretch. There was hardly any traffic so I didn't need to concentrate very much. I thought it was a case of my thoughts wandering."

She sensed a chill in the car. She reached over and turned on the heating. It helped to some extent.

But now the chill was on the back of her head. An eerie atmosphere was pervading the car. The coldness crept into her shoulders, ran down her back and all the way to her ankles. As she sped over the motorway, Kelly was assailed by feelings of dread. She also had the impression that she was no longer alone in the car. She became convinced that somebody was sitting behind her. She resisted the urge to check her rear-view mirror. The sensation grew.

At last she could stand it no longer. She looked in the mirror. There was nothing: only the rear window and the headrests of black upholstery.

Yet still the coldness intensified. She couldn't understand it. The heater was blowing out hot air but she was freezing. She thought she was going crazy.

She kept stealing glances in the mirror. At one point she actually turned around in her seat to look behind her.

"It was horrible," she says. "I wanted to stop but I was scared of even doing that. I thought I'd be even more vulnerable than if I stayed on the road."

She felt that she had to talk to somebody. She reached into her handbag on the passenger seat and found her mobile. The first number in the memory was her parents'. She called it. Her mother answered.

Kelly, in a rush of words, explained the situation. Or thought she did. Her mother didn't understand. Not at first anyway. But after about a minute she said something that, if anything, increased Kelly's fears.

"That sounds like what I felt that night, love," Mrs Mitchelson said. "The night I spent in your bed and you were in the spare room."

Kelly stopped the car on the hard shoulder and got out. Immediately the coldness that she'd felt all over her body left her. Her teeth were chattering. Her words were barely coherent, but she felt safer.

"All I wanted to do was to leave the car there," she says. "But I couldn't; I didn't know where to go. I begged my mum to stay on the line and talk to me. I left the engine running."

But the worst had passed. When she sat back in the driver's seat the chill had gone. The atmosphere in the car had returned to normal. There was no discernible trace of the thing that had intruded. The car was "clean" again.

Her parents were waiting for her when she finally pulled into the yard of the house she knew so well. She was never so glad to be home at last.

"We have a visitor," Mrs Mitchelson said. "Father Conway."

At first Kelly attached no significance to this. The priest was an old friend of the Mitchelsons. He'd baptized their daughter and had often celebrated the Eucharist on their behalf, in both joy and in sorrow. But Mrs Mitchelson sat Kelly down at the table and spoke urgently to her.

"Your father and I talked it over," she said, "right after the phone call. It was him who suggested that we should call Father Conway. And I agree with him. There's something not right about all of this, love. Maybe you should think about getting another place."

"What! But, Mum, I've only after moving in. And I'm just settling in."

"I know, and that's a right shame, Kelly. But don't you see? It's not safe for you to be there."

"Mum, nothing happened in the flat," Kelly lied. The thought of finding another place and uprooting all her stuff seemed too stressful. "It was in the *car*."

"That's not what Brian said. He rang to say he was very worried about you. He says he felt something in that room, and I did too, but I didn't want to tell you for I didn't want to worry you. There's something bad in that flat. And now it's followed you here."

That was the last thing Kelly had considered. When the "presence" left her car she'd imagined the episode to be over. But now that she thought about what her mother said, she saw no reason why the ghost should not have made the entire journey from Belfast to County Tyrone. She didn't know the first thing about ghosts; she'd thrilled to them as a child; as a teenager she'd watched a number of spooky films through latticed fingers. Yet never once had she entertained the possibility that ghosts might actually exist in the real world.

In *her* world.

"Will you have a word with Father Conway?" her mother asked.

Reluctantly she agreed.

The priest was chatting to her father when Kelly went into the parlour. He got up and shook her hand warmly. They engaged in chit-chat for a minute or two before getting to the reason for his visit. Mr Mitchelson excused himself and allowed them their privacy.

"Tell me what you experienced in the car," Father Conway said.

Kelly told him as much as she could. It was hard though. It's one thing to describe things we see and hear – even touch and smell. It's quite another to try to describe a feeling or an emotional experience. But she did her best.

"It was like somebody was trying to get inside my head, Father," she told him. "He seemed to be in the back seat. I felt so cold all of a sudden, but not everywhere at once.

It started in my head and spread down to my feet. It was weird."

"And it seemed to be threatening?"

"Yes. I got the distinct feeling he was threatening me, yes."

The priest seemed to consider this. "Why do you say it was a 'he'?"

"It, er, felt like it was a man, Father. Don't ask me to explain it – I just *knew* it was a man."

"Fair enough. Do you have enemies, Kelly? I don't mean people you don't get on with. We all have *those*. But is there somebody who really hates you?"

"No, I don't think so. Why do you ask?"

"I'm asking because it's not often we actually come across real hatred," he said. "People can dislike us for one reason or another, and very often it isn't personal. You may have something that somebody else doesn't have and they resent you for that. More money, more success, that sort of thing. But real hatred: that's very unusual in the ordinary run of things. So I'm asking you now: Why do you think this . . . er . . . presence hated you?"

"I don't know. I just knew."

"Well, that's good enough for me." He stood up. "I'll tell you what I'm going to do, Kelly. I'm going to say a few prayers in your car." He smiled. "I know it's unusual and we don't do it very often. We used to, mind you. We'd bless an aeroplane, or a ship. No harm in having the protection of Our Lord. The roads can be dangerous places."

It was one of the oddest rituals Kelly had ever seen enacted. Her parents agreed. None had ever seen a car being blessed before.

It was a little after nine in the morning. Kelly's car stood parked in the yard close to the back door. The priest emerged from the house, carrying a prayer-book in one hand. In the other he held a transparent plastic squeeze bottle, of the type Kelly associated with washing-up liquid. The contrast between the modern car and the old-fashioned paraphernalia of blessing could not have been starker.

Father Conway began his ritual. He walked slowly about the car, beginning with the bonnet on the driver's side. As he went, he sprinkled water from his little container and intoned prayers of blessing. When he'd reached the other side of the bonnet he shut the prayer-book and turned to Kelly.

"If you could open the doors now," he said.

He continued the blessing in the soft glow of the interior lights, this time giving the upholstery a light sprinkling of holy water. Kelly noted that he paid particular attention to the back seat. Lastly he sat into the driver's seat. He sprayed the steering wheel and the dashboard.

When he'd finished, he took from his pocket a small object. Kelly saw that it was a plaque of St Christopher with a sucker pad attached. Father Conway affixed it to the still-damp dashboard next to the CD player. He was done.

"There," he said, stepping out of the car. "That should do it."

Sure enough, when Kelly left for Belfast on the Sunday evening, the car felt somehow "different".

"I know this will sound stupid," she tells me, "but it actually felt holier. I'd been half-expecting a repeat of the previous day but nothing happened. No presences, no ghosts. I was so relieved. I had the same kind of feeling when I let myself into the flat in the Holyland. Even that felt different. I wondered if Father Conway's blessing had made its way there."

The coming night was to disabuse Kelly of that fanciful notion.

The first thing she noticed was a sense of utter quiet. From the time of her arrival, the tenants in the apartment below had been listening to their music. They seldom had the volume up: Kelly felt rather than heard the muffled notes of an electric bass. But at about ten o'clock the music was switched off. She guessed they'd gone to bed.

No sounds intruded from the street. That was unusual; even for a weekday. It was as though the world were holding its breath – or the city of Belfast at any rate. The silence made her uneasy; it gave her a sense of foreboding. For the first time in a long while Kelly wouldn't have minded a bit of noise.

She put down the book she'd been reading. It was a textbook on psychology and as such was heavy going at the best of times. Its content had tired her out and had, to a certain extent, depressed her. She'd found herself wondering, as she perused the lines of dense type, if she were actually cut out for psychology. It seemed to her to fit the personality of another. She reached for the remote control and switched on the TV.

But the picture was bad. She hadn't got round to having a proper aerial installed. There was one on the roof but it had been out of action for some time, according to the man who lived across the hall from her. She switched the set off. The silence settled over her again.

Kelly was weary. It had been a long day. She debated with herself whether to put on some music, the radio even, but decided against it. She decided to go to bed.

In the bathroom she filled the sink to wash her face. The rushing of the water sounded loud in the silence. After finishing up, she pulled the plug.

As the water spiralled down the plughole she thought she heard somebody sobbing.

The bathroom was big – bigger than the one she'd been used to in her parents' house. It was fully tiled as well, and therefore tended to echo. She looked down at the last of the water disappearing down the plughole – and decided she'd heard no more than its gurgle reverberating off the bathroom walls.

She went into the small bedroom and climbed into bed. Slightly uneasy now, she lay down and decided to leave the bedside light on a while.

She heard the sobbing again.

It seemed to be coming from the bathroom. Steeling herself, she got up.

But when she pushed open the bathroom door the sobbing stopped.

There was a shower unit above the bathtub and a rail from which a shower curtain hung. It was new; she'd bought it in the course of the shopping expedition she'd embarked on with her mother. The old curtain had been vintage 1960s, stained and tattered. Its replacement was white with a pattern of yellow and green flowers. It was half drawn, the way Kelly had left it.

She had the overpowering feeling that something was lurking behind it.

Kelly's first impulse was to dash out of the bathroom and slam the door behind her. She even considered whipping out the key on her way out and locking the door from the outside. Her own breathing was so agitated now that it was almost drowning out the sobbing.

But she rallied. And her fear began to turn to anger. This was *her* apartment, *her* bathroom, and she was damned if any ghost was going to drive her out of it. She tiptoed slowly towards the bathtub and its concealing shower curtain. The sobbing was growing fainter.

She reached the curtain. She hesitated. Would she have the nerve to do it? She steeled herself, reached out a hand, took a deep breath . . . and pulled aside the curtain.

Nothing. There was nobody. A white ceramic bathtub stared emptily back at her. Everything was still in its proper place: her sponges, her loofah, her soaps, her bath salts . . .

Kelly stood staring dumbly at the tiled wall. She felt foolish. She considered phoning her mother and describing what she'd heard in the bathroom, but she knew her mother would only advise her again to move out; besides, she'd be in bed by now.

Kelly left the shower curtain as it was, crossed to the door, and eased it shut behind her. When she reached the door to her bedroom she hesitated at the light switch for the hall. She decided to leave it on.

She slipped into bed and lay for a few minutes, staring at the ceiling. The apartment continued to be unusually quiet. Eerily quiet.

She reached out a hand and switched off the bedside lamp.

Sleep did come eventually. But when Kelly awoke in darkness some time later she was in the grip of a truly terrifying ordeal. There was someone – or something – lying on top of her. The weight was crushing her. She panicked, tried to kick out with her feet, thrash with her arms. She tried to scream, but could not. The weight had rendered her utterly immobile.

The pressure on her chest was bad enough but the constriction on her throat was even more intense; it felt as if something was trying to choke the life out of her. She could hardly breathe.

Kelly's eyes were wide open but she could not see her assailant. All she saw was the white ceiling above the bed, grey in the early morning light. Her heart was racing and she was screaming, but no sound came.

She sensed a wave of coldness descending on her. It resembled the sensation she'd felt in the car on the way to Tyrone. With one important difference: this "presence", this ghost, was unmistakably female. Kelly cannot say why she was so sure of this; she believes it was something instinctive: the faculty common to all living creatures that enables an individual to recognize the sex of another and to respond to it. Her fiancé Brian was a second-year biology student but his interest extended to the animal kingdom. He'd told her that various creatures use the sense of smell to identify a potential mate. Gorillas, he said, are particularly good at this; elephants can do the same. Brian thought it had something to do with male and female pheromones, those tiny secretions we release but are unconscious of.

Whatever it was, it had convinced Kelly that she was dealing with a woman. A very angry woman. She sensed the stranger's presence on the bed. She could feel the pressure on her torso.

She was deathly afraid. She began to pray. She tried to grapple with the thing that gripped her but could not. Her hands only made contact with thin air. She tried to scream again.

This time she succeeded. She'd found her voice.

The phantom pressure began to ease, to slowly subside. Kelly coughed. She gulped in mouthfuls of air. Her head felt as though it were about to burst. The presence was departing.

She sat up, sweating. She couldn't come to terms with her dreadful ordeal. It had all appeared so real. Had it been a nightmare? Or a spirit visitation? Similar, in fact, to what Brian had experienced.

She got up and staggered, shaking and trembling, to the bathroom. All looked more or less as she'd left it the previous night. She stole a nervous glance at the bathtub in the corner, with its partially drawn shower curtain – and looked away quickly. She wished to splash cold water in her face. She ran the tap, and raised her eyes to the mirror.

Kelly jumped back in fright. She looked again. There were red marks on her throat.

It hadn't been a nightmare after all. The weals could only have been made by fingers gripping her throat. She wanted to scream again.

She looked down at her hands. Her mind was desperately seeking to rationalize what her eyes were seeing. Could she have done it herself? Somehow, in her sleep, had she tried to strangle herself? And was that why she couldn't prise the phantom fingers from her neck? They were her *own* fingers. There's always a rational explanation.

Five minutes later, however, as she sat drinking coffee in the kitchen, Kelly came to appreciate the wrong-headedness of her thinking. She was reminded of two facts she'd learned a long time before: we can't tickle ourselves, and we can't strangle ourselves. She couldn't recall the explanation for the first, but she knew that strangulation entailed a gradual loss of consciousness. Hands that throttle need consciousness to sustain them.

So what had caused the marks on her throat?

Kelly made up her mind quickly. She reached for her phone and called her mother.

"I need Father Conway here," she said, trying to control her sobbing. "I need him to come and bless the flat."

It may be instructive at this point in Kelly's story to look at the phenomenon of "night terrors". A nightmare is defined as a frightening dream that occurs during sleep. A night terror or sleep paralysis, on the other hand, is a nightmare that continues into the waking state. The phase between sleeping and waking is referred to as the hypnopompic state (its opposite is known as the hypnagogic state, when we go from waking to sleeping).

Unlike nightmares, night terrors are accompanied by potent physiological effects; profuse sweating, heightened heart-rate, the urge to scream. Victims also report experiencing a sensation of being suffocated or choked. Kelly was subjected to all of these.

In less enlightened times, prior to scientific investigation, night terrors were believed to be attacks by evil spirits intent on having sexual intercourse with the sleeper. The female demon that assaulted men was known as the succubus; the incubus was its male counterpart.

Kelly remains convinced that the attack on her was of a paranormal nature. And given what she'd experienced up to that point, this is understandable. She is also certain that the spirit was female and that the attack had no sexual connotations.

It is noteworthy, however, that night terrors occur more frequently in people who are undergoing periods of change or emotional upheavals in their lives. Kelly's life had certainly entered a transformative phase. One has to ask whether her new circumstances were inducing some kind of illusion or if, indeed, the apartment was haunted. The fact that Brian reported the same kind of phenomenon lends rather more weight to the latter possibility.

But for now we'll go back to Kelly's story.

In the event, Father Conway had taken ill the previous day. He was elderly and not in the best of health. But as soon as he received the distress call from Mrs Mitchelson he telephoned a good friend of his in Belfast: Father Francis Donoghue, a somewhat younger man but, he assured Kelly's concerned mother, a priest well versed in paranormal issues.

Kelly had temporarily abandoned her apartment and moved in with Brian. Father Donoghue promised her that he'd be along that very evening at about eight o'clock. At the appointed time, the couple heard a car draw up in the street below. Kelly looked out of the window and saw a burly figure in black emerging from a taxi. The priest had arrived.

Father Donoghue resembled more a GAA midfielder than a man of the cloth. During some chit-chat with Brian he confirmed that he had indeed helped his county win a trophy or two before his ordination. But when the conversation turned to the more serious topic of Kelly's ghosts he quickly dropped the easy manner of the footballer and adopted that of the concerned clergyman. He didn't like what Brian and Kelly had to report, and told them so.

"Whatever it is, it has to go," he said. "It seems to have attached itself to Kelly. Why I don't know. I'm not saying you've attracted it," he added quickly. "These things tend to strike at random. We don't know what they are or what their purpose is. All we can do is pray for them – and for the people they torment as well of course."

Kelly appreciated the priest's candour. She found it refreshing. She'd been expecting somebody who'd have hard and fast ideas on what it was she was experiencing, and it took her slightly aback to learn of his uncertainty.

"He was so honest about it," she tells me. "It was nice to meet a priest who didn't pretend he knew more than you did about spirits and that kind of thing. I felt sure he'd be the one to help."

Father Donoghue prepared for the Eucharist with a minimum of fuss. It was a short service. Brian and Kelly joined in the responses and she took Holy Communion. Brian, the man who believed in "nothing", did not. When it was ended, the priest went through the apartment and blessed each room with holy water, in much the same way Father Conway had blessed the car.

"Well, that's that," he said when he was done. "I don't think you'll be bothered by those ghosts again."

Ten days passed. Kelly continued with her studies at Queen's University; Brian returned to his. The couple met every other day. Brian came and stayed for a weekend. They met two days later, had a meal in a restaurant, and returned to Kelly's apartment at about eleven o'clock. She invited him to stay the night.

Brian was a little nervous to be in Kelly's bed again. He recalled all too vividly his experience on the previous occasion. She assured him that the apartment was back to normal, and all had been tranquil following the priest's visit. Brian was not convinced. He didn't believe in blessings and Masses: to him it was all so much mumbo-jumbo.

They retired after midnight. Kelly went to sleep immediately; it took Brian a little longer. Sometime later he woke up. He judged that no more than an hour had elapsed since he'd fallen asleep. At first he noticed nothing untoward in the bedroom. But that was to change.

The presence manifested itself gradually. So gradually, in fact, that Brian wasn't conscious of it until several minutes had passed. He'd assumed that the breathing and soft, sleeping sounds he'd been hearing were Kelly's. But as they grew louder it struck him that they were coming from his left; Kelly was asleep on his right. The sounds seemed to be made by two individuals, not one. As he strained to listen, Brian could clearly distinguish two distinct sounds: the deep breathing of a male, and the faint sounds of a woman moaning.

Then Kelly woke up.

"Brian?"

"Do you hear it?" he asked in a whisper.

"What!" she cried, sitting up in alarm. "What the hell *is* that?"

She was hearing what Brian had heard and it filled her with dread.

"I felt so scared at that moment," she says. "It's one thing to hear about a ghost somebody else sees. You're inclined to only half-believe them. I didn't really take Brian seriously that first time and I'm sure he felt the same way when I told him about *my* ghosts. But now we were together – and we were both experiencing the same things."

The heavy breathing and whimpering gained in volume, by times going away from the bed, by times returning. Brian and Kelly saw nothing.

But they didn't need to; the sounds had been enough. As one, they leaped from the bed. There was only one thing to do: leave, and as quickly as they could.

Kelly and Brian returned to the apartment the following afternoon to collect their things. The previous night had severed her attachment to the place.

There were other apartments to rent, she told herself. Within two days she'd found one. It was slightly smaller and a little farther away from the university, but it was newer. Much newer. The last thing Kelly wanted was another house with a "history".

I put it to her that her apartment in the Holyland wasn't all that old. She agrees. She also suspects that the ghost – or ghosts – most likely predated its construction.

Kelly surmises that the woman met a violent death at the hands of a man, perhaps by strangulation. The throttling sensation she felt about her throat and the woman with the disfigured face whom Brian saw would seem to bear this out.

I wonder what became of the haunted apartment.

"I don't know who's living there now," she says. "I know somebody is because I'm down that way now and again; I've a friend at Uni who lives nearby. If it's in the evening I'll see a light on. Sometimes I'm tempted to ring the bell to see who answers. Maybe it's a girl, who knows? A student at Queen's. I often wonder if she sees anything, if the ghosts are still there."

I ask Kelly if she thinks the ghosts have left.

"Who's to say?" she says with a shrug. "If prayers and a Mass couldn't shift them then maybe they don't want to go."

I can't help wondering about the car. This was so unusual in the sense that it didn't follow the "normal" pattern of ghosts. They tend to remain in the same locality, and will only be seen there. I hint that perhaps Kelly was imagining that particular episode. Unlike the ghosts in the apartment, it never returned.

"That's true," she says. "My car was 'clean' from the minute Father Conway blessed it. Brian and I talked about it a lot. I don't know why it should have followed me in the car . . . but it did, for whatever reason. Brian thinks it wanted me out of the flat and that it was trying to persuade me to go back home to Tyrone again. It sure wanted me out of the flat. And it got its wish."

And that appears to be the case. The entities that came to haunt Kelly Mitchelson seem to have obeyed their own rules, and were not too concerned with the effect they had on the living. They appeared to be re-enacting a drama they played out in a bygone time, perhaps before Kelly's apartment was even built in the district called the Holyland. One can't help but conclude that those entities appear to be as confused as Kelly, her mother and her boyfriend were – that they were unable to separate reality from what is no longer there.

We do not know the nature of the world that lies beyond the death of the physical body. At best we can make educated guesses using the information gleaned from sources both reliable and suspect. Arthur Ellison, in his 1988 book *The Reality of the Paranormal*, suggests that passing "from the physical world to the next might be thought of as a change of consciousness, like waking from a dream." He believes that ghosts – or as he calls them, "discarnate minds" – may be in "a state of perpetual delusion."

He urges caution, however, with our definitions. We say delusion

> only because the experiences would be different from those of the physical world. People in the next world would be deluded only in the sense that their bodies and their world were not really physical though they might mistakenly think so. But it is another world, as it should be, having different space and laws . . . Such a world would be mind-dependent. It would be dependent on the memories of those who experienced it . . .

Desires, he concludes, "unsatisfied in earthly life might play an important part."

It could well be that the female phantom that haunted Kelly's apartment was possessed by an unsatisfied desire: a lust for revenge on the man who'd wronged her in life. We can but hope that she finds her rest one day.

9

Áine Synnott and the Haunted Chapel

O Death, rock me asleep,
Bring me to quiet rest,
Let pass my weary guiltless ghost
Out of my careful breast.

ANNE BOLEYN

They called it a chapel but in truth it wasn't much more than an oratory. It was tiny as houses of worship go: a room the size of a spacious sitting-room. In fact, that's precisely what it had been at one time.

The building that would become the nursing home had been bequeathed to the parish by an elderly lady on or around the turn of the twentieth century. She was the last of a minor branch of an ancient family; she knew that on her death the branch would die with her. During her final months she'd been cared for by an order of nursing sisters and she wished to repay their kindness. She felt that by

241

donating her family home to the order she'd be helping many other people in their twilight days.

The building was the former "Big House" of the locality. It stood in about 200 acres of farmland a little distance from the main road between Bandon and Cork. The family were Church of Ireland and well respected in the area. It was unusual, however, for a Protestant lady to leave her property to a Catholic order of nuns, and she had done so with one stipulation: that the nursing home would be open to the elderly of all faiths and none. For this reason, the oratory had only the minimum of Christian symbolism. There was a large but simple cross behind a plain altar, no statues, and unadorned seating for about two hundred worshippers. A small harmonium provided sacred music when required.

The oratory was a quiet room of meditation and prayer, a retreat from the sometimes impersonal atmosphere of the nursing home. Not surprisingly, it also served as a "wake house" on the death of a patient. Old friends and family could take a dignified leave of the deceased prior to the removal of the remains.

Áine Synnott was nearing her eighty-second birthday in July 2005. By then she'd been a resident of the nursing home for over two years, and had already seen the "departure" of five fellow-residents, had prayed over them with family, friends and funeral staff. Among the departed was Judy Fitzpatrick, an infirm patient who'd been bedridden from the time of her admittance. The two women had taken to one another at once. They had much in common. Both had led difficult lives. Judy had married young but had lost her husband to a form of cancer incurable at the time of his illness. Less than a decade later medicine had progressed so far that the condition wasn't even regarded as life threatening. But Judy was so devastated by her untimely loss that she resolved to remain single rather than risk further heartbreak. She came from a small family and by the time of her admittance to the nursing home was all but alone in the world.

Áine's family was also a small one. She too had remained single, though not by choice. She was a shy woman, very private. In Judy she'd found a kindred spirit and would pass most of her days by Judy's bedside, chatting quietly or reading to her bedridden friend. In their short time together they'd discovered that they'd many mutual friends and acquaintances dating back to their schooldays, even though they'd grown up in different villages and had attended different schools. They'd frequently express regret that their paths had not crossed sooner.

I met Áine Synnott for the first time towards the end of 2007. She'd written me a lovely letter, having heard through a friend that I was preparing a book on true ghost stories. I visited her several times at the nursing home. She was eager to share her experience and I believe I understand why. Hers is a heart-warming story and will, I feel, strike a chord in women of all ages.

It's my first visit to the nursing home. Áine has arranged with the day-sister that I should meet her in the oratory. I consider it an unusual request, but am happy to oblige. A porter escorts me there.

She is taller than I'd expected, perhaps five foot six. Most octogenarians I know are tiny women, frail and delicate. Áine Synnott greets me with a firm handshake. A stout stick seems to be her only concession to her advanced years.

Yet her voice is soft and I recognize the gentleness that came through in her writing. We've been seated together in the oratory for no more than four or five minutes when I begin to appreciate why she chose this venue for our "interview". Even when she talks excitedly I have to strain to understand her. In that respect the oratory is perfect for our private conversation. But there's another reason.

"They'd think I was loopy," she says with a twinkle, "if they heard what I'm going to tell you. I haven't told anybody else. I wouldn't dare."

She wants to know if I'll be using her real name. I assure her I won't be, and that I'll be disguising important details of the case, including people and places. She seems happy with this arrangement.

Áine has the demeanour of an independent woman, a woman used to managing her own affairs. I notice that her hair is cut and styled impeccably, her make-up understated. The tweed suit she's wearing looks new and is finely tailored. We engage in some small talk. She's very articulate, and I find myself wondering why she's in the nursing home in the first place. She supplies the answer unasked.

"I suffer from epilepsy, you see. They diagnosed it a couple of years ago, and my GP told me I couldn't be on my own any more. Too risky, he said. He was right of course. The first I knew of it was when I woke up one day to find myself lying on my bathroom floor. I must have fallen and passed out. Couldn't remember a thing." She taps her stick. "I broke my hip; had to have a replacement. My GP said I was putting my life in danger. He said I might be standing over a hot stove or a pot of soup and lose consciousness, and then where would I be?"

Her doctor recommended a care home. Áine didn't like the idea one bit but saw the sense in it. I can understand her reluctance.

"So here I am and here I'll stay," she says. "I've got used to it and the staff are lovely. I've had one or two turns here but there's always somebody on hand, and that's a great comfort."

We go on to discuss my reason for coming here: Judy Fitzpatrick. Áine points to a table set to one side of the oratory.

"That's where we said our goodbyes to poor Judy. She had a lovely send-off from the people here. It was a very small funeral too but I know that's what she wanted. She hated people fussing over her. A brother of hers came over from Lancashire and he led us in a decade of the rosary before the removal. It was very moving. I never saw him again."

"But you saw Judy again."

"I did. Right here."

Áine was very distressed when she returned from Judy's burial. The nursing home had laid on a minibus to take a number of the residents to the church and back. It had been a sad occasion, she says, but there'd been a general sense of resignation among the passengers in the bus. Yet another of the community had passed on. It was the nature of the care home; it was a place where one came to die. That was in the order of things.

Yet Áine found it impossible to come to terms with Judy's absence. That night she cried herself to sleep. In the morning she went absentmindedly to Judy's room. On opening the door she was taken aback by the empty bed, with its bare mattress and all signs of her friend gone. There was not a thing of Judy's left in the room. Her pictures, her prayer books, her little statues of the Virgin Mary, her bottle of Lourdes water, her dressing-gown, her toiletries. All gone.

Áine went at once to the oratory. She found it silent. The table on which Judy's coffin had lain was disturbingly bare. She chose a pew halfway down, took out her rosary beads – which she carries with her everywhere – and began to pray, her face uplifted to the cross.

Áine had no way of knowing how much time had passed but believes it was ten minutes or more when she sensed a subtle change in the atmosphere of the chapel. The lighting is subdued at the best of times. There are halogen spots set into the four corners of the ceiling; together with two wall lamps with dark shades, they provide a very intimate and serene ambience. But now it seemed to Áine that the room had grown darker than usual. She put this down to her imagination and her attention having been on her prayers. She studied the lights one by one but could see no discernible reason why the oratory should have become dimmer.

The door opened, and Áine heard somebody walking slowly up towards the altar. She did not turn round. The person passed her. It was an elderly woman. Seen from behind, she was not immediately familiar. Her hair was grey and cut in a neat style that required little maintenance. Her clothes were nondescript. In fact she resembled so many of the elderly ladies who shared the nursing home with Áine.

As Áine sat looking at the woman a thought occurred to her: she realized that old age tended to iron out the differences in women that were so apparent in youth; old age seemed to make all elderly women look the same, in much the way that it can be difficult to tell newborn babies apart. It is as though we grow towards a second childhood.

The woman stopped at the table to the right of the altar. She bowed her head in the manner of one praying. Áine was intrigued, but not greatly. After all, Judy's coffin had lain there only the previous day. It was not altogether unusual that a resident would wish to return to repeat a prayer she'd offered up for the deceased. And what better place to recite it than in the oratory?

Áine was just about to resume her own prayers when her rosary beads slipped from her grasp and fell to the floor.

"I bent down to pick them up," she says, "and when I looked up again, she was gone." She clicks her fingers. "As quick as that. I was stunned."

I voice the obvious: Couldn't she have gone out a side door?

Áine draws my attention to the door at the back. It's the only door to and from the oratory.

"In order to leave she would have had to come down the aisle past me again," she says. "That didn't happen. I would have heard her footsteps. I just didn't know what to think. One part of me was telling me that I was seeing things, but I had the strangest feeling that it was Judy. Another part was reminding me that I'd never seen Judy on her feet but always lying down in her bed. I realized also that I'd rarely seen the back of her head because it was always on her pillow."

Áine had no alternative but to conclude that she'd witnessed a ghost or apparition. Yet the apparition was nothing like the insubstantial entities she'd read about in books, or heard being discussed by the more superstitious of the residents. To all intents and purposes the woman standing by the table had been a woman of flesh and blood. Áine had heard her come in, had plainly heard her footsteps.

The next Áine knew she was lying in bed in unfamiliar surroundings. She opened her eyes to find the resident doctor leaning over her, a stethoscope pressed to her chest. One of the nursing sisters was standing to one side, looking concerned.

"How is she?" the nun asked.

"She's fine. She had a bit of a turn. No, she's fine." He leaned closer. "How are you feeling, Áine?"

Áine was to learn later that her "bit of a turn" was yet another epileptic seizure. She had, in effect, lost consciousness in the chapel. This followed the pattern of her previous attacks.

There are, broadly speaking, four types of epileptic seizure. The so-called "petit mal" is the most benign. It's a "staring spell" or "absence seizure" lasting less than fifteen seconds. Less benign is the simple partial seizure. The patient can go into the convulsions associated with the illness but will remain fully conscious throughout. She will lose control of her limbs and be incapacitated. The part of the brain that controls our motor mechanisms will have been affected, hence the patient's paralysis. More serious is the complex partial seizure. The patient may lose consciousness and cannot remember much or most of the experience.

The generalized seizure is the most serious form. The patient loses consciousness completely. Both hemispheres of the brain are affected. The patient convulses, hence the old term "epileptic fit", but at the same time will black out. Áine had twice suffered this fourth type of seizure, the severest. It was for this reason that her GP had recommended she be admitted to the nursing home, where she could be monitored around the clock.

It was not the first time that the resident doctor had treated her following a seizure, nor was it the worst he'd seen. He was concerned, however, because there had been no one on hand when Áine suffered her attack. She'd lost consciousness for an unknown period of time. Anything might have happened to her. As it was, she learned that the porter had looked in on the chapel and found her slumped on the floor. He'd alerted the medical staff at once.

The doctor confined Áine to the infirmary for twenty-four hours. During that time she'd ample opportunity to consider what it was she'd seen in the oratory. She concluded that her "vision" had been nothing more than a hallucination brought about by her epileptic seizure.

Epilepsy is indeed known to elicit hallucinations. The celebrated American scientist Carl Sagan summed up a number of situations and medical conditions that are known to trigger them:

> by a campfire at night, or under emotional stress, or during epileptic seizures or migraine headaches or high fever, or by prolonged fasting or sleeplessness or sensory deprivation (for example, in solitary confinement), or through hallucinogens such as LSD, psilocybin,

mescaline, or hashish. (Delirium tremens, the dreaded alcohol-induced "DTs" is one well-known manifestation of a withdrawal syndrome from alcoholism.) There are also molecules, such as the phenothiazines (Thorazine, for example), that make hallucinations go away. It is very likely that the normal human body generates substances – perhaps including the morphinelike small brain proteins called endorphins – that cause hallucinations, and others that suppress them.

Áine could not even be certain that she'd consciously seen the ghost or if it were no more than a false memory which had found its way into her psyche.

For Áine Synnott was a sceptic as far as ghosts were concerned. She'd always mistrusted the accounts provided by those women in the care home who claimed to have seen one. By and large they were women whom Áine regarded as being a little "batty" – women who suffered from dementia or simple forgetfulness. Some of them couldn't even remember what year it was, or failed to recognize family members when they came visiting. Áine had no wish to be placed in the same category as those women.

And so she kept her singular experience to herself.

A fortnight passed and Áine had put the ghost firmly behind her. She'd settled back into life in the nursing home. It was, she was to find, far less pleasurable without her dear old friend's company. She missed their little chats, their reminiscing about their younger years and the people they'd known. Áine had retreated into herself, and would spend her days alone in her room, reading or listening to the radio. No one paid her a visit – but she'd received very few visitors since coming to live in the home.

Late in the evening of the eleventh day, Áine was engrossed in a book she was reading for the second time. It was a particularly good book and it held her attention. In fact, she'd hoped that it might have the opposite effect. She'd been sleeping badly but had no wish to request extra medication; sleeping pills left her drowsy and irritable the following morning. She was now wide awake, seated in her armchair under the floor lamp.

Without warning, her hands began to tremble. At first she suspected that a draught might be the cause; but the evening was mild and she could feel no draught.

The trembling became a shaking. She could no longer hold the book; it fell to the floor. Áine felt her body convulsing. She was filled with dread. She jerked her head up and prayed she would not lose consciousness – or worse.

Fortunately, she didn't pass out. Instead she felt a paralysis stealing over her. She could no longer move her limbs. Nor could she even shut her eyes. She was forced to stare straight ahead of her, at the window. Standing to the right, just by her bed, was the same figure she'd seen in the oratory. Again it had its back to Áine.

"*Hello, dear,*" a voice said. It seemed to come from within Áine's head. The voice was that of her deceased friend, Judy Fitzpatrick.

Áine, shocked beyond words, nevertheless tried to reply. But she discovered she could not. The paralysis affecting her body extended to her vocal cords. She could not utter a word.

251

She heard the voice again. "*Don't worry*," it said. "*Help is on its way*." But the ghost still did not turn around.

Moments later there came an urgent rapping on the door and a female voice called out. On receiving no response from Áine, the caller opened the door and entered the room. It was one of the nurses; she was followed by another.

"Oh, Áine!" the first nurse said.

Áine continued to stare at the figure across from her as the two sisters busied themselves, examining her. One took her pulse while the other lifted her left eyelid and checked the pupil. She heard them tut-tutting. All the while, "Judy" stood by the bed with her back to the scene.

"I couldn't believe they couldn't see her," Áine tells me. "She was standing across from me as real as you are now. But the sisters were just ignoring her, like she wasn't there at all. And of course she wasn't. It was only later on I realized I was the only one who could see her."

One of the nurses summoned the doctor and Áine was hurriedly wheeled to the infirmary for the second time in less than a fortnight. The doctor expressed his concern.

"He was worried that my condition was deteriorating," she says. "And so was I, if truth be told. To be honest, I thought I was going mad."

Again Áine found herself recuperating in the infirmary. She was miserable, not knowing when the next seizure would strike. She feared that it could be at any moment. She feared that the next seizure could herald her death. She was eighty-two, a patient in a care home where the average age of those who died within its walls was close to her own. She had already prepared herself for the "inevitable" as she called it.

She felt she had to talk to somebody. And what better person, she decided, than the home's chaplain, Father Mulcahy? She knew him quite well and liked him very much. He was a gentle, understanding soul, who was never condescending or patronizing. She asked a sister if he could be sent for. She'd resolved to unburden herself.

"I hope you don't think I'm a foolish old woman, Father," she said, without too much preamble, "but I believe I've seen a ghost."

Father Mulcahy seemed unfazed. He asked her to expand and she told him all she knew.

"You're certain it was Judy?" He'd known her very well, having prayed with her often and offered the communion host at her bedside. He'd administered Extreme Unction in her final hours.

"Quite certain, Father. She even spoke to me yesterday. I'd know that voice anywhere. What do you think it all means?"

The priest was thoughtful – and non-committal. "What do *you* think it means, Áine?"

"I believe she was helping me. I believe she helped me yesterday, when I had the seizure. I talked to the sisters about it. They said the alarm went off in my room. That's why they went there, to see what the matter was. But I hadn't gone near the button, Father! It's over next to my bed where Judy was standing. I was on the other side of the room. I was paralyzed; I couldn't move. How could the alarm have gone off?"

He shrugged. "Who knows, Áine? It could be that the sister was mistaken – that it was somebody else's alarm she saw lighting up. It's not that unusual, what with the number of residents we have here." He smiled. "I like to think it was Himself Upstairs who was watching over you. Have you thought of that?"

"I have indeed, Father. And you're probably right. You don't believe in ghosts then?"

"I do not! And you shouldn't either. There's no such thing as ghosts."

It was then that Áine told the priest about her first "sighting" of the late Judy Fitzpatrick in the oratory. He frowned, and she suspected what he was thinking. He'd been chaplain at the nursing home for many years, and was used to the delusions brought about by old age and the mental health problems associated with it. He didn't come right out and voice his suspicions to Áine but it wasn't necessary. His demeanour spoke volumes.

The Church in general views all ghost sightings with scepticism. In keeping with Bible teaching, ghosts are either good or evil. In other words, on a par with angels and demons. Many clergymen share the conviction that the spirits of the deceased do not come back to haunt the living.

"You get some rest now," Father Mulcahy said. "You've had a turn, and rest is the best thing for it. You'll be as right as rain tomorrow. You'll see."

He reached for his breviary.

"We'll say a little prayer now, Áine. We'll pray for your recovery." He paused. "And we'll pray that you don't see any more of those things."

But the priest's prayers appear not to have had any effect. Before the week was ended, Áine had her third brush with the paranormal. As with the first, it took place in the little chapel.

Áine hadn't been feeling well the whole day. It was nothing serious; more a general sense of being run down and listless. She'd also had a brief argument with another resident at breakfast, which may have led to her feeling out of sorts. The other woman, Margaret Dunleavy, had made disparaging remarks about Áine's solitary ways. She'd accused her of being "snobby" and "antisocial". Since Judy's death, Áine had kept very much to herself. This was due in equal measure to the grieving process as to her withdrawn nature. Before losing Judy she seldom had much social contact with anybody else; now she had practically none.

"You need to cop yourself on," Margaret told her. "Who do you think you are anyway, Miss Muck? You're no better than the rest of us. And don't think we don't know what you and Judy Fitzpatrick were saying about us behind our backs!"

"You leave Judy alone!" Áine was upset. "She did nothing to you. The only gossip around here is you. Show a little respect for the dead."

"Oh, that's rich coming from you," Margaret had retorted. "It wasn't me who was seeing a dead woman in my room, was it?"

Áine was lost for words. How could Margaret Dunleavy have known about Judy's visit? The only living soul who knew was Father Mulcahy. . . .

Margaret's unkind remarks had hurt Áine, causing her to seek the solitude of her room, only emerging for dinner.

She'd skipped lunch, explaining to the sister that she'd no appetite.

At about eight in the evening, when dinner was ended, she decided to make her way to the oratory. She felt she needed a spiritual lift. A few minutes of quiet prayer would be the answer.

As usual, she found the oratory silent, all its pews unoccupied. This time, she chose to sit at the very back and off to one side. She reached into her bag for her rosary beads, shut her eyes and began to pray.

She'd scarcely completed the Apostles' Creed when she heard a loud tap, as of metal being struck. She opened her eyes at once. It came again. It was hard for her to make out where the noise was coming from. When it came a third time, she knew: the tapping was coming from the radiator set against a side wall, the one close to her.

"I wasn't frightened or anything," she tells me. "It wouldn't have been the first time I'd heard a noisy radiator. So I ignored it as best I could."

But no sooner had she returned to her rosary than she heard more taps. This time they came from the radiator against the opposite wall. As if that wasn't bad enough, the tapping began to emanate from both radiators at the same time.

"That's when I knew there was something very wrong," she says. "It wasn't natural. It sounded to me like there were two invisible people hitting the radiators. One minute they'd be struck at the same time, the next they seemed to be taking it in turns. Like they were sending some kind of signal to each other."

It was obvious to Áine that she couldn't continue her prayers. The racket from the radiators was too distracting.

She returned her rosary beads to her handbag and headed back to her room.

But no sooner had she walked the length of the corridor than she heard a commotion. A porter was pushing a trolley down towards the infirmary. A nun – Sister Brigid – accompanied it, head bowed over the trolley's occupant while she recited prayers aloud. The patient on the trolley was Margaret Dunleavy.

Her fatigue forgotten, Áine hurried after them. She was on hand when Margaret was lifted from the trolley and placed gently on a vacant bed. A nurse hurriedly drew the curtains about her. Áine went through, ignoring protests.

"Is she . . . ?"

"Yes, I'm afraid she's passed away," Sister Brigid told her. "It was quick. She didn't suffer much at all, the lamb."

Áine had to know more.

"When did it happen?"

"Not ten minutes ago," the nun said. "She was playing whist with three other ladies down in the TV room. She said she was feeling the cold, even though the heating was on full. She wanted somebody to turn the radiator up for her. But she was right up against it."

At the mention of a radiator Áine was at once alert. She was thinking that it was too much for chance alone that Margaret died in the same moments when the radiators in the oratory were acting up. And that a radiator in another part of the home figured in her death.

"Sister Brigid could see I was in a bit of a state," Áine tells me. "I suppose she didn't want to see a second death that evening. She helped me down to my room and made me comfortable. She asked if I'd like the doctor in but I told her I was all right. I asked her to stay with me for a minute or two."

Áine had to know the details, if only for her own peace of mind. Sister Brigid had tea brought and they settled down for a little chat. Margaret's story came out.

She'd suffered for years from chronic arthritis combined with a hardening of the arteries leading to the heart. It was not unknown for her pulse rate to slow to far below normal. This would be accompanied by a feeling of intense cold in her limbs. Margaret had already undergone emergency treatment on two occasions before being admitted to the home.

On the evening of her death, the other ladies noticed that she appeared to be distracted. She'd difficulty in keeping track of her cards, and made several mistakes when trying to follow suit – most unlike her, according to a friend. She seemed to be feeling the cold very badly. One of her fellow card-players would say later that her face appeared "ash grey" at one point.

"I asked Margaret if she wanted to stop, have a lie down," she says. "She didn't look well at all. We told her we'd stop the game and it didn't matter. But she was determined to finish the rubber. She said she had a great hand." She sighs, remembering. "It turned out she didn't."

Poor hand or not, Margaret didn't get to play it. She placed her cards in her lap and wrapped her shawl more tightly about her shoulders. She was shivering. One of the whist players asked if there was anything she could do. Margaret wondered if she could turn up the heating.

"Oh, you know we're not allowed touch those," her friend said. "We'd get into trouble. You'll have to ask the nurse."

Margaret then left the group, took her chair and went down the room to sit by the radiator.

The door opened and a nurse came in with a little trolley laden with medication. It was Sister Brigid. She went first to the residents grouped around the television set. Somebody had turned the volume up to accommodate those who were hard of hearing. A quiz show was in progress.

Sister Brigid was passing to and fro in front of the TV. Margaret reached for her elbow crutch, propped against the wall and within easy reach. She raised it and waved it at the nurse, but Sister Brigid was preoccupied. She then started hitting the radiator with her crutch to attract the nurse's attention.

Sister Brigid looked her way and indicated that she'd attend to her soon. But Margaret kept banging the radiator. Since she'd always been a brusque and demanding sort nobody paid much attention. Next thing, the crutch clattered to the floor and Margaret sat slumped in the chair.

The resident doctor would pronounce her dead a few minutes later.

"I never saw Judy's ghost again," Áine tells me. We're still in the chapel, and despite having listened to Áine's story, I find nothing creepy, or even unsettling, about the place. It has an air of tranquillity. I imagine it would be a wonderful place for meditation.

"But I still didn't understand about Margaret," Áine continues, "I kept asking myself if Judy had a hand in that."

I wonder aloud if she believes she had. She shakes her head.

"Oh no," she says with determination. "Absolutely not. That wasn't Judy at all. But I think she knew that Margaret's time was up and she wanted me to go to her, perhaps to make my peace. Who knows? I think Judy was trying to get my attention in the same way Margaret was trying to get the sister's. I don't think she wanted me to try and save Margaret's life. She knew that was futile. And she was right, as it turned out."

I put to Áine the question that's uppermost in my mind: Did she imagine it? After all, she'd had an epileptic seizure at the time of each of the first hauntings. She was the only one to see Judy's ghost in her room. I suggest to her that the mind can play strange tricks on us.

"That's true," she concedes. "And if I'd heard this from somebody else I probably wouldn't believe it." She gestures about the oratory. "I know what happened here. I was wide awake. I can account for every second. I know what I heard and I know what I saw."

She leans forward slightly and lowers her voice. She's barely audible, despite the quiet of the room.

"The other thing that bothers me is how Margaret knew," she says. "How did she know that Judy came to see me in my room? Judy never left her bed when she was alive. She couldn't. So why would Margaret say that? Did someone tell her?"

The priest, I venture. She again shakes her head defiantly.

"Out of the question. Father Mulcahy wouldn't break the secrecy of the confessional if they threatened to martyr him. He's the old-fashioned type. Anything you say to him is in the strictest confidence."

I see a flaw here, and tell her. The priest wasn't hearing her confession when she told him about Judy's visitations. She chuckles merrily.

"No, that's true," she says. "It wasn't a confession in that sense. But that wouldn't count with Father Mulcahy. As I say, he's a priest of the old school. Nevertheless I asked him about it. I had to know. Wouldn't you? He took me by the hand and smiled. Then he said something that still makes me laugh.

"'Áine,' says he, 'it's probably the wrong thing to say in the circumstances, but as far as keeping a secret is concerned, I'm like the grave itself.'"

10

Strange Goings-on in the Attic

*There are mysteries which men can only guess at, which
age by age they may solve only in part.*

BRAM STOKER, *Dracula*

Ciara Mulhern does not scare easily. Nor does her young
son Evan. In ways this is not hard to understand; life has
not been easy for the two.

I meet mother and son in their home. Ciara insisted on
this. I believe it was her attempt to convince me that all is
well in the little council-built terraced house in Bray,
County Wicklow. I can tell, practically from the moment I
step over the threshold, that this pleasant young woman is
keen for me to understand that the worst is behind her.
That the peril has passed.

"You hear that?" she says, urging me to stand still in
the little hallway. She's looking up the stairs. Evan, aged
six, is holding her hand.

"No," I say. "What am I supposed to hear?"

"That's it. You can't hear a thing now. They left."

They. I'm about to hear about the entities Ciara refers to by no other name. She cannot put a name to them because she doesn't know what they are – or rather what they were.

But let us go back to the very beginning. Ciara's story begins a little over two years before the time of writing, in April 2008.

She'd come through the loss of her husband Bob, the father of her son Evan. Ciara is reluctant to talk about him, and will only give me the bare bones of what occurred in her marriage. He was two years her senior when they married in 2003. They'd known each other since their schooldays, and were neighbours; Bob lived in the next street.

"I still can't believe I didn't know him at all," she says. "The Bob I knew before we got married was a different Bob altogether. He was always kind and generous. He treated me like a lady. He wouldn't let anybody insult me or anything like that. I always felt safe when he was around."

But that changed almost as soon as the couple returned from their honeymoon in Cyprus.

"He was a different person," Ciara says. "He'd turned into a control freak overnight. He didn't want me going out, only to do the messages or when we went out together. And he started to lay down the law. I was his wife now and he was the boss."

She hesitates before continuing. I can tell she's choosing her words with care.

"I know you've probably heard this a million times," she says. "And to be honest so had I, but I never thought it would happen to me. I honestly don't know what comes over some men when they get married. But Bob changed and it was horrible. It was like living with some kind of tyrant. Nothing I did was ever right. He didn't want me seeing my mates, not even my best friend Jackie. And I always thought he got on so well with her.

"Then I got pregnant with Evan. I genuinely thought that was going to change things, that being a father would make Bob see some kind of sense. But it didn't. As soon as Evan was born it was like as if he was some sort of rival. Which I suppose he was, to his warped mind. He kept on accusing me of spending too much time with Evan. Imagine! He was my baby. Didn't he know that a mother has to be with her newborn child practically around the clock? I mean, who's going to take care of him? Certainly not Bob. He could barely even take care of himself."

A bad situation was about to deteriorate even further. As the weeks passed it became obvious to Ciara that Bob would never accept the child as his. Not that he had any doubts about its parentage; he simply could not face up to the responsibility that fatherhood had placed upon him. He spent less and less time at home. He invented excuses for seeing his pals, and carousing with them into the small hours. Weekends were worse; Ciara seldom saw him from early on Friday evening to late on Sunday.

Inevitably his work began to suffer. He was given a warning: shape up or ship out. He took it seriously for a time, but fell back into his old ways. His drinking got worse. It was out of control. He received a second warning. He lost his job soon after.

The couple found themselves on the dole with a growing son to feed and clothe. Bob continued to drink heavily. He was a disaster waiting to happen.

It happened in the early hours of a morning in late summer. Ciara was roused from her sleep by the ringing of the doorbell. She turned in the bed. No Bob. The doorbell rang again.

"I knew it was bad news as soon as I saw the two Guards," she says. "A man and a woman. They were very nice, quiet-spoken, but I knew they'd come about Bob. I didn't break down or anything. I think I'd been expecting something bad to happen. They wanted me to go with them to St Vincent's Hospital on Merrion Road. He was dead, and they needed me to identify the body."

The accident had involved two cars, both being driven at speed on the main road between Stillorgan and Donnybrook. It was clear that the car Bob was travelling in had been heading homeward, to Bray. He and the driver were killed outright. A third man was in critical condition, as was the driver of the other car.

Ciara phoned her friend Jackie, who lived close by. She agreed to babysit Evan while Ciara performed the distasteful duty of accompanying the Guards to the hospital mortuary.

She freely admits that the death affected her less than it should have. She even suggests that it came as a relief. She'd brought up the subject of divorce several times with Bob, but he wouldn't hear of it. She suspects that it would have wounded his male pride, that his ego would have taken a battering and he'd have been seen as a man who was unable to hold a family and a home together.

The funeral took place three days later, when the police gave permission for the corpse to be released. It was a short service. Bob's mother had arranged a "funeral dinner" in a small hotel, but Ciara didn't attend. She'd no qualms about declining. As far as she was concerned a distasteful part of her life had ended, and she was glad. A door had shut, a veil had been drawn down. She could start again. She could look forward to a peaceful, and more fulfilling, life.

As it turned out, those aspirations were short lived.

It started in little Evan's bedroom, about a week following his father's funeral.

A rustling sound.

A quiet rustling that was barely perceptible at first. Ciara had just tucked the boy into bed, kissed him goodnight, and left the room, leaving the door ajar as Evan insisted. She was in the bathroom brushing her teeth when she heard him call out. She left off what she was doing and went to him. Evan had not sounded frightened. Not in the least.

"What is it, sweetheart?" She switched on the bedside lamp.

"Somebody's scratching."

"Maybe they have fleas. Go to sleep now."

"But don't you hear it, Mammy?"

Ciara thought she'd humour the four-year-old. She made a big show of cocking an ear as though listening intently.

"No," she said at last. "Now go to sleep or I'll be cross."

She kissed Evan, switched off the lamp and left the room. But she'd hardly returned to the bathroom when the child called out again.

This time Ciara was irritated. She seldom, if ever, had any difficulty in getting Evan off to sleep. This was out of character. She went through the procedure again: lamp on, scolding, pretending to listen . . .

But this time she too heard the scratching.

"Mammy, I told you there was –"

"Shush, Evan! Let me listen."

Ciara moved away from the bed and made a circuit of the room. It was hard to say where the noises were coming from. At first she thought they came from under the child's bed but on bending down she could hear nothing from that quarter. It was definitely scratching. To Ciara it sounded as though somebody was using a small strip of sandpaper.

"Do you hear it now, Mammy?"

What could she say? She went to the wall opposite the window. The sound seemed to be coming from that direction. She opened the cupboard. It was filled with Evan's toys. She put her head in. Nothing. The scratching was coming from elsewhere. She shut the doors again and went to inspect the skirting board.

The scratching stopped.

"It went away, Mammy," Evan said.

"I know."

"What was it, Mammy?"

"It was nothing. You go to sleep now."

Some minutes later Ciara climbed under the covers of her own bed and switched off the light. She lay for a while trying to figure it out. A mouse maybe? Yes, it must be a mouse. But *inside* the skirting? Well, she knew it was possible.

Having been raised on a farm, she wasn't unduly nervous of the little pests and knew they could fit themselves into the tiniest of holes and cracks. She resolved to set traps the next day. Thus reassured, she drifted into a light sleep.

But after a few minutes she was wide awake again.

Something had roused her. A sound very close at hand.

Nervously, she switched the bedside light back on and sat up. Perhaps it was something outside – or even in the house next door; the walls of certain council-built houses were notoriously thin. Perhaps she'd been dreaming. But she didn't believe that.

She sat very still, hugging her knees, heart thumping, mind racing, conscious of the night pressing about her, of Evan asleep in the next room and her own solitude. She heard the clock ticking away the seconds, her own rapid breathing, but that was all.

Chiding herself for being silly, she lay down again. But barely had her head hit the pillow than she was sitting up again.

She swore that something had touched her hair.

She wondered if it might have been the pillow; that she'd shifted against it. She was about to lie down again when she heard a by-now-familiar noise: the scratching she'd heard in Evan's room. It was very distinct – and it was coming from the headboard.

My God, she thought, there's a mouse in the bed!

She leaped out, switched on the main light, and stripped off the duvet and pillows.

Nothing.

Trying not to wake Evan, whose room adjoins hers, she checked under the bed and behind it, inspected the wardrobe, the dressing-table drawers, even went through the bin. But of the mouse there was no sign.

Exasperated, she stood in the middle of the room wondering what to do. Go downstairs and try to sleep on the sofa, or return to bed and put in earplugs? That is, if she could find them. . . .

She was rooting about in the locker drawer when she heard the scratching again. But now it had moved. It appeared to be coming from the wall a little above the skirting board. She got down on one knee and pressed an ear against the plaster. The scratching sounds seemed to be growing louder. She flung the earplugs back in the drawer and went downstairs.

Ciara got no sleep that night. Early next morning she was sitting in the kitchen, nursing her sixth cup of tea, when Evan appeared. She was bleary-eyed and exhausted, and could barely make the child his breakfast. It was an ordinary school day, and she walked him to school as usual. But before she collected him again she decided to do something she hadn't done in a while: she'd pay a visit to her brother Seamus. She needed advice. No, more than that: she needed help.

Seamus, the eldest of her siblings, is in his early forties. An illness contracted in childhood had left him unable to work for long periods at a time. He was at home when Ciara called that morning. Over a cup of coffee she told him of her sleepless night.

"I think we have mice, Seamus."

"Have you set traps?"

"I didn't have time. It only happened last night. Will you come and have a look?"

"If you think it'll help . . ."

They stopped off at a hardware shop, bought a half-dozen mousetraps and made their way presently to Ciara's house. It was silent – as it usually was at that time of morning. They went through to the kitchen. Seamus declined his sister's offer of tea. He didn't like the house and was anxious to get the job over with as soon as possible.

He didn't like the house for a good reason. Eighteen months before, he'd answered his sister's cry for help. It had been late in the evening but Ciara had been desperate. She'd decided to enlist his help instead of relying on the Gardaí. Bob had come home drunk and spoiling for a fight. There'd been a scene. Bob had come off second-best.

Weeks would go by before he misbehaved again. The incident had been virtually a re-run of the first. Again Bob backed down under threat from Seamus, yet the altercations had soured Seamus's relationship with his sister. He had his own problems, he told her. She'd hesitated before calling on his help again. Bob's death had changed matters, of course. The siblings had patched up their differences.

They heard the scratching as they were going up the stairs.

Seamus stopped and listened. The noise was very audible in the silent house. It sounded exactly as Ciara had described: mice running about behind – or within – the wall.

"Did you look for mouse-holes?" he asked. "You know: places where they can come and go?"

She shook her head. She'd never seen any. The house, although having been built more than twenty years before, had undergone a complete modernization the previous year as part of a renewal scheme. The skirting boards had been replaced throughout. Nevertheless Seamus made a thorough inspection of those on the ground floor. All were pristine and intact.

He explored the stairs. No sign of any mouse-holes. He went up to the bedrooms and bathroom, even inspected the airing cupboard. All seemed in order. It was while he was on the landing with his sister that he heard further scratching, and the unmistakable scurrying of tiny feet.

This time they were coming from above his head.

"Have you got a loft?" he asked.

Ciara shrugged. "I suppose so. I've never even thought about it."

"You have, you know," Seamus said, pointing to a trapdoor set into the ceiling. "Do you have a torch?"

Ciara fetched it, along with a stepladder. Within minutes her brother had opened the trapdoor – but only with effort; the decorators had painted it shut. He climbed up into the attic.

"You'll be careful, won't you?" she called out.

There was no answer.

"Seamus?"

Still no answer. Ciara was growing concerned. Then she heard his footsteps almost directly above her head. His face appeared at the opening in the ceiling, upside down and looking incongruous. Even so, she could tell he was bothered by something.

"What is it?"

He seemed reluctant to reply. He waited until he'd rejoined her on the landing.

"You have a problem," he said.

"Is it mice?" Her voice shook slightly.

"No, not exactly. I can't explain. Some crazy has been painting up here. Come and see for yourself."

"So Seamus helped me up the ladder," Ciara tells me, and I can see that the memory is disturbing her. "I'd never been up in the loft before – to be honest with you, it had never even crossed my mind to look up there. Out of sight, out of mind, I suppose you'd say. I don't mind telling you I was a bit on edge."

Seamus helped her up into the attic space. The flashlight was very weak and it took a moment or two for Ciara's eyes to adjust. What she saw shocked her.

"I couldn't take it in at first," she says. "It was all so unreal. Somebody had been busy with paint. Black paint. The decorators had painted the ceiling white, but somebody had taken a brush and painted graffiti. Only it wasn't the sort of graffiti you see on walls around the town. This was horrible. It was all disgusting stuff about sexual perversion, and there were things like crosses . . . and strange eyes . . . painted along with the words. I don't even want to describe any of it, it was that bad."

The first mystery was how – and when – the graffiti got there. Ciara assures me that as far as Seamus could tell, nobody had opened the trapdoor to the attic since the decorators had been in. I ask if it was possible that somebody could have done it while she was away. She shrugs off the suggestion.

"That would have been impossible," she says with conviction. "I've never left this house for more than a day at a time. I never went off on a holiday; I didn't have the money. And even if I did, I'm sure I'd have noticed that something wasn't right when I got back."

Seamus had to assist her down the ladder again. She was trembling with fright. Even when he'd replaced the trapdoor and put away the stepladder, Ciara found that she couldn't remain in the house, not even downstairs. In her mind's eye she still saw the frightful things daubed on the attic walls. She gladly accepted Seamus's offer to return with him to his house. His wife Nicola was out at work – she had a part-time job in a supermarket – and Ciara could stay until she got home. He phoned Nicola and asked if she could collect Evan from school. Ciara was too upset and didn't feel up to it.

"I couldn't go back there," she says with emotion. "I couldn't bring Evan back there either. I kept thinking about those horrible things in the roofspace. I felt threatened."

I ask her whether she thought of going to the police. She shakes her head.

"I didn't want to involve the Guards. What would I say to them? And I didn't want anybody else seeing those awful things. I didn't want a stranger involved."

Seamus left her in his house and went to the hardware shop, where he bought a big drum of white emulsion. He borrowed Ciara's house key and set off for her home. It was late in the evening when he returned. Nicola and Ciara had already put the children to bed; Evan was sharing with one of the boys.

Seamus looked exhausted.

"All done," he told her. "You'd never know anybody had been."

"Seamus is good like that," Nicola said proudly. Seamus beamed.

"What do you want to do, Ciara?" he asked his sister. "You're welcome to stay here for a couple of days if you'd prefer that."

She agreed. It was Thursday. Evan would have another day at school. Then they could all spend the weekend together.

"I'll need to get a few things," she said.

"I'll come with you."

The house was as quiet as ever when they let themselves in. Ciara was nervous. She hung back in the hallway.

"You wouldn't mind checking the traps first?" she said. "I can't stand the sight of dead things."

Seamus checked the ground floor first, before climbing the stairs.

After a couple of minutes he was back on the landing, shaking his head. "Nope. Nothing."

"What, you mean we haven't caught any?"

"Doesn't look like it. The coast is clear. Come on up."

Ciara mounted the stairs uneasily. "But that means the scratching wasn't mice."

"No, Ciara. It means we haven't caught them yet. Now hurry up. I haven't got all day."

On the landing she paused and looked up instinctively. The blank oblong of the trapdoor looked somehow ominous. She smelled fresh emulsion.

Quickly she packed a small suitcase and an overnight bag, and joined Seamus downstairs.

"I'm all right now," she said, not wanting to appear silly. But inside she felt far from all right.

The weekend passed pleasantly at her brother's house and Ciara was able to forget her troubles. Being away gave her a fresh perspective on things.

Everything had a logical explanation, she told herself. The graffiti was the work of a former tenant. It really had nothing to do with her and Evan. Mice could get into cavity walls. Seamus had said as much. The traps would get them – eventually.

Thus reassured, she left her son off at school on the Monday morning and returned to her home in a more positive frame of mind. She'd said nothing to Evan about the graffiti; he was too young to understand. He hadn't asked why they'd spent the weekend at his uncle's home. He'd had a nice time; that was all that mattered.

She'd brought her suitcase with her. It contained essential items. She'd decided to collect the overnight bag from her brother's house later that day.

All seemed normal, just as Seamus had promised her. It was a bright, sunny morning and the kitchen was cheerful as she put the kettle on for tea. The mousetrap by the backdoor was still empty, but she didn't really care and put it from her mind.

But as she was about to reach for a tea bag something in the atmosphere changed. All at once she had a strong sensation that she was not alone, that there was someone behind her, standing in the doorway.

Ciara could not bring herself to look round. She was afraid to move.

She was conscious of the sounds from outside: bird calls in the back garden, traffic out on the road. She heard a child wailing and a ball being kicked against a wall somewhere close by. Life was continuing as normal – but she felt anything *but* normal.

"It was a very strange sensation," she recalls. "I'd never experienced anything like it. I just *knew* that there was someone in the doorway, but at the same time, a logical part of me was telling me there couldn't be anyone there."

I put it to Ciara that she may have been suffering the effects of an overactive imagination. After all, she'd been convinced that there were strange goings-on in the house. Could it not be the case that her mind was playing tricks on her, that the sensation of being watched was nothing more than the power of suggestion? She concurs. I ask her how long the sensation lasted.

"Not long, mind you," she says. "A minute at most, but then I thought: I'm nervous about coming back and it's just my imagination, as you say."

Nevertheless, she checked the hallway and opened the front door. There was no one there; she was alone in the house.

She made her tea, drank it at the table, picked up the suitcase, and climbed the stairs.

The smell of paint still lingered on the landing, but that was to be expected. She'd taken care to leave the bathroom window open to help to disperse it. She was conscious of the trapdoor above her but refused to look up, not wishing to be reminded.

In her bedroom she threw open the window. She noted that the mousetrap lay undisturbed, and thought no more about it. There were more important things to be getting on with. She busied herself with unpacking. But no sooner had she taken the first few items from the case than she felt the same odd sensation taking hold of her again. She felt certain she was being watched. This time, however, she decided to fight it, and not be cowed.

Summoning up a great effort of will, she turned to face whatever might be there, intruding upon her private space. But again there was nothing to be seen. Yet still she sensed a presence, a baleful one.

"Go away!" she shouted, dashing out to the landing. But yet again there was nothing.

Wearily she turned back to the bedroom. This time, however, she *did* glance up at the trapdoor.

It was open.

Ciara was horrified. Her worst fears had been confirmed – there was someone, or something, in the house after all. The sight of that dark opening unnerved her completely. She ran downstairs as fast as she could, snatched up her handbag and fled.

She didn't slow her step until she'd reached Seamus's house. When he opened the door he found her almost incoherent.

"D-did you . . . did you leave the trapdoor open?" she managed to blurt out, trying to catch her breath.

"No . . . I don't think so. Why would I do that?"

"Because it's open now!"

"No, I'm sure I didn't."

"Really sure?"

"Yes."

She told him about what she'd just experienced and about there being no mice in the traps.

"I'm phoning Nicola," he said. "She was talking about this very thing last week, when I told her about the graffiti. She said you should get the house blessed."

"Blessed? Why should I do that? You know I'm not religious. Neither are you, come to that." Ciara knew that Nicola was a bit of a "Holy Joe" but hadn't expected that her brother would go along with her suggestion.

"Okay, I'm not religious," he said, "but maybe a blessing would help, who knows. Well, let me put it this way: it won't do any harm, will it?"

Father Boyle met Ciara and her brother at her home three days later. It was only the second time she'd returned following her encounters with the "presence". Seamus had also been with her on the first occasion. She dared not return alone. Once again he'd helped her to collect clothing and other necessities. She'd ordered a taxi that time.

The priest was affable – if, thought Ciara, not overly friendly. She wondered how often he was called out to bless a house. She had a feeling it wasn't too often.

She also found it curious that he didn't ask many questions about her ghosts – she was convinced they were ghosts; she had no rational explanation for them. She decided that Father Boyle's silence on the matter was due, not to a lack of religious faith, but to his refusal to believe in superstition. He seemed to Ciara to be a "sensible" man, from his carefully brushed grey hair to the toes of his finely polished black shoes.

The blessing did not take long. Father Boyle left them in the living-room while he went through the small house, prayer-book in one hand and holy-water sprinkler in the other. They heard him intone the same prayers over and over. In Latin. Ciara felt there was something very medieval about the whole thing.

She thanked him profusely when he was done. He declined her offer of tea, explaining that he'd other duties to perform. He left her with a prayer leaflet, which she looked at only when he'd gone. She was surprised, but delighted, to find it contained the words of a hymn she'd heard in childhood. It was *Bless this House*:

> *Bless this house, o Lord, we pray.*
> *Make it safe by night and day.*
> *Bless these walls so firm and stout,*
> *Keeping want and trouble out.*

Bless the roof and chimney tall,
Let thy peace lie over all.
Bless the doors that they may prove
Ever open to joy and love.
Bless the windows shining bright,
Letting in God's heavenly light.
Bless the hearth a'blazing there,
With smoke ascending like a prayer.
Bless the people here within,
Keep them pure and free from sin.
Bless us all, that one day, we
Are fit, o Lord, to dwell with Thee.

She and Evan returned to the house the following day. It seemed normal. No mice, no scratching, no invisible presences. And presumably nothing up in the attic – or so she fervently hoped.

It was Evan who sounded the alarm, as he'd done when the first manifestations occurred. They'd spent two peaceful nights and days in the house, and Ciara had put the worry of it all behind her. She'd said the prayer for three days running, and had convinced herself that the house was well and truly blessed.

She awoke to find Evan at her bedside, tugging at the duvet.

"There's a man in my room!"

Ciara's first impulse was that of any mother: to tell her child that he'd had a bad dream and to take him back to bed. But something about Evan's demeanour told her that she should take it seriously. On top of that she was recalling the events of the past few weeks. It might, she reasoned, be nothing at all. But then again . . .

"What sort of man?" she asked.

"A big man."

"Is he still there?"

"Don't know, Mammy."

She climbed out of bed and took the little boy's hand.

"All right," she said soothingly. "We'll have a look, will we?"

The only light in Evan's room was from his Peppa Pig night-light. Ciara stiffened as soon as she entered. The watcher was back: the presence she'd felt so strongly in the kitchen. She could *feel* it standing in the corner. She knew it was the same entity; she sensed an intelligence that seemed to be following her every move.

She couldn't let Evan see how terrified she was in those moments. It wouldn't be fair on the child. What he needed then, she told herself, was a mother to protect him, and not one who fell to pieces for no good reason. Swallowing her fear, she switched on the main light. The atmosphere in the room changed immediately.

"See, there's no one," she said. "Where was this man supposed to be anyway?"

Evan pointed to the corner. Ciara wished he hadn't. Anywhere, she thought: anywhere else in the room, but not in that corner.

"Don't want to sleep here, Mammy."

Ciara didn't argue. Back in her bedroom she tucked Evan into bed beside her; he quickly fell asleep. She lay awake, sleep refusing to come. She'd locked the bedroom door and kept the bedside light on. On the one hand she needed darkness to sleep; on the other she was frightened of what that darkness might bring.

Her eye fell on Father Boyle's prayer. It was on the locker, where she'd placed it. She picked it up, recited it softly a couple of times, felt slightly more reassured, and lay down again.

Some minutes later a noise out in the corridor had her fully alert. She sat up. Listening; hoping to have her terrors dispelled. She heard the regular breathing of little Evan beside her. She *had* imagined it, then. Heartened, she was about to settle down when it came a second time. Now she heard it clearly.

It was the sound of the trapdoor being pushed open.

She clapped a hand over her mouth. She began to sob. Evan must not be woken up. He could not be made a party to this. She had to protect him.

The ceiling directly above her creaked. Something was moving across the loft. Something very heavy was being dragged.

"Like a bag of cement," Ciara recalls. "Or somebody pulling a big piece of furniture. I was terrified because I knew there was nothing up there. When I'd been up that time with Seamus the roof-space was empty."

Didn't she want to flee the house immediately?

"Of course I did, but it was two o'clock in the morning. I really couldn't impose on Seamus and Nicola again, and especially not at that hour. Besides, Evan was asleep. And to be honest I was petrified to leave the room. Believe it or not it felt safer to be locked in than brave it out and go out to the landing."

The unsettling noises continued throughout the night. There were the scratching sounds she'd become accustomed to. But there was a new addition: odd thumps.

"Like something being dropped," she says. "A small object, not very loud."

She rang Seamus at first light. "They're back," she said.

"They?" came his sleepy voice.

"There's . . . something in the attic. Tell Nicola I'm sorry, but we're going to have to impose on you again."

It appeared that Father Boyle's blessing hadn't worked. Ciara blamed herself. Perhaps she didn't believe sufficiently in prayer.

"I'd get a psychic in if I was you," Jackie said.

Over a few drinks in their local, Ciara had bared her soul to her best friend. She'd had the feeling that Jackie would scoff at the blessing by the priest; she'd no time for such things. Yet she'd surprised Ciara by mentioning a psychic. It was most uncharacteristic of her.

"If you change your mind," Jackie said on leaving the pub, "I can give you a phone number."

"I'll think about it."

Ciara did more than that. Her mother came to visit her the following day. She was concerned, not having seen her daughter for some time. To Ciara's surprise she agreed with Jackie's suggestion.

"I don't want a psychic," Ciara told her. "That sort of thing gives me the creeps. Maybe if the priest offers a Mass this time, and with more people there."

Her mother was doubtful. "I knew a lady who had the same sort of thing," she said. "She was pestered for months on end. Nearly went out of her mind. In the end she called a psychic in and she was rid of it the same day."

Ciara considered this. She's a cradle Catholic, as are most of her friends, family and acquaintances. Although not a staunch believer, she doesn't hold the Church in high regard. Nevertheless she was wary of placing her trust in what she held to be superstition – if not downright deception.

Yet the more her mother spoke of her friend's experience – and the resolving of her problems by a psychic – the more she warmed to the idea. She kept telling herself that it couldn't hurt, despite the dire warnings she'd heard from childhood against dabbling in the occult.

"I kept thinking it was somehow wrong," she says. "But I suppose when you stop and think about it there's really no difference in believing in the power of a priest and the power of a psychic. At the end of the day they're not much different, are they? We're brought up to believe that the one knows more about the supernatural than the other, but is that really true? I wasn't sure."

She considered the alternative. By this stage she had the distinct feeling that she'd overstayed her welcome in her brother's house. The strain of having two families under the one roof was beginning to show.

"But I knew I couldn't go back to my own house," she says. "Not with those . . . *things* in there. I'd have lost my mind, and of course I had to think of Evan as well. He's a good kid, very strong-willed. He takes after me that way. But I couldn't have him being scared to death by those things. We'd talked about them when we got to Seamus's house and I asked Evan to describe what he'd seen. I wondered if it was Bob he'd seen in his room, but I couldn't ask him that. But he kept calling it 'the man'."

"And what did this man look like, sweetheart?"

"Don't know."

"Well, was he old or young?"

"Don't know, 'cos his face was all fuzzy."

"And what about his clothes? What was he wearing?"

"They were black clothes, but they were all fuzzy too."

At any rate Ciara's mother, together with further coaxing from Jackie, won her over to the proposition of contacting a psychic. On an impulse her mother telephoned her friend; she learned that the woman who'd been of such help to her had retired from her "practice" but was still available for what she termed "an emergency". Ciara's case seemed to meet that requirement very well. Within the hour an appointment had been made. The psychic, whom we will call Janet, agreed to come to the house in Bray. But she was very elderly by that time and unable to travel. And so it was arranged that Ciara's youngest brother would collect her in his car and take her to the house. There was only one last thing Ciara wished to know: how much would Janet charge for her services?

"Are you mad?" her mother said. "Sure you'd insult her if you offered her money. Janet doesn't charge people. She does it out of the goodness of her heart. She's a saint."

Her words had a profound effect on Ciara. She'd become so accustomed to people wishing to make money from victims of the paranormal that she expected nothing else. She freely admits that that, for her, was the deciding factor. To be sure, Father Boyle hadn't charged for his services either, but it could be argued that the blessing of a house was a part of his duties as a priest.

Ciara reasoned that a psychic who provided her services for nothing had to be bona fide.

Janet turned out to be a fiery old lady of indeterminate age. Ciara guessed she was in her mid-eighties. She was tiny, and seemingly so frail that Ciara had second thoughts about engaging her to "cleanse" her home. She hoped that whatever Janet encountered would not tax her too much.

She needn't have worried. What Janet lacked in physical strength she more than made up for in force of personality and will. She entered the house as though it were her own, as though she'd been there many times before.

Ciara led the way into the front room; it was the quietest part of the house, facing as it did onto a little square of similar houses with a patch of grass in the middle.

"Did somebody die?" the psychic asked. "Somebody close to you?"

"My husband," Ciara told her. "It was a while ago."

"Not for him it wasn't," Janet said at once. "They have no idea of time, you see."

"They?" Seamus said.

"Ghosts in general." She turned to Ciara. "What was his name? Your husband."

"Bob."

Seamus then related what he'd found in the attic. Janet frowned on learning about the nature of the graffiti.

"Was Bob involved in anything dangerous?" She saw Ciara's incomprehension. "The Dark Arts?"

She'd no idea what the woman was talking about. Janet, in words that did nothing to alleviate Ciara's unease, explained about black magic and related occult practices.

"No, never anything like that," Ciara assured her.

"And before his death. Did you see any changes in him?"

"He was drinking very heavily."

"I see. Did he have blackouts?"

"Well, after one of his binges he'd remember next to nothing the next day. Sometimes he'd forget who he'd been even drinking with."

"Someone died here," Janet said with conviction, "and there was drink involved."

"But Bob didn't die here—"

"I didn't say it was your husband."

Ciara hadn't expected that. She was startled. "Who then?"

"Someone who lived here in the past," Janet said. "If a man drinks heavily he can attract all sorts of bad influences to him. There are a lot of things out there that are hanging around and waiting for an opportunity to come in. Drink's the connection here – your husband and this one. God only knows," she glanced up at the trapdoor, "God only knows what he was up to – up there."

"But a young family lived here before me," Ciara said. She believed the psychic was really taking things a bit far.

"No, way back, way back," Janet said dismissively. "There's a lot of negative energy in this house. Something bad happened here and your husband's death didn't help things. I hope I'm not frightening you."

"Well . . ." Ciara was scared half out of her wits. She was beginning to regret having allowed the strange woman in, wished she hadn't listened to Jackie and her mother. "Maybe it's better if we just move house then." But even as she said it, Ciara knew she'd be compounding one problem with another. She'd have had to put herself on a waiting list and had no idea how long it would be before she could be rehoused. Nor could she be sure they'd even take her seriously. "My house is haunted; I need another one," was not an explanation that would meet with a sympathetic response.

"No, *they* have to move, not you," Janet said. "That's why I'm here. Now, let me see upstairs."

Ciara showed her the two bedrooms, the bathroom and a box-room at the back used mainly as a storeroom. Janet returned without delay to Evan's bedroom.

"There's a spot here," she said.

Ciara was dismayed to see her go to the corner where Evan had pointed out the apparition of "the man".

The psychic went back onto the landing and glanced up at the trap-door. "And here. Something happened here just at the top of the stairs." She shut her eyes and sighed heavily. Seamus and Ciara exchanged nervous glances, not knowing what was coming next.

"A young man." Janet continued. "Not in his right mind . . . a young man. He's falling . . ." She grasped the banister and opened her eyes. "I'm sensing . . . I'm sensing he fell and . . ."

She didn't finish the sentence and Ciara was too afraid to ask. They followed her down the stairs again and into the front room.

Without further ado the psychic made her preparations. She drew the curtains in the living-room and instructed

Seamus and Ciara to join her at the table. From her handbag she took a small oil-burner, lit a tea-light and set it in place. She took out a small packet of ground herbs and sprinkled them on the burner dish. Almost immediately there arose a wonderful fragrance that Ciara could not identify.

"White sage," Janet told her. "Highly efficacious. They don't like it one bit."

They again. Ciara was dreading even hearing the word spoken aloud. It chilled her. But a minute later Janet said something that chilled her even more.

"Your aura is weak. We'll have to do something about that. They could be using it as a doorway you see. I'm going to work on your chakras. You won't feel anything different but I guarantee you'll be a changed woman when we're done."

On Janet's instructions the three held hands, forming a small group in the middle of the room. Ciara heard Janet intone what sounded like a prayer or incantation. It was in a language unfamiliar to her. She thought it might be Hindi or some other Eastern tongue. It was not unpleasant on the ear.

Janet shut her eyes when the prayer was finished. Ciara felt her small, wiry hand tighten its grip. As the psychic had predicted, she felt nothing out of the ordinary.

But she *saw* something. She began to tremble.

"Courage, dear," Janet said, her eyes still shut.

Ciara had thought at first that what she was seeing was connected with the herbs that Janet had burned. For she swears she saw a dark shadow rising on the far side of the room and assuming a shape.

She looked in panic at Seamus. He gave no sign that he was seeing what she was seeing. Was she imagining things?

The shape was just as Evan had described it: it was "fuzzy" and had the appearance of a very tall man. It began to move about the room. Ciara had the disquieting thought that it was seeking a means by which it could enter the circle made by those three pairs of hands.

Then Janet began to intone another prayer. It resembled the first but appeared to be more of a spoken command. Whatever it was, she said it over and over again. Her eyes were still shut tight.

All the while that Janet prayed, Ciara's attention was fixed on the shadowy shape. It held a dreadful fascination for her; although she wished more than anything to be able to look away, she discovered she could not. She was like a mongoose that had fallen under the mesmerizing spell of a cobra.

But eventually the apparition began to fade, to grow lighter and more indistinct. The change was gradual at first but soon accelerated. It finally disappeared completely. Janet opened her eyes.

"There," she said with a smile. "That's that taken care of."

"And, thank God, she was absolutely right," Ciara tells me now. "I don't know how she did it but we haven't been bothered since."

Ciara Mulhern is clearly no fantasist. I have seldom met a more down-to-earth, no-nonsense individual. She likes to talk and has views on a great many issues. She talks a lot of sense.

For this reason I find it hard to doubt her story, incredible though it may appear. Yet the fact remains that she – and only she – saw anything that evening when Janet banished her ghosts. And banish them she did.

I have not spoken to Janet. She did not wish to be interviewed. She is elderly and has an entire career of combating unwelcome psychic phenomena behind her. She neither needs nor desires publicity of any sort.

Seamus reports seeing nothing and hearing nothing out of the ordinary that evening. He does, however, concede that the house seems somehow more "peaceful" than it did before Janet's intervention.

In effect, then, the only witnesses to the appearance of mysterious shapes and the scratching of phantom mice are a young widow and her six-year-old son. And what can we make of that graffiti in the attic, long painted over? Who was responsible for it? A drunken young man – who, according to the psychic, met his untimely death in the house a long time ago? I ask Ciara if she'd looked into the history of the house in order to prove or disprove Janet's theory.

"No, absolutely not. I really don't want to know. The whole experience was just so traumatic. If I discovered that what the psychic said was actually true and that someone was killed here . . . well, it would prey on my mind and be too unsettling. I think it's best not to know."

Father Boyle stopped by again to see how things were. He was pleased to hear that Ciara was experiencing no more problems. She did not consider it prudent to tell him about the visit of a psychic. She felt he'd disapprove.

As I leave the little house in Bray I notice something I missed when I came in. There's a framed prayer in the hall and, next to it, a holy-water font. The prayer is "Bless This House".

"I say it every day," Ciara says. "So does Evan. He loves it. His granny found an old record of it, sung by Perry Como. She plays it sometimes when we visit her and we sing along to it. It's nice."

I agree.

NOTES

Introduction

Page 2 *pookas, haunted graveyards* – It is a measure of how, down through the years, Irish ghost stories have altered in character – and in the "characters" contained within them. Not one person under the age of sixty whom I spoke to during my research had even heard tell of the pooka, yet Irish ghost stories told in Victorian times and even later are replete with mention of this entity.

According to Celtic legend, the pooka (which derives from *púca*, an old Irish word for "ghost") is a hobgoblin that can appear variously as a hare, a goat, a dog, but usually as a horse. It is also cognate with "puck". Shakespeare made use of this character in his *A Midsummer Night's Dream*, calling him Robin Goodfellow. This entity seems to have been known in Scotland, Wales and the southwest of England.

David Rice McAnally, the Victorian collector of Irish ghost stories, was told of a pooka seen by the friend of a jaunting-car driver. It appeared to him in the form of a talking horse. (I have taken the liberty of converting McAnally's "cod Irish" into legible English.)

I never saw it, glory be to God, but there's them that has, and by the same token, they do say that it looks like the finest black horse that ever wore shoes. But it isn't a horse at all at all, for no horse would have eyes of fire, or be breathing flames of blue with a smell of sulphur – saving your presence) [McAnally was a clergyman] – or a snort like thunder, and no mortal horse would take the leaps it does, or go as far without getting tired. . . . He [the friend] knew it was the Pooka because it spoke to him like a Christian mortal, only it isn't agreeable in its language . . .

David Rice McAnally, *Irish Wonders* (1997) Gramercy Books, New York

D R McAnally described in some detail the variations in the wail of the banshee and what each was said to signify:

The Banshee is really a disembodied soul, that of one who, in life, was strongly attached to the family, or who had good reason to hate all its members. Thus, in different instances, the Banshee's song may be inspired by opposite motives. When the Banshee loves those whom she calls, the song is a low, soft chant, giving notice, indeed, of the close proximity of the angel of death, but with a tenderness of tone that reassures the one destined to die and comforts the survivors; rather a welcome than a warning, and having in its tones a thrill of exultation, as though the messenger spirit were bringing glad tidings to him summoned to join the waiting throng of his ancestors. If, during her lifetime, the Banshee was an enemy of the family, the cry is the scream of a fiend, howling with demoniac delight over the coming death-agony of another of her foes.

Page 4 *lies outside the physical* – So accustomed are we to the physical world we perceive with our five senses that it's difficult for many of us to appreciate just how pitifully limited this perception is. Yet physicists now suspect that the electromagnetic (EM) spectrum may well be infinite.

However, for practical purposes we can take the EM to mean the spectrum between radio waves, which have a frequency of about 10,000 Hz, and gamma rays, which have the smallest wavelengths and the most energy of any other wave in the EM.

Gamma waves are generated by radioactive atoms and in nuclear explosions. They have a frequency of 10^{19} Hz – 10 followed by nineteen zeros. Of this astonishing range we can perceive a mere 0.0035%. This means in effect that practically the entire physical universe is beyond the scope of our eyes and ears.

Of the non-physical universe we know nothing.

Page 5 *the ghost has been with us since the bronze age* – There have been attempts to go back even further than this. Some contend that one of the cave drawings of Lascaux, in the Dordogne region of France, depicts a phantom horse. The pictograph, executed about 17,000 years ago by a Cro-Magnon artist, shows a dark-brown animal fading into white. The horse appears to be either appearing or vanishing in a stampede of other animals. "Perhaps the artist just got tired," suggests author Melissa Mia Hall, "but the image is mysteriously haunting."

onto their clay tablets – Most experts agree that in 2700 BC a cuneiform scribe named Shin-eqi-unninni incised in a clay tablet the first account of a human being communicating with a ghost or spirit. On the twelfth tablet of the *Epic of Gilgamesh*, the great Sumerian epic, the grieving hero converses with the ghost of his dead friend Enkidu, who tells him about the afterlife. Gilgamesh has implored the god Ea to allow him to speak to his friend.

> Ea, from his abyss deep, heard Gilgamesh and took pity, saying: "Nergel, hear me now, open a most wide aperture in thy roof, from whence can Enkidu waft like smoke up from your hot fires below." Nergel heard Ea's great voice and did cut a hole in his roof to allow Enkidu's spirit to waft up from his hot fires below.

Page 12 *James Haddock, who lived to the south of the city* – The story is one of the most intriguing in the annals of Irish hauntings, not least because of the intervention of Jeremy Taylor. A Church of England clergyman educated at both Oxford and Cambridge, Taylor (1613–67) was one of the great poetry and prose writers of his time and was even likened to Shakespeare. He was also renowned as one of the finest orators in Ireland.

When the ghost of James Haddock appeared to his friend Francis Tavener, Dr Taylor was Bishop of Down and

Connor. His palace was at Hillsborough, the village Tavener had departed for his ride to Belfast. His horse reared at the sight of the ghost, almost unseating him. "Take Daniel Davis to court!" the ghost urged. "There's something wrong with my will." Davis was the man who'd married Haddock's widow; he'd had a son by her and had altered the will in the boy's favour.

Dr Taylor heard reports about the ensuing trial, which took place in Carrickfergus, and summoned Francis Tavener and other witnesses. He declared the appearance of the ghost in the witness box to be genuine. It remains the only case of its kind on record.

There is a fascinating sequel. James Haddock's tombstone refused to remain upright. Many attempts have been made to right it, and after each attempt it is found lying flat. It remains in that position to this day. It is, however, somewhat difficult to identify as five or six tombstones in the cemetery have fallen, and all face down.

Page 13 *she'd written a note to her uncle* – There are several variations on the Marsh haunting. One has the niece eloping with a seafarer:

> A popular explanation of the archbishop's ghostly appearance concerns a favourite niece of his, a girl whom he had reared from a child. When the girl fell in love with a sea captain, the archbishop strongly disapproved and tried to prevent her from seeing the man. The young couple made up their minds to elope and the girl, doubtless to assuage her

conscience, wrote a note to her uncle, pleading for his forgiveness, and placed it in one of his books in the library.

John Dunne, *A Ghost Watcher's Guide to Ireland* (2001) Appletree Press, Belfast

from the benign to the malevolent – Whether ghosts are in fact neutral, good or evil remains a contentious question. Gerina Dunwich tells us that

there are people from all walks of life who continue to be terrified of ghosts and see them as something potentially harmful.

Professor Hans Holzer, a renowned parapsychologist and prolific author, believes otherwise. In his book, *Ghosts: True Encounters with the World Beyond*, he states, "Ghosts have never harmed anyone except through fear found within the witness, of his own doing and because of his ignorance as to what ghosts represent." Although he does acknowledge that there are a small number of cases of ghosts attacking the living, he believes them to be "simply a matter of mistaken identity, where extreme violence at the time of death has left a strong residue of memory in the individual ghost."

Dunwich, Gerina, *A Witch's Guide to Ghosts and the Supernatural* (2002) New Page Books, New Jersey

Róisín and the Ghost that Drew Blood

Page 36 *the image of herself disappearing in the mirror* – Mirrors and ghosts were inextricably linked in the ancient world. Sir James Frazer, the intrepid Scottish anthropologist (1854–1941) who wrote *The Golden Bough*, a study of religion and sociology, mentioned the fear of one's reflection among the Greeks. He went as far as to say that the legend of Narcissus, who became fatally entranced with his own reflection in water, owed much to this fear and that the Greeks saw in a man's dreaming of his mirror-image an omen portending his death. Frazer made some interesting observations that may have a bearing on the practices surrounding the Irish wake:

> Further, we can now explain the widespread custom of covering up mirrors or turning them to the wall after a death has taken place in the house. It is feared that the soul, projected out of the person in the shape of his reflection in the mirror, may be carried off by the ghost of the departed, which is commonly supposed to linger about the house till the burial. The custom is thus exactly parallel to the Aru [of Indonesia] custom of not sleeping in a house after a death for fear that the soul, projected out of the body in a dream, may meet the ghost and be carried off by it. The reason why sick people should not see themselves in a mirror, and why the mirror in a sick-room is therefore covered up, is also plain; in time of sickness, when the soul might take flight so easily, it is particularly dangerous to project it out

of the body by means of the reflection in a mirror. The rule is therefore precisely parallel to the rule observed by some peoples of not allowing sick people to sleep; for in sleep the soul is projected out of the body, and there is always a risk that it may not return. As with shadows and reflections, so with portraits; they are often believed to contain the soul of the person portrayed. People who hold this belief are naturally loath to have their likenesses taken; for if the portrait is the soul, or at least a vital part of the person portrayed, whoever possesses the portrait will be able to exercise a fatal influence over the original of it.

Page 43 *her "psychic" powers began to show themselves* – The term "psychic" is relatively new to the literature of the paranormal. It is thought that it was first used by the British doctor Sir William Crookes, who wrote in 1871 to a science journal concerning an unknown and invisible agency capable of raising a table: "Respecting the cause of these phenomena, the nature of the force to which I have ventured to give the name of *Psychic. . . .*"

Crookes would, at about the same time, speak of a medium as a "psychic", perhaps because it was suggested by EW Cox, a fellow experimenter and author of *Animal Magnetism*, in discussing the mysterious powers that "sensitives" or mediums possess, who wrote to him thus: "I venture to suggest that the force be termed the *Psychic Force*; the persons in whom it is manifested in extraordinary power *Psychics*; and the science relating to it *Psychism*, as being a branch of Psychology."

The Little Shop of Hauntings

Page 61 *say a few prayers for the ghost* – It is frequently asserted that prayer has the power to banish a ghost. Not in the sense of exorcising the entity but helping it in its passage to the next life.

Catherine Crowe, writing in the nineteenth century, recalled a ghost seen in Germany by a peasant woman. The apparition was in the company of "two smaller spectres". It disappeared when the woman said prayers on its behalf. She briefly examined the role of prayer within Christian denominations.

If these things occurred merely among the Roman Catholics, we might be inclined to suppose that they had some connection with their notion of purgatory, but, on the contrary, it appears to be among the Lutheran population [of Germany] they chiefly occur – inasmuch that it has even been suggested that the omission of prayers for the dead, in the Lutheran church, is the cause of the phenomenon. But, on the other hand, as in the present case, and in several others, the person that revisits the earth was of the Catholic persuasion when alive, we are bound to suppose that he had the benefit of his own church's prayers.

Catherine Crowe, *The Night Side of Nature, Or Ghosts and Ghost Seers* (2000) Wordsworth Editions, Ware

Edel Delahant and the Family Poltergeist

Page 85 *make fools of people* – It is generally assumed that the poltergeist is an entity that does not interact with humans in quite the same way as other paranormal visitors do. We tend to think that the "communication" is very much a one-sided affair. Yet there is a well-documented case of a Dublin poltergeist that manifested, towards the close of the nineteenth and the beginning of the twentieth century, in a house near St Stephen's Green. According to reports the poltergeist used to converse with the family that occupied the house.

They referred to it, or him, as "Corney", and he answered to the name. His voice was said to sound as if it came out of an empty barrel. The servants, who slept in the kitchen, were afraid of Corney and asked to sleep in the attic instead. However, the first time they slept in the attic room, the doors of its cupboard burst open and Corney said: "Ha! Ha! You devils, I am here before you! I am not confined to any particular part of the house!" He was seen only twice, once by someone who apparently died of fright as a result, and once by a seven-year-old boy, who described the figure to his mother as that of a naked man, with a curl on his forehead, and "a skin like a clothes-horse".

Corney had somewhat a warped sense of humour; his first manifestation was mimicking the sound of someone on crutches when one member of the household had to temporarily go on crutches with a sprained knee. He would not allow anything to be kept in one of the kitchen cupboards, tossing out whatever anyone tried to put in there.

On one occasion, he announced he was going to have "company" that evening, and if the residents wanted any water out of the soft-water tank, they should draw it before going to bed, as he and his guests would be using it. Next morning, the water was a sooty black, and there were sooty prints on the bread and butter in the pantry.

When a clergyman came to investigate him, the crafty Corney kept quiet, and on being asked later by the servants, "Corney, why did you not speak?" he said, "I could not speak while that good man was in the house."

Corney made life so lively for the family that they resolved to leave the house and sell the remainder of their lease. But each time someone came to look over the house, his antics speedily drove them away, until at last the lady of the house appealed to him to stop troubling prospective buyers. Corney relented. In fact he said, "You will be all right now, for I see a lady in black coming up to this house, and she will buy it." Within half an hour, a widow had called and agreed to take over the lease, and the family thankfully left Corney behind.

Page 89 *a weight pressing down on him* – It appears as though Granddad had fallen victim to what is called the Old Hag syndrome, or night terror. It is as yet unexplained. The symptoms generally follow a familiar pattern; the victim awakens suddenly and feels suffocated, as though an invisible force is weighing down upon him. He is unable to move or even cry out. Sometimes strange odours and even apparitions accompany the phenomenon. It usually dissipates immediately before the victim loses consciousness.

Medical research shows that about 15% of adults have had this bizarre experience at one time or another. It has certainly been with us for some time, possibly throughout our entire evolution. In the second century AD the Graeco-Roman physician Claudius Galen diagnosed the Old Hag syndrome as simple indigestion – which it may well be. Physicians of our own time agree that it may well be a symptom of chronic indigestion. Others attribute it to narcolepsy or other sleep disorders. Still others blame stress, sexual anxiety, or indeed any of a number of physical or psychological disorders.

Perhaps we should leave the last word on the matter to ghost-hunter Christopher Balzano:

> People have been reporting the 'floating ghost' for centuries. She sits on your chest and paralyzes you as you helplessly wait for her to go away. Ever since people have started writing down haunted tales, the old hag has been stealing people's air. . . . Your brain wakes up before your body does, and you open your eyes but can't move your legs. Your mind is still coming off of a very vivid phase of images due to REM and dream stages, and you create a ghost holding you down in your bed. . . . Of course, we all dream differently, so maybe we just choose the face of our tormentor.

Page 95 *unresponsive to prayer* – Experts at *Our Sunday Visitor*, the American non-profit media group, outline the Catholic position on the poltergeist and how it should be regarded within the context of the paranormal. They state that problems stemming from the activity of demons and ghosts appear to be resolved by prayer but poltergeists "don't seem to respond to these spiritual remedies".

Ghosts – departed human spirits that have been allowed by God to visit earth – usually cease their hauntings when they receive the help they seek from the living. Demons recoil from sacred words and objects. Yet poltergeists, when confronted with these responses, usually continue their mischief, sometimes even laughing or scoffing.

If poltergeists aren't demons or ghosts, what exactly are they? One possibility was suggested by Father [Herbert] Thurston: "It is . . . possible that there may be natural forces involved which are so far as little known to us as the latent forces of electricity were known to the Greeks." (*Ghosts and Poltergeists*, p. vi). I take it that he meant here impersonal forces of nature.

Most poltergeist activity seems to be sporadic and temporary, and dependent on the presence of a particular person – usually an adolescent or child. This last element of the pattern has led some observers to suggest that perhaps such phenomena are actually being caused, unknowingly, by the person in whose presence they keep taking place. (This could also be one explanation for other well-publicized types of paranormal activity.)

Aoife and the Mischievous Ghost

Page 124 *the proctors heard boxes* – From Brad Steiger's *Things That go Bump in the Night* (2005) Bounty Books, London.

going through its entire "repertoire" of tricks – It is curious that the entity which tormented Aoife did not include in its repertoire what belongs to by far the largest single category of poltergeist phenomena: the pelting with stones or pebbles. It even has a "scientific" name: lithobolia, the "stone-throwing devil". Natural scientist Ivan T Sanderson cautioned researchers against using the term "throwing" when speaking of poltergeist activity. According to Sanderson's observations, the stones are "dropped" or "lobbed" or "just drift around" rather than being thrown. "Stone-dropping is a purely physical phenomenon," states Sanderson, "and can be explained on some physical principles, though not necessarily on Newtonian, Einsteinian, or any others that concern our particular spacetime continuum."

Again, I find it a little surprising that Aoife experienced nothing of this nature, given that it's one of the most reported forms of poltergeist activity. On the other hand, none of the other victims of poltergeists I interviewed made mention of it. I have no explanation for this.

The Haunting of Aisling, age Eight

Page 151 *the victims were sacrificed* – Aisling's "little man" seems to conform to some extent with other such finds. They are by no means confined to Ireland but appear to be a phenomenon common in the Celtic world, particularly across northern Europe. In the absence of written records, any interpretation of the bog bodies must remain guess-work. Archaeologists suggest four different explanations: punishment, scapegoating, augury and sacrifice.

Their very dating has been notoriously fraught. Remains from bogs have been placed at periods from later prehistory up to the nineteenth century. When Graubelle Man was found in Denmark, it could not be ascertained whether the remains were those of a local peat-cutter who'd disappeared in the region around 1887 or if the corpse was considerably older. Similar difficulties have been encountered in Britain and Ireland.

The British archaeologist Melanie Giles tells us that bog bodies "continue to present funerary and forensic archaeologists with a particular series of problems."

First, they are often found in circumstances which lead the public and police to believe they are dealing with a modern – or at least historically recent – murder. Second, they are often discovered as part of mass peat extraction, which in the process removes all trace of the original landscape in which the bodies were interred. For both reasons, exhumation is mandatory, both to avoid the complete despoliation of the remains (many are already significantly damaged), and aid forensic investigation.

Giles goes on to report the finding of a number of severed heads in Irish bogs, as well as the so-called Oldcroghan Man, of whom only the upper torso and arms were found interred in the bog. Carbon dating carried out by the National Museum of Ireland placed the corpse within the middle Iron Age, c. 361–175 BC. The remains were those of "an adult male, whose body bore few signs of physical labour or injury until the time of his death." He had stabs wounds to the chest and lung. He'd been disembowelled and dismembered, his lower body had been removed below the ribs and the head was severed.

The well-fed and manicured appearance of many "bog men", together with a lack of evidence of manual labour, has led some to theorize that we are dealing with high-status captives or hostages, who were sacrificed after their seizure in tribal warfare or following insurrection against a chief. Eamonn Kelly, the Keeper of the Antiquities division at the National Museum in Dublin, has suggested that many of the Irish bog bodies were buried close to barony boundaries, which, he argues, may well preserve much older tribal boundaries underneath. This would tally with Sheila's interpretation of Aisling's very own "bog man".

Page 152 *belief in what they called the ka* – The ancient Egyptians thought that, upon death, the soul splits into two distinct entities. One, the *ba*, belongs to the individual, while the other, the *ka*, is more a component of the group consciousness of the human race. The occultist Borce T Gjorgjievski explains Egyptian belief in more detail.

Man was considered to be consisted of nine parts: a physical body, a shadow, a double or *ka*, a soul or *ba*, a heart or *ib*, a spirit or *khu*, a power, a name, and a spiritual body. The *ka* was the double of the physical body and it remained around the grave after death. In the graves of the pharaohs there were special places built for the *ka*, called "The Temples of Ka". The *ka* was usually shown as two upward hands. The *ib* or the heart had great influence after the death when the earthly deeds of the individual were judged. The heart was measured against a feather, and if it showed heavier, the person was thrown to a crocodile-like monster to be eaten. In the *Book of the Dead* there are special prayers with which the person prays to his heart not to testify against him. The *ba* or the soul leaves for heaven after death, and it might visit the grave from time to time. It was depicted as a bird with the head of the person.

Similar beliefs were present in other cultures. In ancient China it was held that the soul splits into two or three parts. Elsewhere in the Far East, in Indonesia for example, it was believed that the soul will split into a good and evil spirit, each of which goes on to dwell in its own realm of the afterlife.

The Night the Veil was Rent

Page 184 *able to impersonate her* – It seems that certain entities are adept at pretending to be the souls of the departed. In *The Dark Sacrament*, my book on exorcism in Ireland, I recounted a frightening haunting that persisted for more than fifteen years. The woman concerned had joined her children one evening to experiment with a Ouija board. It had all been in a spirit of fun. Great was their astonishment when before too long they received communication from an entity purporting to be a Frenchman who'd lived in another century. He told the woman that he wished to join her, despite her protests. There followed years of persecution until finally a deliverance ritual carried out by a clergyman succeeded in driving out the entity. Its true nature has remained a mystery.

The Unquiet Spirit of Hazel Quinn

Page 189 *The third type of ghost* – There is also a fourth type: the ghost of a living person. Brad and Sherry Steiger tell us that psychical research has identified seven different situations in which the "astral body" or "body of light" will detach itself from the physical body, thereby creating a ghost or phantasm that may in certain circumstances closely resemble the entity which we consider to be the spirit of a deceased human being. Such out-of-body experiences (OBEs) or astral projections are classified as follows.

1. Projections that occur while the subject sleeps.
2. Projections that occur while the subject is undergoing surgery, childbirth, tooth extraction, etc.
3. Projections that occur at the time of an accident, during which the subject suffers a violent physical jolt that seems, literally, to catapult the spirit from the physical body.
4. Projections that occur during intense physical pain.
5. Projections that occur during acute illness.

6. Projections that occur during near-death experiences (NDEs), wherein the subject is revived and returned to life through heart massage or other medical means.

7. Projections that occur at the moment of physical death when the deceased subject appears to a living percipient with whom he or she has had a close emotional link.

In addition to these spontaneous, involuntary experiences, there also seem to be those voluntary and conscious projections during which the subjects deliberately endeavour to free their spirit, their soul, from their physical body. It would appear that certain people have exercised this peculiar function of the transcendent self to the extent that they can project their spiritual essence at will and produce ghosts, apparitions, of the living.

Brad E Steiger and Sherry Hansen Steiger, *Gale Encyclopedia of the Unusual and Unexplained* (2003), Thomson Gale, Missouri

Page 209 *That belief is shared by many* – Varied and wonderful are the stories put out by the more flamboyant of the psychics and mediums. They range from a vague belief that the dead can return to exert some little influence on the physical world to a conviction that we are literally surrounded on all sides by ghosts. The celebrity American psychic James Van Praagh would even have us believe that he overhears ghosts conversing at their own funerals.

After the dead leave their physical body and realize that they are no longer attached to their body, they move into the membrane [*sic*] between earth and the next dimension closest to earth. At this time, ghosts make up their mind whether they want to remain close to the earth as earthbound ghosts or cross into the light. During this window of opportunity, ghosts usually attend their funeral to see how they are being laid out, who shows up, the various preparations, and so on. I have heard many odd remarks by ghosts while attending their funeral. *Why did they put that dress on me? Who picked those flowers for my casket? I want to be in a bronze urn, not a wooden box*. Often I have heard ghosts say that they do not like having an open casket. Some male ghosts have communicated that they do not like being "made up" for their funeral. Many a ghost has caused plenty of havoc at his or her funeral in order to help the loved ones "get it right". Then there are those who don't give a second thought to the details of their funeral and are very surprised by all the fuss being made over them.

James Van Praagh, *Ghosts Among Us: Uncovering the Truth About the Other Side,* (2008) HarperOne, San Francisco

The Dead Girl who Sought Revenge

Page 215 *his "psychic ether" theory of hauntings* – Professor Price's theory held that the collective emotions or thought images of a person who has lived in a house some time in the past may have intensely "charged" the psychic ether of the place – especially if there had been such powerful emotions as fear, hatred, or sorrow, "supercharged" by an act of violence. The original agent, Price theorized, "has no direct part in the haunting. It is the charged psychic ether which, when presented with a percipient of suitable telepathic affinity, collaborates in the production of the idea-pattern of a ghost."

He was saying in effect that any building in which human beings have lived or been otherwise active will be saturated with the "residual traces" of many emotions, good and bad, joyous and fearful. And thus are so-called ghosts produced.

At the same time it could be the case that owing to the plethora of mental images so produced, there will be over-saturation and therefore no distinct ghost can take form. We would have what amounts to an "overkill" of images and impressions. As Brad Steiger puts it: "It is only when an idea-pattern that has been supercharged with enormous psychic intensity finds the mental level of a percipient with the necessary degree of telepathic affinity that a real ghost can appear."

Áine Synott and the Haunted Chapel

Page 249 *American scientist Carl Sagan* – Sagan (1934–1996) devoted an entire chapter to hallucinations in one of his books: *The Demon-Haunted World: Science as a Candle in the Dark*, (1997) Ballantine, New York. He also noted that: "Such celebrated (and unhysterical) explorers as Admiral Richard Byrd, Captain Joshua Slocum, and Sir Ernest Shackleton all experienced vivid hallucinations when coping with unusual isolation and loneliness."

Strange Goings-on in the Attic

Page 276 *certain she was being watched* – This sensation occurs very frequently, yet may be no more than the imagination playing tricks. Anthropologists sometimes explain it as a defence mechanism with which we are born, a throwback to primitive times when our survival depended on our ability to sense the presence of a predator. But very often the sensation may be an indication of the presence of a ghost. The parapsychologist Rosemary Ellen Guiley has this to say:

> If you are near ghosts, your first clues are most likely to be physical. Your skin tingles or crawls, or the hair on the back of your neck and on your arms stands up. These are age-old, primitive responses alerting us to the unseen presence of potential danger. While most ghosts are not dangerous, most are unseen, and their invisible presence may change the atmosphere of a place and trigger our automatic body responses.
>
> You may also feel a strange tightening or unpleasant sensation in the gut. Or, you may have a generalized, overall feeling that "something" you can't see is present. There may be a ringing or buzzing noise in your ears."

Rosemary Ellen Guiley, *Ghosts and Haunted Places* (2008) Chelsea House, New York

SELECT BIBLIOGRAPHY
AND FURTHER READING

Belanger, Jeff, *Encyclopedia of Haunted Places* (2005) New Page Books, New Jersey

Corcoran, J Aeneas, *Irish Ghosts* (2001) Geddes and Grosset, New Lanark

deFaoíte, Dara, *Paranormal Ireland* (2002) Maverick House, Ashbourne

Dunne, John, *A Ghost Watcher's Guide to Ireland* (2001) Appletree Press, Belfast

Dunwich, Gerina, *A Witch's Guide to Ghosts and the Supernatural* (2002) New Page Books, New Jersey

Ellison, Arthur J, *The Reality of the Paranormal* (1988) Harrap, London

Fanthorpe, Lionel and Patricia, *Death: the Final Mystery* (2000) Hounslow, Oxford

Fennell, Desmond, *Haunted: A Guide to Paranormal Ireland* (2006) Poolbeg, Dublin

Fodor, Nandor. *The Haunted Mind: A Psychoanalyst Looks at the Supernatural* (1959) Helix Press, New York

Greer, John Michael, *Monsters: An Investigator's Guide to Magical Beings* (2001) Llewellyn, Minnesota

Guiley, Rosemary Ellen, *The Encyclopedia of Ghosts and Spirits* (1992) Checkmark, New York

– *Ghosts and Haunted Places* (2008) Chelsea House, New York

Lendrum, William H, *Confronting the Paranormal* (2002) WH Lendrum, Belfast

Ogden, Daniel, *Magic, Witchcraft, and Ghosts in the Greek and Roman Worlds* (2002) Oxford University Press, New York

Ogden, Tom, *The Complete Idiot's Guide to Ghosts and Hauntings* (1999) Macmillan USA, Indiana

Seymour, St John D and Neligan, Harry L, *True Irish Ghost Stories* (1914) Hodges, Figgis, Dublin

Steiger, Brad, *Things That Go Bump in the Night* (2005) Bounty Books, London

– (with Sherry Hansen Steiger) Gale Encyclopedia of the Unusual and Unexplained (2003) Gale, Michigan

INDEX

317